Sweet
Carolina

Heroines of the Golden West
BOOK ONE

SWEET CAROLINA

STEPHEN BLY

CROSSWAY BOOKS • WHEATON, ILLINOIS
A DIVISION OF GOOD NEWS PUBLISHERS

Sweet Carolina

Copyright © 1998 by Stephen Bly

Published by Crossway Books
       a division of Good News Publishers
       1300 Crescent Street
       Wheaton, Illinois 60187

Cover design: Cindy Kiple

Cover illustration: Dan Brown

First printing, 1998

Printed in the United States of America

Library of Congress Cataloging-in-Publication Data
Bly, Sephen A., 1944-
   Sweet Carolina / Stephen Bly.
     p.   cm.
   ISBN 0-89107-973-4
   I. Title. II. Series: Bly, Stephen A., 1944- Heroines of the Golden
West: bk. 1.
   PS3552.L93S9 1998
   813'.54—dc21   97-49183

11	10	09	08	07	06	05	04	03	02	01	00	99	98
15	14	13	12	11	10	9	8	7	6	5	4	3	2	1

For Jill Carter

It's the men who walk straight
who will settle this land,
the women with integrity
who will last here.

PROVERBS 2:21,
THE MESSAGE

~ One ~

CAROLINA CANTRELL DETERMINED that handsome men possess similar characteristics.

Wide, square shoulders.

Eyes that tease and tempt.

A relaxed smile that reveals an honest heart.

A deep voice that causes a flutter in a woman's heart.

But ugly men are each one unattractive in his own repulsive way.

She knew that it wasn't exactly the way Tolstoy began *Anna Karenina*.

But it was true.

The man who hunkered across the grimy, sticky table from Carolina was uniquely ugly. Her instant evaluation was based on more than his tobacco-stained vest, unwashed shirt, and ragged canvas trousers.

His eyes danced.

But it was a wild, explosive, unpredictable, frightening, promenade.

His nose was big and crooked. His smile came only from the left side of his face, which allowed him to grin and size her up all at the same time. His eyes were too narrow for such a wide head. They were beady and reflected a blue-gray ambivalence. The cracks and lines around his eyes were hardened from years in the sun and caked with dirt. The faintly white skin above the hat line on his forehead hinted of true flesh tones, but a jagged scar there marked him like a brand of violence.

The wide-brimmed hat pushed back on his head sagged, revealing a tear near the right ear. It looked as if it had been burned, or at least held close to a fire. The four-button off-white cotton pullover shirt no longer had any trace of buttons nor any hint of its original hue. The two-week beard sported flecks of black, red, gray, and grease in an almost comical pattern.

His teeth were crooked, yellowed, and reflected some gold. His hair was uncombed. His fingernails seemed permanently packed with grease.

Carolina knew that it was not going to be a pleasant conversation.

Just a necessary one.

Her gloved right hand smoothed the folds of her forest green dress and then returned to her lap to clutch her leather purse. "Mr. Starke—," she began.

"Ma'am, you can just call me Hardrock."

His alcohol breath seethed only slightly more loathsome than the musty, stale odor of the unkempt mercantile store. "Why would I want to do that?"

"You and me bein' friends and all. My Christian name's Horatio, but most of my friends call me Hardrock."

"Mr. Starke, whatever gives you the idea that you and I are friends?" *Relax, Carolina . . . you knew it would be this way. This is not Paris or London. It's not even Christiansburg or Omaha!*

"Me and your brother goin' back a ways and havin' partnered up for years. That makes you and me pals, don't it?" He punctuated the question with an uncovered belch.

"As far as I can tell, you and my brother were partners—at least until the day he was murdered—although there is no mention of you in his letters home. How friendly you were toward each other remains to be discovered. Tell me again where you were when the outlaws attacked the store."

"I was sick. Real sick."

She thought about placing her hands on the table but spied a thick, greasy film on its top. She pointed to the ceiling of the store instead. "You were in the sleeping quarters in the loft?"

"Eh, no, ma'am, I was over in the saloon. Actually, there's a loft over there too. But I was downstairs at the time."

Carolina fought back the urge to stomp over to the window to let some fresh air in. She reached up her sleeve and tugged out a lace-edged, embroidered handkerchief to wipe the perspiration from under the black curls that ringed her forehead. "You were thirty feet away, and you didn't hear any gunshots?"

"I told ya, I was real sick. But your brother done good, like I said in my letter. He plugged 'em both and kept them from rifling the cash box. Davy was a brave man. You can be proud of him for that." Starke leaned back in his chair. His generous stomach protruded even more.

"I am aware of my brother's attributes. David Lee was brave, reckless, adventuresome, self-centered, and stubborn beyond reason. But you haven't told me how it was that several gunshots inside a building failed to wake you up." She raised her head and stretched her neck as she spoke and quickly lowered them as she heard her mother's scolding words: *Carolina, your neck is way too long already; don't make it look worse.*

"I guess I was so sick I passed out," Starke explained.

"Sick and passed out in a saloon?" *Drunker than a Prussian private on payday, no doubt. Perhaps Mother and Mr. Franklin were right. I should have just written off this whole affair and stayed in Maryland.*

Starke picked his teeth with a dirt-crammed fingernail. "You just ask ol' Tap Andrews—he'll tell ya."

"Andrews?"

"He runs the Slash-Bar-4 Ranch up the road a piece. He rode up just as your brother got shot and found me in my sickly condition."

"I will definitely have a talk with Mr. Andrews. Now, Mr. Starke, the reason I've rumbled, bounced, jostled, and ricocheted off trains, stages, and wagons for almost two weeks in order to find this place, wherever we might be—"

"This here's Yellowstone County, Montana Territory."

"I've come here to see that my brother is properly buried and to settle his affairs. I have no intention of staying any longer than necessary to accomplish those tasks. If I sound short with you, Mr. Starke, it is because I am neither used to this country nor accustomed to dealing with grief. I suggest we settle things up, and then I'll be on my way back to the train depot in Billings."

"I'll be happy to show you his marker up there on the bluff. His personal things is up in the loft. That was his office and bedroom."

A puff of fresh air drifted into the room like a delightful cottonwood perfume. "Before I look at those things, Mr. Starke, I believe we should settle up the matter of this joint venture."

He crashed his oak chair back down to the floor. "Excuse me, ma'am?"

"The business partnership—Starke and Cantrell's Mercantile Store. Now you seemed to indicate that you and my brother were equal partners—is that correct?"

"Yes, ma'am . . . built her up from nothin', we did. Me and Davy scratched for gold in the Big Horns and purtneer starved to death. Then we heard about the Northern Pacific tracks comin' through. So we hightailed it to the Yellowstone and staked out this property. Built this here buildin' with our own bare hands, me and Davy."

Carolina glanced at the far wall and thought she could see May daylight shining through. "I see you spared no expense."

"This is a rough land. Besides, we was in a hurry. The train crews were headed this way. That's no time for finish carpentry. And them was good times. Train crews and cowboys who didn't want to travel to town just stopped off here to spend their pay. Why, they bunked twenty to a room in those days."

She looked around at the scattered barrels, wooden boxes, and crude shelving. "Room? What room? You ran a hotel in this building?"

"Well, in the winter time they was right here on the floor. Bedrolls, blankets, and saddles stacked almost on top of each other. It was really somethin'. You should've been here."

A room full of Horatio Starkes? Lord, deliver me from ever having to experience that. The odor alone would shorten one's life span. "It's hard for me to imagine."

"Yes, ma'am, we were sackin' up money like a mine owner back in them days. But they're gone . . . all gone now."

"And what did you and my brother do with the profits you made in those glory days?"

The man's blue-gray eyes darted around the room, not focused on her at all. "I invested mine, of course. Buy more product, I always say. But Davy, well, he was a big-hearted man."

"Oh?"

"He kept grub-stakin' prospectors and cowboys in hope that they would strike pay dirt. Mainly, he took a bunch of worthless mining claims for collateral. I wanted my half in cash. Yes, ma'am, I told him he was tossin' his future away. I'm mighty sorry there ain't more funds left for you."

"From your letter, I didn't expect there would be much. Let me get to the point, Mr. Starke. I presume you want to buy out my brother's half of the business."

"Buy out? Well, ma'am . . . if we're talkin' about this store, I surmised that with Davy gone to his heavenly reward, the store rightly belongs to me."

She rapped her fingers on her purse. His brazen assumptions reminded her of that Russian wool merchant in St. Petersburg. "You surmised wrong. David Lee sent title papers to this property with my name listed as heir and assign. Your name, on the other hand, is not recorded anywhere. I believe that gives me some legal ownership. However, I have no intention of staying in this desolate land and certainly none of remaining your partner. So what will you offer me for David's half of this business?"

"Oh, well now, if you're talkin' buyin' out, you do know that we had that holdup, and they took . . . "

A large fly buzzed around her head, and she brushed against her left ear and felt her single pearl earring. "You stated in your letter that no money had been stolen."

"I did? Oh, yes, ma'am . . . well, that's true. But times ain't been so good lately. Now that the railroad's finished, the reservation settled down, and the soldiers went back to Fort Laramie, business has been poor lately. Me and Davy was a strugglin' just to keep beans on the table."

Her green dress had black lace at the high collar and at the wrists. The lace fluttered in the air as she pointed across the room. "That explains your appalling lack of inventory."

"Yes, ma'am. You bein' an observant woman, you kin see business ain't exactly thrivin'."

"With such lean times, perhaps you could explain the liquor that you were unloading from the wagon onto the front porch when I drove up. There must have been $500 worth of merchandise in that order."

"Oh, that. Actually, it only cost me about $350, delivered. I know how to drive a bargain. Well, that's where we make our profit, so naturally—"

"You spent all available money on alcohol?" *Does he intend to sell it or drink it?*

"I figured it was our last chance to make the business go."

"I find it hard to believe that my brother was ever your partner." Carolina's light breakfast at the Billings hotel seemed long ago. *Surely, I will not have to eat at this place. I should have listened when they told me to pack a dinner with me.*

"It's right up there on the front of the building—Starke and Cantrell's. We worked real good together, your brother and me. He took care of this side of the store, and I took the other."

"Mr. Starke, I'm confident that you would like to get back to your side of the building as soon as possible. I, certainly, would like to be on an eastbound train. So what will you give me for my brother's share of the business?"

"You said you got the papers right there?"

"Yes, in my purse."

"Well, I reckon . . . just to honor poor Davy's memory, I could give you $100 for your half. Not that I have it all in cash, mind you. I'd give you some now and mail the rest to you back east as soon as it comes in. Yes, ma'am, the first $100 that comes into the cash box is yours."

At the sound of boot heels and jingling spurs, her head spun toward the open doorway. A gaunt-faced cowboy with battered shotgun chaps sauntered inside and pushed his brown felt hat to the back of his highly soiled head. Behind the beard and dirt were weak brown eyes. His right hand was wrapped in soiled linen and sported a good-sized dried bloodstain. "Excuse me, miss, I'm lookin' for Cantrell. Have you seen him?"

"What do you want?" Starke barked.

The man fixed his eyes right on Carolina while he talked to Horatio Starke. "I want Cantrell. I've got something for him."

Carolina stood and brushed down her long, dark green dress. She could feel the grime on the floor grind under each step of her lace-up black shoes. Their heels made her appear taller than her five feet, six inches, but she was still several inches shorter than the man. "David was murdered. I'm his sister. How may I help you?"

"You're Cantrell's sister? Excuse me for staring, miss." He took off his hat and held it in front of him with both hands. "I jist haven't seen a gal scrubbed up and wearin' such a purdy dress in a long, long time. I been starin' at longhorn cattle so long you have the appearance of a heavenly vision."

"Thank you. Such a lovely line. Now did you have something for my brother?"

"Yes, ma'am." He tipped his hat and stepped closer to her. She couldn't tell if the smell came from him or Starke, who still slouched at the table. "Your brother loaned me twenty dollars last summer, and I promised to pay him back." He held out a double eagle gold piece.

"That goes in the cash box!" Starke jumped to his feet and scooted toward the cowboy's outstretched arm.

"It came out of Cantrell's vest pocket, not the cash box," the man protested. "So I reckon I'll just give it to his sister. Sorry about your brother, ma'am. He always treated me square."

"I appreciate hearing that," she acknowledged. He dropped the coin into the palm of her beige-gloved hand. "Is there anything else I can do for you?" Carolina's eyes glanced up at the thin-faced cowboy's, and she realized that he was carefully studying her every word. Her face warmed. "What I-I mean is," she stammered, "do you need any supplies today?"

A wide smile washed across his thin, dusty face. "Oh . . . supplies? I reckon I could use a twenty-five-pound bag of pinto beans and some salt pork."

"We ain't got no salt pork," Starke blurted out. "The beans is over there in that stack, but they are in fifty-pound sacks. The scales is broke, so you got to buy fifty pounds or nothin'."

Carolina strolled over toward a counter cluttered with half-full small glass jars. "You don't need scales to divide a sack in half," she objected. "Pour yourself out half a sack, Mr. . . . ? "

"Porter. Rawbone Porter's the name, Miss Cantrell."

"Well, Mr. Porter, if you need something to go in those beans, I'd suggest you might like one of those chili blocks and some spices."

His voice grated, yet was soft and apologetic. "Eh, yes, ma'am, but I ain't no cook. I mean, I don't know much about spicin' up food." He stepped up beside her, and she was glad for the heavy aroma of cinnamon and cloves.

She didn't move away from him but glanced down at the jars. "I'll select a blend that will make them a lot tastier than plain pintos. Mr. Starke, split a bag of beans for Mr. Porter, please."

Within minutes a small cotton sack corralled a fistful of selected ingredients. Porter paid for his goods in coins and then ambled out to the porch. Cantrell and Starke followed.

"You ain't goin' to leave before you buy a drink, are ya?" Starke challenged.

"It's got to be a mighty just cause to get me to drink before noon. I'll jist pass this time." Porter strapped the grub sack on behind his worn Texas saddle.

Carolina tucked her folded gloves into her purse, which she held at her side. "Now, remember, just a three-fingered pinch for every pot of beans. Any more than that will melt your tongue."

"Yes, ma'am." His grin exposed a wide gap between his two front teeth. Porter forked his mount and then rode up to the edge of the porch. "You aimin' to run this store permanent?"

She shaded her eyes with her hand. "No, I need to return to my home in the States."

"Well, that's too bad, Miss Cantrell. You'd surely make this place a pleasant sight to visit."

"Thank you."

Porter looked over at Starke. "Did you know another Texas herd is comin' this way? The boys should be here by the first of next week."

"I'm glad to hear that! Tell 'em I have special prices for Texas men. As you can see, I jist got in a big order." Starke swept his arm toward the barrels on the porch.

"I'll tell 'em." He tipped his hat to Carolina. "Good-bye, Miss Cantrell. You brightened up my day. I'm grateful to the good Lord for that."

She watched the cowboy ride through the cottonwood trees toward the river.

Lord, I'm not sure my smile has ever brought You any thanks before, but I'm glad it did this time.

She handed $2.10 to Starke. "Write this down in your books."

He quickly crammed the coins into his vest pocket and then rubbed his beard with the palm of his hand. "What books?"

"You do record sales, don't you?"

"Why?"

"For inventory control and so you have an idea what's in the cash box."

"I'm real sharp about business, Miss Cantrell. I just keep it all in my head."

"Well, my memory is less than perfect, Mr. Starke. So if you'll return the funds, I'll record it and place it in the store's cash box, which seems to be otherwise empty."

He handed her two dollars, but she kept her hand out until he produced the dime. She entered the store, found a ledger with her brother's handwriting, and inscribed the sale. By the time she returned to the porch, Starke had rolled the liquor barrels into the saloon part of the building. He plopped down on a rickety wooden bench and wiped his forehead with a highly soiled red bandanna.

"I believe we were trying to establish a price on half of this business, Mr. Starke."

"I told you I'd give you $100."

"You just bought $350 worth of alcohol, and you tell me half the business is only worth $100?" she challenged.

"Oh . . . well . . . I wasn't figurin' inventory, of course. Why don't you take the goods in the store, and I'll keep what's in the saloon? Plus I'll give you $100 dollars like I said."

"You are sure that's all it's worth?"

"Yes, ma'am, and I'm tryin' to be just as fair as I can be."

"I don't suppose I could convince you to offer me more?" She raised her eyebrows and lilted her voice.

"Ma'am, that's the best offer I have. You'll just have to trust me."

Mister, I've spent the past five years in charge of my father's import business, and I'd still be in control if it weren't for good old Mr. Franklin.

A creaking wagon wheel caused her to turn toward the roadway. An older woman, wrapped in a dark dress with a red and black shawl over her head, drove a worn farm wagon pulled by two thin dark mules to the front of the store. Several barefoot children rode in the back.

"I need to buy some ground wheat flour and sugar," the woman called, the reins still in her hand.

"Go on!" Starke waved his hand and shouted. "We don't sell to your kind."

Carolina spun on her heels and stared down her narrow nose at the man. She could feel her teeth grind. "What do you mean, we don't sell to her kind?"

"Mexicans. We don't sell to Mexicans," he blurted out.

"That's absolutely ludicrous. Of course we do."

"What do you mean, we?" he growled.

"Until you buy me out, this business is half mine." She turned and called out to the woman, "We'll sell you flour and sugar. And anything else you want. . . . Unfortunately, we seem to be a little low on supplies. But please come in and look around."

Starke sulked into the saloon half of the store while Cantrell waited on the woman and her three children. It was at least thirty minutes later before the customer left.

Carolina carefully jotted down the purchases in the ledger. Starke blustered through the doorway that separated saloon from store.

"Where's the money?"

"In the cash box, of course."

"I decided I don't need two cash boxes."

"And I decided we do."

"We? Why do you keep sayin' 'we'?"

"You still haven't purchased my half of this enterprise."

"I told you I'd give you $100 plus inventory on this side of the wall. Now sign them papers, and you can be on your way."

Carolina stared at the man's narrow eyes. "Before we make any agreement, we'll need a witness."

"A witness? What fer? Don't you trust me?"

"Why on earth should I, Mr. Starke?"

"You ain't goin' to get no witness out here!"

"Why, Mr. Starke, you do plan to have more customers today, don't you?"

"No way of knowin'. I told you, business has been poor. We might not have another . . . "

She pointed to the trail up from the river. "Sounds like a rider to me."

"Probably just some drover who wants to wet his thirst.

"If he's sober, he can be our witness."

"You know, I could just yank them papers away from you if I wanted to. What would you do then?"

"You could try. But you need to determine if the reason I carry this purse with me is because I have a small revolver in it. Then you need to ask yourself, 'Is she the type who would use it, if necessary?'"

"You cain't bluff me!"

"Believe me, Mr. Starke, I have no intention of bluffing you."

"Well, I didn't say I was goin' to steal them papers. I just said I could if I set my mind to it. You did agree to $100 fer your half, right?"

"All I agreed on was that we need a witness."

The dust-covered cowboy rode a black horse with a Slash-Bar-4 branded on its hip. Carolina noticed his broad, strong shoulders and his easy smile. She thought his eyes danced a little as he climbed down off his horse and tipped his hat in her direction.

"Howdy, ma'am . . . howdy, Starke." It was almost a laughing voice. For the first time all day, Carolina had the urge to check her hair in a mirror.

"Which side of the place you comin' to buy from, Odessa?" Starke quizzed.

"Hardrock, you haven't properly introduced me to this lady."

"Oh, this here's Cantrell's sister from back in the States," Starke huffed.

The cowboy pulled off his hat and nodded at her. His hair looked neatly trimmed. The off-white starched collarless shirt looked fresh. "Pleased to meet you, ma'am. I presume you have a name? I'm Lorenzo Odessa. I foreman up on the Slash-Bar-4."

"I'm Carolina Cantrell."

He's the first halfway clean man I've met in a week. If he had a French accent, he'd remind me of Henri. When I was a little girl, I made a list of qualities I admired in a boy. At six years old, I listed cleanliness above godliness.

"Sorry to hear about your brother. I'm new in the country and hadn't met him yet, but from what folks say, he was a brave and just man."

"Thank you. I appreciate that eulogy, even if it did come secondhand. Did you need to buy some supplies?"

"Yes, Miss Cantrell, I surely did." His revolver was strapped high on his waist, like he spent most of the day in the saddle.

Starke blustered through the door into the store ahead of them, but Odessa waited for Carolina to enter, still holding his hat.

Why couldn't David's partner have looked like Mr. Odessa? He is slightly bowlegged, needs to file his nails, sports a little trail dust, and his left ear looks lower than the right, but I'm not a critical woman. All-in-all, not a bad-looking man, if looks mattered—which they don't. Certainly not to me. There is no one of interest to me in Montana. Nor in Maryland, for that matter.

"Ma'am, here's what I need. Maybe you can help me. My missus is gettin' sort of . . . well, she's big . . . I mean to say, she's great with child."

"Congratulations!" *Married? Children on the way? Somehow it doesn't surprise me. "I told you all the good ones are taken!" "No, Mother, that's not true." Is it?*

"Thank ya. It's all sort of new to me. This will be our first child. But Selena—that's my wife—she woke me up about three in the mornin' askin' if I could ride down here and buy her an airtight of those little pickled peaches. I bought her one a couple weeks ago, and she's been houndin' me ever since."

Odessa paid for two cans of pickled peaches and studied a glass case that contained one dusty beige woman's straw hat with a short peacock feather.

"Would you like to purchase the hat as well?" Carolina asked.

"It's a mighty handsome one. Don't you think so?"

A voice like a peaceful brook. The tone of a man's voice speaks volumes. Most seem hurried or angry or lustful. Some sound all three. But his is confidently serene. Maybe he has a brother. Which is, Carolina, an absolutely stupid thought. I quit playing this game years ago. "Mr. Odessa, to be honest, it's a lovely hat, and I'm extremely surprised to see it in a store this remote."

"I reckon I'd like to buy it, but I don't have the cash. My Selena likes to dress purdy, and it would tickle her to have that hat. But we need to save our pennies for the baby."

"I understand." *Works hard, frugal. Straightforward. No sign of guile. Perhaps I judged this land too quickly. Even in the wilderness some trees grow straight and true.* "Mr. Odessa, we need you to be a witness on a legal document. Would you be willing?"

"I don't know many legal terms. What's it about?"

"I'm not interested in continuing this partnership, so we need to establish the value of this establishment."

"One of you sellin' out?"

"That's right," Starke crowed.

"And Mr. Starke insisted that half interest is only worth $100."

"Look at this place. It ain't much," Starke chimed, and he waved his hands in the air.

Odessa shook his head. "Doesn't look all that bad to me."

Carolina held up her thin white fingers to silence him. "No, Mr. Starke is the one most familiar with the business. And if he says half of it's only worth $100, then I will trust his word."

"I did say she could also have the inventory on the store side." Starke shuffled his scuffed brown boots.

Odessa glanced around the room. "Miss Cantrell, you're not really going to sell out for $100, are you?"

Carolina Cantrell opened her purse, withdrew five gold coins, and shut her bag up quickly. "No, I'm not selling out. Mr. Starke, since you are unable to produce $100 cash, I'd like to buy your half."

The word exploded out of the man's bearded face like a bull-frog's last croak. "What?"

"You did say it was worth $100, didn't you?"

"I said your half was worth $100. I didn't say nothin' about sellin' my half."

"Mr. Odessa," Carolina reached over and placed her hand on the cowboy's arm, "didn't Mr. Starke just say that one-half of the business is worth $100?"

Odessa smiled widely and revealed straight white teeth. He patted her hand. She could feel rough calluses and a strong grip. "He surely did, ma'am."

"Then doesn't he have to accept my money?"

"I ain't sellin' for less than $1,000!" Starke fumed.

Carolina stuck her face within inches of his and raised her dark, sweeping eyebrows. Any trace of a smile had been replaced by a straight-lipped glare. "And, Mr. Starke, neither am I!"

Odessa jammed his thumbs into his vest pockets and shook his head. "Whoa . . . sounds like you two have locked horns. I reckon you won't be needin' my signature today. Is there anything else I can do for you, Miss Cantrell?"

She stalked across the store to the doorway that connected to the saloon. She stared into the dark den and allowed the stench of alcohol and sweat to flood around her.

Relax, Carolina . . . calm down. Make a good business decision. What would Father do? He'd say, "Sweet Carolina, you're in charge. Don't let them take that away from you. You've always been in charge. You have to be. It's in your nature." No one on earth can force me to do what I do not want to do! Nor will they force me to a quick decision. I do not make quick decisions.

Help me, Lord.

She turned back and glanced at the two staring back at her. *Always too many Starkes and never enough Odessas. It's the same all over the world.*

"Mr. Odessa, would you see if you can find some nails and please hammer that door shut between the saloon and the store? Until I have been given a fair price, I claim this end of the building."

"You can't do that!" Starke protested. "That door has always been open! This business is half mine!"

"You get that half." She pointed to the open doorway that led to the saloon. "Does that sound fair, Mr. Odessa?"

"Yes, ma'am. I reckon it does," he laughed. It was a teasing laugh, one that a woman could quickly get used to. "Unless he wants the store and will give you the saloon."

"Give her what?" Horatio Starke's eyes glinted with anger, and he cursed.

"Mr. Odessa, would you please escort Mr. Starke out of my store?" Carolina requested. "His language is blasphemous and insulting."

"*Your* store?" Starke screamed.

"She's right and you know it. Foul language in front of ladies don't impress me much either. You better go on, Hardrock." Odessa waved his hand. "You haven't got a chance in the world once a woman's made up her mind on something."

"You can't make me leave my own business!" he hollered.

Odessa rested his right hand on the worn walnut grip of his holstered .44. "No, but I can sure enough throw you out of Miss Cantrell's store."

"I ain't packin' no gun," Starke whined.

"I am." Lorenzo Odessa's voice rolled like a tidal wave across the room.

Horatio Starke sulked and cursed his way into the saloon. Odessa slammed the solid wood plank door between the two rooms.

"Miss Cantrell, I don't reckon ol' Hardrock is a happy man. I hear he ain't very pleasant to be around when he gets drunk."

"He's not exactly charming when he's sober." Carolina glanced around at the dust that hung in the sunlight that broke into the store from smudged windows and an open front door.

Odessa scooped up a handful of nails and a hatchet and nailed tight the rough, unpainted door that joined the two ends of the building. As he worked, Carolina climbed the stairs at the back of the room and inspected the loft that served as her brother's bedroom and office. Wooden boxes stuffed with clothing, papers, and ledgers lined the wall where the roof line slanted to the floor. A large four-poster bed stood beyond the boxes. Each post was the size of tree trunk. On a dust-covered dresser was a photograph of two small children posed in front of a tall white column.

David Lee, I don't know why you had to come out here. And I don't know why you had to die out here. A man should die with his family when he's old—with a wife and grown children at his side—not from some assassin's bullet in a wild and filthy place like this.

She glanced at the interlocked hands of the two children in the photo.

You were twelve and I was eight. The world was perfect. We sailed to England, and you assured me you'd look after me. Big brother, where have you gone? I need you. There's none left but Mother and Mr. Franklin. He's made life impossible, you know. . . . No, you don't know. You left before mother remarried.

I cried the whole summer when you left us in Paris. You promised to come back soon. That was nine years ago. David Lee, I did not cry when I got the letter about your death. This is the life you wanted to live.

I will not cry now.

Lord, help me not to cry.

She wiped the corner of each eye with her handkerchief. The hammering in the room below ceased.

"Miss Cantrell, is there anything else I can do for you?"

She walked to the half wall of the loft and looked down at the store below. "Mr. Odessa, could you explain to me why my brother has a heavy iron plate on the floor underneath his bed?"

"Stray bullets, ma'am."

"How's that?"

"Well, if someone was down on this level, hurrahin' the place—you know, shootin' it up just to celebrate—a stray bullet might accidently blast right through the floorin'. So lots of upstairs rooms have iron plates under the bed."

"Oh."

"Are you sure you're going to be all right here by yourself?"

Carolina held the rough pole banister as she descended the steep staircase. "Yes. Mr. Odessa, I wonder if I could hire you to do a few chores for me? I know you need to get back to your wife and your job, but if you could do a few things, I'd like to pay you by giving you that woman's hat."

Odessa glanced over at the glass case. "I suppose no one's countin' on me moseying back for a while anyway. That surely would tickle my wife. What else can I do for you?"

"I'd like you to put my horse in the corral, push my buggy to the side of the building, and help me carry in my bags."

"You thinkin' about stayin'?"

"I have no other choice but to abandon ownership completely. And that doesn't make very good business sense, does it?"

"No, ma'am, I reckon it don't. But then I'm not much of a businessman."

"Well, I am a businesswoman. Now I'll need to rearrange the merchandise. There seems to be no pattern to the products. If you could help me for two hours, the hat is yours. Is that a fair trade?"

"Two hours for a three-dollar hat? I'd say you are a mighty generous lady, Miss Cantrell." Odessa sauntered toward the door. "I'll go put up your rig."

For the next two hours Carolina did not see any customers nor Horatio Starke. By the time Lorenzo Odessa mounted his black horse, with a beige hat tied to his saddle horn, and trotted off in the direction of the Slash-Bar-4, the store was swept, the merchandise arranged in neat rows, and the windows washed.

Carolina had pushed her sleeves up to her elbows, and the top two buttons on her high lace collar were now unfastened. She dragged one of two oak chairs out to the roofless porch where she plopped down and let out a deep sigh.

The midafternoon sun was half past straight up, and the clear sky was a delightful blue. Carolina heard birds chirp and twitter in the tall, light-green-leafed cottonwood trees that separated the store from the Yellowstone River.

She was tired.

And hungry.

All right, Carolina Katherine Cantrell, world traveler and college graduate, do you have any idea what you are doing out here? This is like work for a charity in the city. It's difficult and grimy, but there's a satis-

faction upon completing it. Now it's time to go home, clean up, and join some friends for supper.

It feels like I should hitch up my pony and ride off. Carolina, are you actually going to run this store? You aren't really going to spend the night in a musty loft attached to a saloon.

Are you?

It's just been a game. You played well, but you lost. Now go home and find something worthwhile to do with your life.

I don't lose well, Lord.

I don't lose.

Ever.

But just what exactly am I trying to win? It's like playing jacks by myself in the closet. Who cares if I win or lose? Lord, why is it I always have to prove something, but I never know whom I am proving it to?

It's like every moment of every day is a schoolroom test.

And I never have any recess.

With a snare-drum rattle and a cloud of dust, a large wagon rolled up the road next to the river. Carolina Cantrell jumped to her feet. Horatio Starke lunged to the porch in front of the saloon's outside door. One glance at him and she knew he had been drinking or sleeping, or both.

Pulled by four teams of mules, the freight wagon creaked under an obviously heavy load. A young boy in a tattered straw hat rode on top of the tarp-draped wagon. A bearded teamster swung down off the peeling green-painted seat.

He shouted an unintelligible sentence at the mules, tossed the reins up at the boy, and whacked the dust off his canvas trousers with his wide, floppy hat.

"You selling something to cut the dust?" he hollered.

Starke bounded down off the steps in front of the saloon. "Welcome, partner. I've got some of the finest sipping rye whiskey this side of Billings."

"You've got the only whiskey this side of Billings!"

"Well, you're right about that. Is that where you're headed? Billings?"

"Yeah, and I'll go broke at this rate. An old boy came in and placed a big order two weeks back. Said he struck some rich ore across the line in Wyoming. He left a deposit and promised to pay the rest in gold if I delivered it to the state line. Said he'd come and meet me. I've been camped up there for five days, and no one showed. Finally, this boy staggers in and says they got jumped by Indians, and the old man got himself kilt. Don't that beat all? I'm stuck with a wagon full of goods and no customer. I should have demanded full payment in advance—that's what I should have done."

As he climbed the steps to the saloon, he tipped his hat at Carolina. "Howdy, ma'am."

She strolled toward them. The teamster seemed to have a dried stream of tobacco from his chin whiskers to his knees. He was a little shorter than she, and Carolina stared right into his leather-tough eyes.

"Excuse me, but before you enter Mr. Starke's establishment, I wonder if I might have a word with you?"

"He's *my* customer. You ain't got nothin' in there to slake his thirst," Starke protested.

"Shoot, you can roll me in the grave the day I don't have time to talk to a purdy lady." The teamster's grin disclosed two silver teeth. "What can I do for ya, miss?"

She pointed toward the wagon. "I was curious about what you are hauling."

"Mainly food and mining gear. Flour, sugar, salt, potatoes, airtights, coffee. Then there's shovels, picks, axes. Some trade goods too. He must have figured he'd have to negotiate with the Indians. But I reckon it's too late for that."

"I wonder if you'd be interested in a business deal?"

He slowly stared at her from her shoes to her black curly hair. "Depends on what kind of business you're in."

She didn't blink an eye. "I'm the owner of this store."

"Store? I thought this was a saloon."

"That end of the building is a saloon. This end is a store."

"Kind of isolated out here for a store, ain't ya?"

"It was my brother's business. I'm determined to run it until someone offers me a fair price." She glared at Starke. "Would you leave your entire load here at the store and allow me to sell it on consignment? I'll give you 70 percent of whatever I can get for it."

The teamster stared at her again. This time he watched only her eyes.

"That's a fierce temptation, ma'am, but I don't even know you."

"That's right!" Starke shouted from the open door of the saloon. "She might be some hurdy-gurdy girl who's tryin' to rob you. Why, she tried to steal my own store from me."

The teamster glanced over at Horatio Starke, then at Cantrell, back to Starke, then back to Cantrell. "Mister, where I come from, it's a serious offense to slander a lady. And whatever else this woman might be, it should be obvious even to a drunk that she's a lady. But he's right about one thing, ma'am. I don't know you at all. I just can't go leavin' my goods with a stranger. Anyone around here who can identify you? You know any folks in Billings that can stand for you?"

"No. I'm from Virginia. . . . Well, lately I've run my father's business in Chestertown, Maryland. I just came in today and haven't met . . . Wait! Mr. Odessa. Mr. Lorenzo Odessa. I believe he's foreman at the Slash-Bar-4. I do know him."

The teamster's bushy eyebrows raised. "So you know Odessa and Andrews and them? Well, why didn't you say so? A man can bank on the word of that Slash-Bar-4 bunch. I hear Mrs. Odessa's . . . you know, with child."

"Yes, Lorenzo was in today and said Selena sprouts bigger and bigger by the day. I believe it's some weeks before her time. But she sure covets pickled peaches. I sold him my last two airtights. Do you have any in the wagon?"

"I do believe so. Well, shoot." He paused and glanced out at the freight wagon. "A man's got to take a chance now and then if he's goin' to make a dollar. Tell you what—I've got an invoice right up there in the wagon. You read through that and tell me what you want. If you can give me 10 percent now, I'll let you pay me the rest in ninety days. I'd rather sell them out here than have to haul them all back to town."

"Thank you very much! I'll review the bill of lading and draw up the paperwork."

"July," he hollered to the boy on the wagon, "after you water them mules, you hep this lady dig through the goods. Anything she wants, pack into the store for her." Then he turned back. "I'll settle up with you after I cut the dust out of my throat."

Carolina Cantrell sat on the porch, hands folded in her lap, and watched the boy with the blue denim canvas trousers and long-sleeved, collarless gray cotton shirt haul water to each of the mules and wait patiently for each to slurp its fill.

Carolina, you're not making this any better. You should leave, yet you've gone and spent your travel money on goods. It seems that you keep undertaking things that you have no intention of doing. Lord, it's like my stubborn will, my calculating mind, and my romantic heart never talk to each other anymore. They keep utterly surprising each other.

When the boy finished with the last mule, he hiked over.

"Did you want to look at the goods?" He had a smooth, fairly clean face and a voice that was too high for his size.

"Yes, actually I decided to take all of them. But you look a little warm. Why don't you sit here for a moment."

"Thank you, ma'am." He plopped down on the step next to her chair.

"July—that's an unusual name. Is it a nickname?"

"No, ma'am. I was born in Independence, Missouri. So my mama named me July. My last name is Johnson."

"Well, my name is Carolina Cantrell. How old are you, July?"

"Fourteen, I reckon. I sort of lost track, bein' on my own and such."

"Where's your family?" she quizzed.

"In heaven. Where's yours?"

"Well . . . I hope some of them are in heaven also."

"Ain't that somethin', ma'am?" he chuckled. "Here's you and me sittin' here strangers, and our kin might be the best of friends."

"I never thought of it that way. I understand your former . . . employer was killed. That must have been terrible to witness."

"Yes, ma'am. He was walkin' over to the fire and dropped dead before we ever heard the report from the rifle. They must have been a long ways away."

"You mean others were there?"

"I was just the camp tender, but there was six men diggin' on the claim. Mr. Howard—that was my boss—he hired the others but wouldn't let anyone leave camp for fear that they'd tell someone where the strike is. The next day after he was shot, the Indians swooped down about daybreak, and them other five lit out toward the four winds."

"Were they all killed?"

"I don't know. I hid out in the grass near a prairie dog town. Figured the Indians wouldn't ride in there after me. Then, when it was dark, I lit out toward Red Rock Butte. I knew Mr. Howard was going out there to meet a supply wagon. I hitched this ride back to Billings with Mr. McGuire. He said he'd feed me 'til we get to Billings if I'd take care of the mules."

"It sounds dreadful—watching a man get killed like that."

"I've seen worse. It's just the way life is."

"July, what are you going to do once you get to Billings?"

"Get me a job somewhere, I hope. A man's got to eat."

And so do boys. She studied his worn clothing. "How would you like to go to work for me?"

"You own this saloon?"

"I own the store at this end of the building. I need someone to help me run it for a while. I can't guarantee I'll own it very long, but then . . . who knows?"

"Would I get paid?"

"I'll give you a place to sleep and meals, plus thirty dollars. If I sell the store in a week, you still get the whole thirty. If I don't sell it after a month, you get the thirty, and you can go on down the road if you want to."

He pushed his straw hat back. "I don't have to kill no one, do I?"

"Of course not! I just need someone to tend my horse, clean the store, haul supplies in and out, and wait on customers when I'm busy."

"You want me to clerk in the store? I ain't never been a clerk for anyone, but I can read, write, and count money."

"Well, you'd be more than a clerk. I think of you as the assistant manager."

"July Johnson, assistant manager? Yes, ma'am . . . I like that."

"Then you'll work for me?"

"I reckon so. When do I start?"

"Right now."

He vaulted to his feet. "What's the assistant manager's first job?"

"First you need to go in there and grab a piece of stick candy for yourself. An assistant manager can't go around hungry."

"Yes, ma'am. And what do we do after that?"

"We'll unload that wagon."

"Do you live way out here all by yourself, Miss Cantrell?"

She laid her hand on his shoulder as she walked him into the store. "Not anymore, Mr. July Johnson . . . not anymore."

— *Two* —

BOTH THOUGHTS THAT FLASHED through Carolina Cantrell's mind the moment she opened her eyes disgusted her.

The bedding is filthy.

And so am I!

You could never live in the West, Carolina. There's just too much . . . dirt!

The cobwebs lacing the rafters above her loft bed caught the morning sunlight that beamed through newly scrubbed windows and gave a decorative ambiance to the musty room. Her long, heavy gown proved extremely warm, and she had spent most of the night under only a single flannel sheet.

At least, she thought it was flannel.

Parisian slippers waited by the bed, and she tucked her bare toes quickly into them to avoid the rough wood floor. Carolina glanced over the half-wall railing down at the store. The front door was open. July Johnson, in a clerk's white apron, was sweeping the porch. His shaggy brown hair looked oiled down from a center part.

Carolina slipped a knit shawl around her shoulders and neck, more for modesty than warmth. The broom on his shoulder and his lips puckered in a whistle, Johnson strolled back into the store.

"Good morning, July," Carolina called from the loft.

Youthful enthusiasm reflected up at her. "Mornin', Miss Cantrell! Did you sleep well?"

She leaned her hand on the well-worn but freshly scoured railing. "Much better than I thought, thank you. How about you? Is that cot sufficient?"

I'm not used to seeing anyone before I've had a chance to fix myself.

I wonder why this doesn't bother me. It's like being out here frees a person from the social customs of the East. But it doesn't free me from being decent and proper!

"Yes, ma'am. It felt like a hotel in St. Louis after sleepin' on the ground for a couple of months. Eh, I built the fire up, got some tea water boilin', watered your horse, and swept the store. What would you like for me to do next?"

He's like a puppy trying to please. "What time is it?"

"If that brass clock with the broken glass at the back of the store is workin', it's quarter to seven."

The aroma of a store full of merchandise mixed with the heat of the woodstove reminded Carolina of the Plaza Central in Veracruz. "Oh, my . . . what are you doing getting up so early?"

"I guess I'm a little anxious. I ain't never been no assistant manager before."

She tugged at her pierced earlobe. It felt raw. "Mr. Johnson, if you ever expect to go any higher than assistant manager, you'll have to improve your language skills."

"Ma'am?"

"'I have never been' is much better than 'I ain't never been.'"

His mouth dropped open a little, and he stared up at her with round blue eyes. In the silence Carolina fidgeted with her shawl and glanced down to make sure her gown was buttoned clear up to her neck.

Even with a shawl, I shouldn't stand here in my flannel gown to visit with a young man. "Is something wrong, July?"

"Oh . . . no, Miss Cantrell. It's just been a long time since anyone cared about the way I talk. No offense, ma'am, but for a minute you reminded me of my mother."

Your mother! Young man, I am only ten years older than you—not twenty or thirty.

"How old were you when she died?"

"About nine, I reckon. Mama and Daddy both got shot dead when Rosto Rollins and his Texas gang tried to steal that big gold shipment in Custer City." His voice slipped into a monotone, a practiced control of emotion.

"How dreadful!"

"Yes, ma'am . . . but I don't like to think about it anymore. It don't do no good."

She stepped back away from the loft wall and blocked her view of him. "I'll be down shortly and fix us some breakfast."

"No, ma'am, I'll fix breakfast. I've cooked for a crew for over a year. I can make you a tasty meal. Do you like your eggs fried or scrambled?"

Carolina padded back over to the edge of the loft and peered down at July. "Do we have eggs?"

His smile reached from ear to ear. "Yes, ma'am. I discovered six layers down in the brush between here and the river. Bein' there ain't no other place around, I reckon they belong to the store. I fetched four big fresh eggs this morning when I packed water up out of the river." He waved his arms enthusiastically as he talked, the long sleeves of the new white cotton shirt held up by the black garters just above his elbows.

"That's wonderful. I'll be down in a few minutes."

She scooted over to the foot of the bed and stared into her open trunk.

Two weeks—you packed for a two-week trip. Now what are you going to do, Carolina? The dress from yesterday is dirty . . . but so am I. I have to have a bath. A hot bath. A very hot bath. And wash my hair. At least I have my curling irons. Oh, my, I probably smell as musty as this room. Fortunately, no one will notice.

I hope.

I definitely need to make a list. I'll bring a mirror up here. Sweep down the cobwebs. Put curtains on that window. Sort through those boxes of David's. Try to make sense of those ledgers. Clean out the dresser. Perhaps I can hang curtains above the rail, like what I used in Venice.

Yes, I'll have to make a list. Do not allow spontaneous whims to dictate your actions. Do everything on the list. Do nothing that is not on the list. It's the way to accomplish anything worthwhile and bring order out of chaos.

That is, if I were planning to live here permanently and run the store.

Which I'm not.

With the aroma of fresh cologne on her cheeks and eggs frying on the woodstove, Carolina descended the narrow, steep wooden stairs that hugged the back windowless wall of the store. The rail felt smooth from the oil on people's hands.

The big room looked brighter and more cheerful than it had on the previous day. The entire wagonload of new merchandise made the store seem sufficiently stocked.

"Did that noise from the saloon keep you awake much last night, Miss Cantrell?" She couldn't tell if July blushed or merely reflected the heat of the stove.

"Not like I thought it would. I was so tired. I don't suppose you've seen Mr. Starke this morning, have you?"

"Yes, ma'am. He was our first customer today. He banged on the door at daylight and wanted to buy a padlock and key. I put the four bits into the cash box. You can go see for yourself."

"Oh, I trust you, July." *I slept through someone banging on the front door? This is not good, Carolina. Things are happening without your oversight, beyond your control. That cannot happen again!*

She inspected the bottom of a gray-tinted porcelain cup and deemed it sufficiently clean. Then she poured it full of hot water. "Is he going to put a lock on his saloon door?" She scooped tea from the small burlap bag into the perforated spoon and clamped it shut. Then she stirred it into her cup.

"No, ma'am. He put the padlock on the pump. That's why I had to haul water from the river."

Her thin shoulders and arms stiffened, and several drops of tea sloshed to the rough wooden floor. "He did what!" she exploded.

July pointed out the open doorway. "He locked the water pump."

Carolina felt the veins on her neck tighten and throb. "He can't do that! That well is for both businesses!"

"It's okay. It don't take me too long to carry water up. It ain't like we was goin' to take baths or anythin'."

Carolina set the teacup on an unopened wooden box of horseshoe nails and snatched up a pick handle from a barrel of assorted handles.

"Your eggs is about ready!" July insisted in a voice meant to still a storm.

"I'll be right back." The words seemed to shoot out of her piercing brown eyes as well as her narrow, thin lips.

"You want me to come with you?"

"No, I can handle this myself, thank you." She scowled.

"Yes, ma'am," July gulped. "You ain't goin' to kill him, are you, Miss Cantrell?"

That remains to be seen! "Of course not!"

The heels of her heavy shoes banged on the wooden floor as she marched out the front door, across the uncovered front porch, and up to the open door of the saloon. She hammered the pick handle against the casing of the doorway.

"Mr. Starke, I want to talk to you!"

A rasped voice rumbled out of the darkness. "I don't want to talk to you!"

With her left hand on her narrow waist, she kept the pick handle raised in her right. "Mr. Starke, would you please come here!"

The answer rolled out, half belligerent, half intoxicated. "Not with you standin' there like Carrie Nation. If you want to talk to me, you come in here."

"I have never in my life entered such an ungodly establishment, and I'm certainly not going to begin now."

"Your brother weren't so picayune."

She held the pick handle like a club in front of her with both hands and took one step into the dark, dirty room filled with whiskey fumes. "Mr. Starke, why did you fasten a lock on the pump?"

"It's my well and my pump. I can do whatever I want. I decided to lock it so nobody would steal my water."

She squinted her eyes and tried to focus on the shadowy figure leaning against the distant bar. He spun the cylinder of a revolver he held in his hand. "Half of that well belongs to me. My brother helped you dig it, no doubt."

"Yes, ma'am, he did. But if you draw a line right out into the yard from the wall that separates the saloon from the store, you'll see that the well is clearly on the saloon side. Therefore, it belongs to me!"

She lowered her hands to her side. "That's ludicrous!"

"I don't know what that means, but you're the one that made up the rules. You said ever'thing over there belongs to you, and the well ain't over there. Now if you ain't going to come in and buy a drink, I'll ask you to leave so you don't scare away my customers."

Short, shallow breaths made each word choppy. "How dare you . . ." *Relax, Carolina. Relax. Don't let him see you flustered.*

"I did dare."

Keep control. You are in charge here. "We are not through with this matter," she fumed.

"Nope. I don't reckon we are. My offer still stands. I'll buy you out for $100."

"I wouldn't sell to you for $2,000!" She spun around and stomped back to the store.

Why did I say that, Lord? Of course I'd sell for $2,000. Starke is a disgusting bug, but a fairly harmless, disgusting bug. Just sell out and go home, Carolina. That's the whole purpose of this trip. You didn't travel all this way just to squash bugs, did you?

After she tossed the pick handle to the floor, she scooped up her cup of tea and slumped down at the small oak table near the woodstove.

"He's incorrigible!"

"Yes, ma'am. I reckon you're right, whatever that nobby word means. I heard ever' word—from both of ya."

She sat with her back perfectly straight, but her hands quivered enough to make her worry about spilling tea on her dress. "How in the world a brother of mine could team up with such a man is beyond me. Perhaps David was ill."

"Here's your eggs, Miss Cantrell. I'm makin' some starter for biscuits, but it won't be ready for two days, so I figured we might eat some of these crackers."

"The right to water is a basic human privilege. Who does he think he is? It's immoral—that's what it is. I shall just have to pay a visit to the sheriff."

July Johnson slid into the chair across the table with a tin plate heaped with fried pork and eggs. "How's your tea, Miss Cantrell?"

"'Draw a line in the dirt,' he said. Where did you say those chickens were?"

"Between the river and the store. You ain't tried your eggs yet."

"Between the store and the river, but not between the saloon and the river?" she pressed.

"Eh . . . yes, ma'am. Say, I did notice some cherry preserves up on the shelf, but they're waxed tight. I didn't know if they was for eatin' or sellin'."

"Then the chickens are ours. Mr. Starke does not get one egg— do you hear? Not one egg!"

"Yes, ma'am. How about them preserves? Shall I fetch 'em down for us?"

"The privy!" she shouted. "It's out back on our side, correct?"

"Eh, yes, Miss Cantrell . . . but it ain't much."

"We'll put a padlock on it and see how he likes that!" she announced.

Johnson put the forkful of eggs back on his plate. "I wouldn't do that, ma'am."

"Why not?" She sipped her tepid tea.

"'Cause I don't reckon Mr. Starke is one of them that cares much whether he does his business in a privy or not. You lock the door, and things could get a lot more rank than they are . . . if you catch my meanin'. No offense, ma'am."

Carolina sighed and set down her teacup. "Yes, of course. You're right, July. No lock on the privy."

"If you want, we could dig another well. I dug one out at camp. In fact, that crate over there has the hand pump we was goin' to install at the diggin's. We got the shovels and ever'thing right here in the store."

She strolled toward a large wooden crate labeled "Chicago, Illinois." "Can we dig one next to this back wall and have the pump right here in the store?"

"I reckon so." July dove back into his breakfast.

"How long does it take to dig a well?"

Johnson swallowed a lump of ham and coughed. "You mean, just you and me diggin'?"

Carolina glanced down at her soft, thin white hands. *I've never dug in a garden, let alone a well.* "Eh, yes, how long would it take us?"

"Depends on where the water level is, but this close to the river, it cain't be too bad. I reckon in three days, providin' the ground's not too rocky and we have the timbers to line it right. I spotted a roll of wire screen over there. We could use it to keep the trash out. We could have a first-class well."

How old is this boy?

"How do you know all these things?"

"Shoot, Miss Cantrell, ever'one knows how to set a well, don't they?" July's fork scraped across the tin plate.

"Perhaps they do in Montana. I can assure you they don't in Maryland." She ground a little pepper onto the eggs and then stabbed a small piece. "These are very good, July."

"Thank ya, Miss Cantrell." He beamed. "I told ya I was a good cook. You want me to start diggin' that well right away?"

"Let me think this through first. You know what the Bible says—we need to count the cost before we begin."

July scratched his head. "It talks about diggin' wells in the Bible?"

"I believe the Bible refers to building a tower, but the same principles apply."

"You don't say!" He scratched the back of his neck and stared down at his plate. "I don't know nothin' about the Bible. It talks about heaven, don't it?"

"Yes, it does. But it talks about lots of other things too. I'm sure you know some of the stories. Everyone knows about Jonah and the fish or Daniel in the lions' den or Adam and Eve in the garden of Eden."

"They was where?"

"You really don't know those stories?" *A young man can grow up in America in the 1880s and never hear Bible stories?*

He finally looked her in the eyes. "No, ma'am, but I can read."

"And you've never heard any Bible stories at all? You've never heard about Jesus?"

"Jesus? Oh, yeah, I've heard about Him all my life, but my mama made me promise I'd never use them kind of words."

"Well, Mr. July Johnson . . . I think we'll just take a little time every morning and read some Bible stories. Would that be all right with you?"

"Yes, ma'am." His beaming smile reflected sincere delight.

Mr. July Johnson, your emotions are always right on your face. Someday you'll be a lousy poker player—and a handsome husband.

She slipped another bite of cold eggs into her mouth. "Now, July, why don't you get us some of those cherry preserves? These crackers are about as palatable as a washrag. I'll go upstairs and get my Bible. We might as well read a little right now."

I hope it won't be the part about turning the other cheek!

Carolina nailed a piece of clothesline high along the wall line of the loft rail and was draping a piece of red and white gingham over it when July hollered from the open doorway, "Here come three men on Texas ponies!"

She secured the cloth with wooden clothespins and scurried down the stairs. "Are they drovers?"

"Nope. They look like bummers to me."

Carolina scooted past a barrel of picks and shovels and stood alongside July. "What do you mean, bummers?"

"Them that always show up too late at a gold camp without a dollar in their pocket. They're the kind that lay around all day and get into trouble at night." His youthful hand rested on the handle of his buckhorn hunting knife in the scabbard on his belt.

"You think they're headed for the saloon?"

"I reckon."

The men walked their horses across the yard toward the building. All three were in their late twenties or early thirties. They wore cheap, soiled suits and vests, with shirt collars buttoned at the top. The man on the lead horse wore a round hat with a pointed crown, and his chin sported a week's worth of beard. From his new leather holster, strapped around the outside of his coat, peeked a black-handled revolver.

The next man's blond hair hung down to his collar from under a black Mexican sombrero with silver-threaded stitching. And the final man looked too big for his horse. His shirttail was untucked, and a tall white feather stuck up from the right side of his wide-brimmed hat.

All three were slumped in their saddles, and they dismounted as if unused to forking a pony for any distance.

Hardrock Starke bolted out the doorway of the saloon. "You boys look mighty thirsty—mighty thirsty. Drinks is a real bargain early in the day!"

The lead man studied Starke briefly and then looked at July and Carolina. "You all got a store there?"

"The store's over on this side," July called out.

"She'll gouge you!" Starke hollered.

The blond man started up the stairs toward the store. "Well, sir, if I'm goin' to be gouged, she's a mighty purdy one to do it." He tipped his hat in her direction. Carolina and July stepped back into the store as all three men entered.

"Gentlemen, what can we get for you?" Carolina asked.

"My name's Bud, and the one with the scroungy beard is Diggs, and the one with the new holster is One-shot McColister."

She backed up toward the far wall as the men spread out into different aisles, their eyes searching the shelves.

"You want me to get the shotgun down?" July whispered, as he slipped back by her.

She shook her head as the one called Bud approached. "Here's what we need. We just got off the train in Billings last night and heard some old freighter talk about a new strike up in Devil's Canyon in Wyoming Territory."

Diggs pulled a watch out of his vest. "Your clock's ten minutes fast," he noted. "We've ridden all night."

"Why?" July asked.

"Because they aren't going to beat us there this time."

"Who?"

"The horde." Diggs jammed his watch back into his pocket.

"What horde?"

"The horde of stampeders that shows up every time someone hollers gold!"

Diggs sorted through a stack of identical gold pans. "This time we're gettin' there first."

"We rode straight through from Billings," One-shot blustered as he made a feeble attempt at tucking in his shirt. "The others waited 'til morning for supplies, but the old man said you'd have everything we need out here."

July stepped up to the blond-haired man. "You payin' in coin or gold dust?"

A wide, gentle smile broke across Bud's face as he pushed the big sombrero to the back of his head. "Your clerk gets right to the point, don't he?"

"I'm the assistant manager of this store," July announced.

"Well, Mr. Assistant Manager," Bud laughed, "we'll pay in gold and silver coin. Is that acceptable?"

"Hey, you men want a drink, don't ya?" the dirty and unshaven Hardrock Starke shouted from the doorway.

"Why in blazes would we want to drink at this time of the morning?" Diggs shrugged.

One-shot pulled a spade out of a barrel and examined the grain in the handle. "Ain't the time to celebrate yet," he mumbled in a voice that reminded Carolina of the waves that crashed into the rocks at Lighthouse Point on St. Simons Island.

"Hah! Teetotalin' bummers! I got no use for 'em!" Starke stomped back toward the saloon.

Bud pulled a list out of his pocket. "Here's what we need, and we'd better divide it evenly into three bundles so we don't load any horse too much."

Johnson stared over at One-shot McColister. "One Texas pony seems to be loaded pretty good already."

The big man scowled and let his right hand drop to his pistol grip.

"July!" Carolina scolded. "Don't be impertinent!"

"Nothin' personal, sir. I was thinkin' your horses might last longer if only two carried the load. You ain't exactly got big old Montana horses."

Bud let his sombrero dangle on his back, held only by the stampede string about his red bandanned neck. "We're going to put the supplies on the horses and just walk ourselves."

A spade. Pick. Three gold pans. Mercury. Pork. Flour. Coffee. Molasses. Raisins. Frying pan. Coffeepot. Three tin cups. Three tin forks. Three tin plates. Small medicine chest. Three large wool blankets. Fifty pounds of beans. Five pounds of sugar. Three Cuban cigars.

When all was paid for, the massive bundles had to be loaded on the horses. With the money secure in the cash box, Carolina and July stood on the porch and observed the men tying down their supplies.

"At least with you walking the horses, they'll be fresh if you run across any Crow or Cheyenne. That's reservation land down there. They don't like prospectors too much. You could always drop your packs and race to the rocks."

"Say, that reminds me," Bud added. "The old man in Billings said there was a little boy out this way that had actually been to Devil's Canyon. We sure would like to talk to him."

Carolyn slipped her hand onto July's shoulder. They were exactly the same height. "There aren't any little boys around here."

"I can see that." One-shot shrugged.

July bounced to the edge of the porch, swinging his legs to the dirt yard. He studied the big man with the new holster. "Can I ask you a question, Mr. McColister?"

"I reckon so."

"How'd you get the name One-shot?"

"July!" Carolina implored.

McColister continued to tie his load. "Ask them." He nodded to the other two.

"Is it because he's such a good shot?" July asked the one with the sombrero.

"It does have somethin' to do with his shootin'," Diggs hooted.

Bud led his horse to the porch as he waited for the others. "McColister there just might be the worst shot west of St. Louis."

He grinned. "Me and Diggs call him One-shot because if he ever did get in a gunfight, that would be all he'd get off—just one shot. After that, he'd be dead!"

Carolina noticed that McColister joined in with the other two in the laughter, and she allowed herself to smile.

Bud pushed his big sombrero back. "Well, Miss Cantrell, next time you see us we'll undoubtedly be rich hombres!"

"Yep," One-shot added, "we just might come back and buy up all your stock."

"I'll sell you the whole store right now for $2,000," she offered.

Bud stared at her for a moment and then pulled his big hat back onto his head. "No, ma'am. Even if we had the money, which we don't, we wouldn't buy you out. A purdy gal runnin' a store is a wonderful sight. Gives a man somethin' to think about on a lonely night. Chances are, we'll have plenty of those."

Carolina felt her face flush.

There are some advantages to a region that is in short supply of women. You get to be the center of attention more often. Of course, I don't want to be the center of attention.

Bud pointed to the south. "We figured on headin' due south until we hit the Big Horn River and then go upstream about thirty miles. Will that get us there?"

"It might also get you an Indian attack or an army escort back to Montana," July informed him.

"Sometimes you got to take a chance to make a fortune, son."

Diggs looked at his watch and then stuffed it back in his vest. "Can't make a penny sitting around wishing. Come on, or they'll gain on us."

"Who will?" July inquired.

Bud tugged on his buckskin's lead rope. "All them other stampeders."

Carolina and July watched as the three hiked up the hillside to the south, each leading a well-loaded horse.

"You think they'll really find gold?" Carolina asked.

"Nope. I'm not sure they'll even find the Big Horn River. But lookin' for gold is kind of like playin' chuck-a-luck. Ever' once in a great while, even a tinhorn strikes it rich. That's why they're all out here."

She looked into July's big blue eyes. "Chuck-a-what?"

"It's a gamblin' game, Miss Cantrell. And it's one that you should never play!"

Is he really only fourteen? "I'll remember that."

July reached around behind his back and retied his apron. "Do you think there will be other gold seekers comin' through here?"

"Perhaps. But these three said the others were going to buy supplies in Billings. I presume everyone will be in a hurry. It's doubtful that they'll stop here."

July walked to the edge of the porch and stared at the side of the store. "Shall I start diggin' that well near the window?"

Carolina paced the planks and scanned the yard. She tapped the toe of her lace-up boot on the rough wood deck. "July, that rain barrel is empty, right?"

"Yes, ma'am."

"Well, hitch up my horse to the buggy. You can pull the seat out and use it like a wagon. Then load up the barrel. Go soak it in the river awhile, then put it back on the buggy, and bucket it full. We'll park the buggy right here by our end of the porch, and that should give us enough water for a couple of days. Perhaps by then I'll decide if we should dig our own well."

"You really goin' to sell the store for $2,000?"

"That would be nice. I told you yesterday I probably wouldn't be here long."

"I'm kind of hopin' it won't be for a month or so." July stared down at his worn brown boots. "I think I'm takin' a fancy to this kind of job."

"You seem to be a natural at it."

His blue eyes sparkled.

A fourteen-year-old girl will have her dreams fulfilled someday.

"Miss Carolina, where do you want me to put that buggy seat while I'm haulin' water?"

"Let's shove it up here on the porch. We can use it for a divan. Do you need help with it?"

"No, ma'am . . . but I almost forgot. I ain't cleaned up them breakfast dishes yet."

"Go on, Mr. Johnson. Fetch the water. I'll wash the dishes. Quite a few things could still use some scrubbing around here."

Including me!

Carolina scoured the table, counter, and dishes. She felt her hands begin to blister as she mopped the rough floor. July stuck his head through the doorway. "There's a peddler comin', and he's got a handsome-lookin' dark-haired woman with him!"

Handsome woman?

Carolina thought about pulling the sleeves of her dress down, but they were so wrinkled she left them pushed up to her elbows. *It is summer. Surely bare forearms are acceptable in this land.* Her dress felt sticky; the black ringlet curls stuck to her forehead. She stepped out to the porch as the high-sided paneled wagon rolled up in front of the store.

"Tell Cantrell I've got his order here!" a middle-aged bearded man shouted from the driver's seat.

Carolina eyed the woman in the tight-fitting gray suit. Her black hair cascaded in curls and waves down her shoulders and almost to her waist. She had dark, full eyebrows that seemed to be slanted in permanent mystery. A wide black velvet and bone choker circled her neck.

A long, dark skirt billowed across the woman's lap and hung to her ankles. Her blouse held Carolina's attention. There were absolutely no sleeves, and the woman's dark-complected arms were exposed completely up to her shoulders. The scooped lace neckline made it difficult to tell which part was blouse and which part woman.

Oh . . . that kind of "handsome-lookin' woman"!

"I said, tell Mr. Cantrell I brought in his order!" the man repeated, and he climbed down from the flat-roofed wagon.

Carolina turned her gaze away from the woman. "July, don't stand and stare. Put that buggy seat over here," she fussed.

July pointed back to the peddler. "He wants to speak to Mr. Cantrell."

She turned to the man, who now stood by the edge of the porch, which was almost three feet higher than ground level. "Excuse me, my mind was, eh, preoccupied. Mr. Cantrell was murdered a few weeks ago. I'm Miss Carolina Cantrell, David's sister. I operate the store now."

He pulled off his wide-brimmed, tan beaver felt hat. "Pleased to meet you, ma'am. My name is Tegan McDoud. Most of 'em just call me Tuffy. What happened to the other man—the one who smelt like a pigsty and was usually drunk?"

She glanced at her short shadow and reached up to brush back her hair around her ears as she avoided looking at the woman in the wagon. "He still runs the saloon. We separated the businesses."

McDoud unfastened the last button on his vest and slapped dust off his trousers with his hat. "This is a mighty tough place for an Eastern lady such as yourself to run a business."

Thank heavens, at least he can tell I'm from the East. "I'm quite experienced at running both retail and wholesale businesses."

"I ain't callin' you to account for that. But are you used to the rough characters that ride up out of the brush? A third of them ought to be in jail, and another third ought to be hung. Don't mean to discourage you. It's your life, not mine." He jammed his hat back on his head. "Now your brother did order some goods, and I—"

"Mr. McDoud, before we go any further, I didn't know my brother had an order with you. I'm not sure I'll have the funds yet to pay for them."

"Well, I don't give credit," he lectured. Then his grin revealed tobacco-stained teeth. "But this is your lucky day, Miss Cantrell. The order is prepaid."

"It is?"

"Yep. Now don't ever say Tuffy McDoud isn't an honest man. I could have fed you a big line and double-charged you, but that ain't the way I do business." He glanced over at July Johnson, who continued to stare at the woman in the black lace blouse. "Boy! Come and help me unload these goods. Miss Cantrell and the 'Marquesa' can sit and visit awhile."

He and July moseyed to the back of the once brightly painted wagon.

The 'Marquesa' of what? Carolina turned toward the woman in the wagon. "We haven't been introduced. I'm Carolina Cantrell."

"I know about you," the dark-haired woman smirked.

"You know me?"

It was a powerful, almost baritone voice. "I know you grew up in Virginia, are used to having your own way, are shocked by my blouse, consider yourself a woman of strong faith, and one year ago were jilted by a man you had set your hopes on."

Carolina felt a sharp reflexive pain shoot down her neck. Her knees locked up. She felt dizzy. "That's ludicrous!" she snapped.

With a wry, noncommittal smile and raised eyebrows, the Marquesa replied, "Which part?"

"In your great knowledge of me, you must know that more than once I was approached by Gypsies in Bavaria who gave me the same kind of prattle," Carolina's small brown eyes narrowed, "after which they either tried to sell me something or steal something. How about you? Are you selling or stealing?"

At that accusation, the Marquesa leaped off the wagon. Her heels slammed into the hard-packed Montana dirt. The woman staggered back a step or two and favored her right ankle. With some obvious pain, she caught her breath and looked up at Carolina. "I will not be called a liar, a thief, or a Gypsy!"

"Nor will I be called a spinster or a shrew."

The woman bent over to brush back her skirt and rub her ankle.

If she comes up with a knife, I'll know I'm in Budapest again. Carolina slipped her hand into the deep pocket of her long green dress and felt the ivory grips of the silver-plated rimfire .41 derringer.

"Do you want us to carry this inside or leave it on the porch?" McDoud puffed as he and July Johnson labored to slide a huge galvanized trough full of packaged goods on the edge of the porch.

The sound of McDoud's voice deflated Carolina's anger. She deserted the confrontation and stepped over to examine the merchandise. "My heavens, what is all of this?"

"Mainly fabric yardage, sewing supplies, and store-boughts. There's some fancy ladies' things in that gold box," McDoud explained.

"No, I meant this zinc trough. Is it part of David's order?"

"Yes, ma'am. It was special-ordered from San Francisco."

"What's it for?"

"It's a bathtub. And a small one at that. Cain't say I know why your brother ordered it, since he was this close to the river. Maybe he had a customer."

A bathtub! Big brother, how did you know I would need this?

McDoud slumped on the porch and wiped the sweat from his forehead with his sleeve. "Shall we leave her here?"

Carolina's head spun toward the peddler. "Leave who here?"

"This bathtub. Do you want it here or inside?"

"I definitely want it inside."

"Well, come on, Mr. Assistant Manager." Tuffy McDoud motioned to July. "Let's tote that in and then go have a drink at the saloon. You are a drinkin' man, ain't ya?"

"No, sir. I'm only fourteen."

"That's good, son. It's a nasty habit. Many a man would have a longer life if he'd never drank liquor or chased loose women. But, of course, that ain't much of a life."

"Mr. McDoud!" Carolina interrupted.

"Eh . . . right. Sorry. It's best you listen to your mama here, son."

"She ain't my mama. We ain't no kin at all."

Mother? I look old enough to be his mother?

"I'll let you and the women visit while I pay a call on the old saloon and try to burn the hide off the inside of my belly."

The Marquesa limped a little as she climbed the stairs, yet waltzed into the store ahead of the others.

Visit with her? We have nothing to talk about! How does she know about me? Have we met before? Why did she say those things?

Carolina led the tub-toting men into the store and motioned for them to set it down near the counter.

"Son, I'll give you two bits if you'll water my two horses and grain them a little."

"Yes, sir." Then he turned to Carolina. "Is that all right, Miss Cantrell?"

"Certainly."

"After I do that, I'll drive that buggy down to the river and fill up the rain barrel," July proposed.

She nodded approval.

Tuffy McDoud stepped toward the middle of the room and then turned back to Carolina. "You blocked off the door to the saloon?"

"Yes. You'll have to use the one out on the porch."

"Cain't blame you none. The alcohol fumes themselves is enough to scare most folks off. I figure someday a man will strike a match, and the whole building will blow like a gas-filled mine shaft." Then he turned to the dark-haired woman. "Marquesa, I'll only be about ten minutes."

McDoud and Johnson shuffled out of the room. The Marquesa surveyed Carolina as she fumbled with the packaged goods in the tub. After she lugged a large string-tied bundle wrapped in brown paper to the counter, Carolina took a deep breath.

"I'm afraid we got off to a poor start. Please, help yourself to some tea on the stove and sit down if you'd like. Make yourself at home while I tend to these bundles and discover what my brother purchased."

As the Marquesa waltzed to the stove, Carolina scooted around behind the counter so she could open the package and still keep an eye on the woman.

"You seem to think you know me; however, I don't know you at all. I don't even know your name."

"I like being called the Marquesa." The words shot out of the woman's mouth like a dart hurled toward a corkboard.

"Marquess is a title, of course. The feminine is marquise. Just what exactly is a marquesa?"

"It's Spanish. You don't think this is merely a tan, do you?"

"Well, normally, a marquise is married to a marquess, who ranks above an earl but lower than a duke. However, in this country we have a habit of disregarding titles of nobility unless they're spoken in jest."

"My real name is no concern of yours," the woman informed her. She sipped her tea from a peach-colored porcelain cup with a dainty, chipped handle.

Lord, I really am trying to be civil.

"All right, you're a woman of mystery. Are you and Mr. McDoud married—or perhaps business associates?"

"I fail to see why that is any concern of yours," the Marquesa announced. She gazed into the bottom of her teacup. "I can read tea leaves. Would you be interested in a reading?"

"I most certainly would not! And I will not have occult activity in my store!"

The package contained ten men's cotton shirts. She carried the stack across the store to a shelf with men's clothing and stacked them on top of an empty ammunition crate. When she turned back around, the Marquesa loomed behind the counter.

"What are you doing back there?" Carolina demanded.

"Making myself at home." She unleashed a very professional smile.

"Well, make yourself at home over by the table, please. I need to stand back there while I open these packages." Carolina gathered several more small ones from the tub and waited for the woman to exit from behind her counter. She caught a strong whiff of lilac perfume.

Did she get into the cash box? I've got to know. I can't look while she's watching me. . . . Just go on, Marquesa. Get in the wagon with the peddler and go away.

The second package contained six flannel nightshirts. They were all a dull solid gray with an embroidered blue diamond on the left side of the three-button, collarless neck. The Marquesa lounged next to the table, her dark eyes circling the room surveying the merchandise.

"Would you please stack these over by the shirts?" Carolina asked her.

The woman shrugged and scooped up the nightshirts. "Rather boring, aren't they?" she mused.

"They're for men," Carolina replied.

"That's what I meant," the woman smirked. She turned her back to the counter and meandered toward the distant shelf.

Carolina hurried to check out the cash box. To her relief, the funds were untouched.

Her back still toward Carolina, the Marquesa called out, "You didn't really think I was interested in your $26.42, did you?"

Carolina glared at the back of the woman's thick, black wavy hair. *Lord, there is something very, very wrong about this woman. I want her out of here. I'd rather not have to force her out at gunpoint.*

"You've given me no reason to trust you." Carolina retrieved another package and unwrapped it. "And perhaps I've given you none either," she added. "So why don't we call it a standoff? You go your way, and I'll continue with my work here."

"Oh, no, I'm staying here until Tuffy's finished his drinking binge."

"No, you aren't."

"You'd kick me out of the store?"

"I'm asking you to leave."

"And if I don't?"

"Why wouldn't you?" Carolina slipped her right hand into the pocket of her dress. She still held the brown paper-wrapped bundle in her left. "We have absolutely nothing to talk about."

"We could talk about Jacob Hardisty."

The package tumbled from Carolina's hand. Her chin dropped. "Ja-Jacob? You know Jacob?"

"You haven't figured it out yet, have you?"

"Who are you?"

"I'm the one Jacob left you for."

Carolina suddenly felt plain . . . dull . . . colorless. "The actress?"

"Yes. How do you like my Gypsy performance?"

"You've been playing a part?"

"Carolina Katherine Cantrell, we all spend our lives playing parts. Some of us do it on stage and get paid, but we are all acting."

"What's that supposed to mean?" Carolina slowly inched out from behind the counter.

"Think about it." The Marquesa moved down a crowded aisle toward the open front door. "But don't pout—he left me too. For a real marquise."

That's how she knew all of that about me! What else did Jacob tell her?

A loud bang followed by a curse and a scream and then two more crashes echoed from the saloon. Both women rushed out to the porch. Tuffy McDoud staggered out of the saloon. Blood trick-led from his nose and matted in his mustache.

"What happened?" Carolina asked.

"He tried to serve me watered-down rye whiskey—that's what happened." He gestured to the Marquesa. "Come on, it's time to get back on the road."

"Where's Mr. Starke?"

"Asleep."

"Oh?"

"I busted a chair over his head. He might be sleeping for a good spell."

McDoud and the Marquesa climbed up in the wagon. He tossed a two-bit piece to Carolina. "This is for the boy."

"We still have things to talk about," the Marquesa goaded Carolina.

"I'm not sure what that would be."

"Jacob's here in the West, you know."

Carolina's mouth dropped open. "He's out here?"

"Nice, very nice. Coy. Puzzled. Naive. That's very good. Come on, Miss Cantrell, he's the reason you and I both came out here, and you know it."

"That's certainly not true!"

"I'll be at the Bella Union in Billings for four weeks. If you're in town, stop by and catch my act. After that, I'll go on to Helena and Silver City. I'll find him sooner or later—unless you find him first."

"I have no intention of looking for Jacob. Why do you want to find him?"

"To kill him, of course. Unless you do the job for me first."

"Why in the world would I want to kill him?"

The Marquesa turned to McDoud. "Isn't she delightful?" Then she whipped back around so fast her hair flowed in the breeze. "You really ought to be in theater. So wholesomely convincing."

"Sorry to break into your chitchat, ladies." McDoud wiped his bleeding nose with a soiled blue bandanna. "But I've got to reach the sutler at the agency before dark."

Carolina watched the dust column of the departing wagon for a long time. *She knew I was here. But how? She came by just to throw out that gauntlet. Lord, how do I know she told the truth about Jacob? You know I didn't come out here to find him. Just the opposite.*

Carolina had all the packages unwrapped, the goods inventoried and stacked on the shelves, the wrapping paper neatly folded beneath the counter, and the string balled by the time July Johnson drove up with the water barrel in the buggy. She stepped over to meet him.

"They leave already?" he called as he pulled up close to the porch. His face had been scrubbed clean and his hair wetted and combed.

"Yes."

"I surely hoped to see the Marquesa again. I reckon I never saw any girl that purdy before."

"Girl? She was twice your age."

"The heart don't know no age, Miss Cantrell."

"The heart doesn't know any age," she corrected.

"Yes, ma'am, I couldn't agree with you more," he sighed.

Oh, great! A sage and frisky fourteen-year-old.

"Pour some more cold water on your face, July. You'll get over it."

"Yes, ma'am. Does it show that much?" He blushed.

"Just a little." She fought to hold back a wide smile. *Lord, I have no idea how to raise a fourteen-year-old boy.*

"Find yourself a snack, Mr. Johnson. Then we'll try to carry that empty tub up to my loft."

"You ain't goin' to sell it?"

"Not as long as I live here."

"But you ain't got a stove up there to heat water," he cautioned.

"I'll just have to tote some water up from down here, won't I?"

"You goin' to take a bath right now?" He rocked back and forth on his toes.

She looked at July and shook her head. *Now there is one enthusiastic young man.* "No, not now. Perhaps tonight . . . or in the morning."

It was almost an hour later before they yanked and pushed the galvanized tub into the loft. The cloth wall made the room seem fairly private, but the fact that there was no door at the top of the stairs led Carolina to cram the tub in between the bed and the dresser.

"You might roll out of bed and drown," July teased.

"I'll remember that."

He is definitely not a little boy.

A loud string of muffled curses filtered through the wall from the saloon as they clomped down the stairway.

"What's wrong with Mr. Starke?" July quizzed.

"I believe he has a headache."

"From drinkin' too much?"

"From breaking a chair with his head."

A wagon clattered into the yard. July raced to the doorway. "It's four men in a loaded-down farm wagon!" he shouted.

"Did they stop?"

"Yes, ma'am. Three of them are headed this way. One's stayin' with the wagon." July scooted back inside the store.

Suddenly the bright light of a Montana summer afternoon reflecting through the doorway was blocked by three tall men crowding through it.

Two wore shotgun chaps, the other a black vest with silver conchos.

One had ears so big they seemed to hold up his hat.

Another had a scar across his forehead that made his right eye look half-closed.

The third grinned, revealing two missing front teeth.

All three stood bowlegged, their revolvers strapped low in well-worn holsters.

I can always tell in one glance what a man is like. It's a gift. These men are bank robbers. Or highway bandits. Or rustlers. Obviously, it's some gang. Why was it I needed to be in Montana? Carolina shoved her right hand into the deep pocket of her dress and clutched the little two-shot revolver.

"Gentlemen, can we help you?" Carolina's voice cracked in a lilting sort of way.

All three wide-brimmed cowboy hats were swooped off the heads. With hat-creased, unkempt hair and mostly white foreheads, they stepped closer.

"Ma'am, we was wonderin' if anyone had come through here yet lookin' for the Devil's Canyon diggin's?"

"Several came this morning." She suddenly felt like a schoolteacher lecturing students on the first day of class.

The blond one with the black vest looked a tough eighteen. He turned to the others. "Then we're on the right trail!"

"We'd be obliged, ma'am, if you could tell us what direction they're headin'."

"Mr. Johnson is the assistant manager here. I believe he could tell you better than I."

July beamed and stepped up to the men. "They was goin' straight south to the Little Big Horn, then upstream to Devil's Canyon."

"How do we find this Devil's Canyon? What does it look like?"

"It looks so rugged only the Devil could live there. . . . I mean, that's what folks tell me," July offered.

"Thank ya." Then the blond man turned to Carolina and nodded. "Ma'am, appreciate your time. Excuse us. We was expectin' some mean, old cuss out here, and you . . . well, you kind of flustered us."

"Purdy women always fluster Larry Roy," the toothless one teased.

The third man spoke up. "The truth of the matter is, if this was a big shindig night, miss, the three of us would probably go out in the alley and beat each other to a pulp seein' who would get to dance with you first."

"Oh, my . . . if this were such an event, I assure you I'd save a dance for each of you." She flashed her totally emotionless smile.

"We might take you up on that. Don't you go backin' out on us. If we find gold up there, we'll come and throw us a big roof-rattlin' blowout right on your porch," Larry Roy insisted.

"Well, I wish you God's speed and His protection. That's reservation land you're headed for. Don't jeopardize your lives. Gold isn't worth dying for."

"Yes, ma'am."

"Do you need any more supplies?"

"We purdy much got our outfits in Billings," the scar-faced one announced.

"I can see that."

"You got any false teeth?" the third man asked.

"I'm afraid not."

"You'll hardly recognize me when I become rich. I'll be sportin' those fancy porcelain teeth."

"You got any tea, ma'am? These two bought supplies, but all we're haulin' is Arbuckles."

"I have one-pound and three-pound sacks of tea."

"Give me a three-pounder and one pound of sugar, please."

When the three men left, they packed out several more bundles of supplies. From his doorway, Horatio Starke tried to yell them back to buy a drink, but they ignored him and tipped their hats to Carolina. *Okay, maybe I was wrong about those three. But they certainly look disreputable.*

Didn't they, Lord?

Sometimes I feel like a rabbit running with a pack of wolves. What am I doing out here in Montana?

"You're ruinin' my business!" Starke hollered. "You standin' there lookin' like a temperance organizer has them all too worried to come in and drink."

"You are welcome to buy me out at any time. Of course, the price goes up with all the new inventory."

He spat a wad of tobacco across the porch. It splashed near her feet.

"Mr. Starke, would you please spit on your side of the porch!"

She hiked inside the store and then emerged with a large piece of chalk. Carolina stooped down and dragged the white chalk across the worn wooden porch.

"That side is yours. This side is mine."

"Yours and mine, yours and mine. This is all just a game to you!" he muttered and stomped back into the saloon.

Several more argonauts stopped by for supplies before the sun dropped below the rolling, rocky hills to the west. All were on their way to the fabled Devil's Canyon claim.

Carolina tallied the day's receipts and toted the cash box up to the loft as July fried potatoes and ham on the woodstove. On her way down the stairs, she wiped the perspiration from her forehead with a towel that lay across her shoulder like a shawl.

"July, it's incredibly warm up in the loft. Cooking on the wood-stove in the summertime is a hot procedure. Let's eat out on the porch tonight."

"Yes, ma'am. Do you want me to hang that Closed sign by the door?"

"I don't think we'll have any more customers tonight, do you?"

"To tell you the truth, Miss Cantrell, I was mighty surprised we had as many as we did. This store ain't on no major trail, no train stop, or nothin'. If it weren't for all of 'em thinkin' they can ride down there to Devil's Canyon and scoop gold nuggets off the ground with a spoon, we wouldn't have no customers at all."

"I do believe you're right, Mr. Johnson. Now how about open-ing one of those airtights of peaches to go with our supper? Whatever the reason, we had a good day. I think we can splurge."

"Yes, ma'am!"

Two men rode in while they ate supper on the porch, but both of them headed straight into the saloon. Carolina dipped a pan into the rain barrel for water to wash dishes. Then she put her hand into the water.

"Even this river water warmed up today. It feels refreshing." She paused for a minute and then glanced at July. "I think I'll take a bath. This water is just perfect the way it is. Help me tote some up there. I'll need several buckets full."

Eight, to be exact.

Carolina banished July to the front porch, but she had him leave the front door open in the hope that some heat in the room would escape. She also had her loft window partially open for the same reason. The quarters were shadowy, but she didn't want to light a lantern.

The water was colder than it had felt on her hand. As she sank into the tub, she gasped and rubbed her bare arms. Then she sank down until the water was almost up to her shoulders.

This might be the best-feeling bath since that four-day train ride from Istanbul to Paris. I don't think I'm cut out for this country. I'll make a

For Sale sign tomorrow. With all the stampeders scurrying to Devil's Canyon, there might be someone who'll want to buy.

She leaned her head back and rested it on the rolled edge of the galvanized tub. Carolina closed her eyes for a minute.

Several minutes.

Clean sheets on the bed.

Clean hair.

Clean body.

What more could a girl ask for?

Well, I suppose I could ask for a husband, children, comfortable home, meaningful life, and exciting challenges. There you go, Carolina. That's what happens when you let your heart override your mind and your will.

I don't intend to let that happen again.

Soon.

July's voice crashed like a cymbal up the stairway. "Miss Cantrell?"

Her eyes shot open. The loft was almost dark. "I'm still getting my bath!" she hollered down.

"Yes, ma'am, but a tall man on a tired horse just rode up."

"Is he headed for the saloon?"

"I cain't tell yet. He's pullin' his saddle and rubbin' down his horse out next to the corral. He definitely plans on stayin' awhile."

Carolina reached over the tub and grabbed the embroidered towel that was neatly folded on the dresser. She quickly began to dry her hair.

"He turned the horse into the corral, and he's headin' for the store, Miss Cantrell," July hollered. "Shall I tell him we're closed?"

"You wait on him, July, but whatever you do, don't let on that I'm up here. I'll be down in a few minutes."

A few minutes later she heard a voice—soft, yet authoritative. "Howdy, son." A tickling feeling slid down Carolina's throat. "Is David up in his office? I need to go up and talk to him."

Jingle-bobs sang as heavy boot heels banged their way across the wooden floor. In the loft above, Carolina Katherine Cantrell pulled a clean flannel sheet straight over the top of her head.

— Three —

"WAIT! MISTER, YOU CAIN'T GO UP THERE!" July Johnson's boot heels crashed across the floor. "There's a lady up there!"

"David has a woman in his loft? So that's the reason for those frilly gingham curtains."

Carolina sank lower into the water. *Frilly? They're as plain as . . . as Pittsburgh.*

"No, Mr. Cantrell is dead. He got murdered some weeks back, and his sister came out from back east to run the place. She's, ah . . . ill-disposed."

From under the flannel sheet, Carolina heard both sets of boots pause at the base of the stairs. *Ill-disposed? If he comes up here, I'll be just plain ill.*

"David's dead? I hadn't heard. I'm mighty sorry to hear that. He was a good friend. Please express my condolences to Mrs., eh . . . "

"Miss Carolina Cantrell." July's voice wavered somewhere between a twelve-year-old's and a twenty-year-old's.

The deep, sturdy voice softened. "A young lady out here operating a place like this?"

"Yes, sir. A very handsome lady."

Carolina tugged the flannel sheet off her head and let it slip to her shoulders. *Thank you, Mr. Johnson, but maybe I shouldn't listen to this conversation.*

She could hear them move toward the front door. Carolina tossed the sheet back onto the thick-mattressed feather bed.

"Son, I wonder—"

"My name's July Johnson. I'm the assistant manager of the store."

"Well, Mr. Johnson," the deep, tired voice sounded laced with a chuckle, "other times when I stopped by, David would allow me to sleep in the hay shed next to the corral. Can I have your permission to do that? Hay's a little softer than the dirt."

"I'll have to ask . . . I mean . . ." July cleared his throat. "Yes, sir. I give you my permission to spend the night out there."

"Thank you, Mr. Assistant Manager. Please tell Miss Cantrell her brother was a fine man who lived in some awfully wild country. I considered him a friend, and I'll miss him."

"I'll tell her."

"Say, just how long has she been runnin' this store?"

"Two days."

"Two days? I'd give her another two days or one big hoo-rah, and she'll be scamperin' back to Virginia, I reckon."

Of all the conceit! You judge me, and you haven't even met me. You think I can't handle this place? Mister, there is nothing on this earth that motivates me more than a man who doubts my ability! Especially coming from a saddle tramp who has to beg a place to sleep. Lucky for you we weren't standing face to face when you said that. I have a glare that can bring strong men to their knees.

Why does he have to be tall? Tall with broad shoulders, no doubt. I wonder how tall he really is?

"I figure Miss Carolina for a stander. She won't chase easy. And she's from Maryland," July corrected. "I think she was born in Virginia but lately livin' in Maryland. Them states is right next to each other, you know."

"Loyalty to your employer is a commendable attribute, Mr. Johnson. I like you standin' up for her like that. For what it's worth, I think you make a choice assistant manager."

"Thank you, sir."

"You wouldn't happen to have any coffee on the stove, would you? I'm gettin' low on supplies."

"No, sir, just hot water. She likes tea."

"Yep. That figures."

What do you mean, "that figures"? What's wrong with drinking tea?

It's certainly more civilized than boiled coffee grounds with broken egg shells! I have never been judged so thoroughly and so incorrectly by someone who's never met me. Mister, there's a good reason you're alone. Obviously, there's only room in your life for one . . . you!

Which is something you know all about, Carolina.

She sat in the luke-cold water in the galvanized tub until she heard July call out, "All's clear, Miss Cantrell."

"Please shut the front door, July, and don't let any more customers in until I come down."

"Yes, ma'am. Was it all right that I let him stay in the hay shed?"

"It's on our side of the corral, isn't it?"

"Yes, ma'am."

With a clean towel wrapped around her, Carolina stepped out of the tub and dried off. "Good. That's fine. We can allow anyone we want to stay there."

"He sure is tall."

"How tall?"

"With his hat on, he had to bend down to come in the door. He looks strong too. Tall and strong. He sure would be a good man to help dig a well . . . if we was goin' to do that."

Carolina picked up a small towel, leaned forward at the waist, and dried her hair. "Thank you for your evaluation, Mr. Johnson."

"One last thing, Miss Cantrell."

She shook her head and felt water drip on her shoulder. "Yes, July . . . what is it?"

"Can I bust open a sack of Arbuckles and take him a little coffee? A man like that likes to have his coffee at night."

"July, we can't just provide—"

"I'll take it out of my wages, Miss Cantrell."

Practice hospitality, Carolina. The graciousness of a fourteen-year-old puts you to shame. No matter how egotistical the man might be, he was your brother's friend.

"Miss Carolina?"

"Definitely take him some coffee, and, no, you don't have to pay for it."

"Thank ya, ma'am."

She waited for the sound of the door to close before she started to get dressed.

"Eh, hem!"

"What is it now, July?"

"I reckon the rest of the fried taters and ham will spoil before daylight, don't you?"

"Yes, I believe you're right. It would be nice if we had an ice room to store things. What's your point?"

"Since I'm goin' to toss them anyway, how about me offerin' them to the tall man on the tired horse?"

"That's fine, July. Is there anything else?"

"No, ma'am."

"Shut the door behind you."

"Yes, ma'am."

July Johnson lounged on the buggy seat on the front porch with only the stars above and kerosene lamps in the saloon for light when she finally opened the door to the store and signaled him in.

"It's cooled down out there, hasn't it?" she remarked.

"Yep. Soon as the sun goes down, that west wind picks the cool air right off the river and blows it up here like a big fan," July reported. "Did you ever see one of them electric power fans? I saw one down in Cheyenne. It sure was somethin'."

"Yes, I met Mr. Edison in New Jersey last fall."

"Who's he?"

"The man who invented the electric light."

"Never heard of him."

"You will." She continued to stand in the darkened doorway. "Sounds fairly quiet over at the saloon."

"They ain't got no piano and no women, so I reckon there ain't—there isn't nothin' much to do but drink, fight, play cards, and cuss."

"Sounds like a rather pitiful evening. Did he go in the bar?"

"Who?"

"The tall man with the tired horse."

"Nope. He built him a little fire out by the willows and boiled himself some coffee and cleaned his revolver. I don't think he's got two bits on him. He sure had a beaut of a Colt. It's sort of silver-plated and has etchin' all over it. Probably has his name on it."

"What is his name?"

"I don't know. I couldn't get close enough to read and was too embarrassed to ask."

"Embarrassed?"

"Men like that—it ain't proper to ask their name."

"Men like what?"

"A man whose .44 is well used and is stayin' in the willows. No, ma'am, you don't ask him his name."

"I'll introduce myself in the morning. Perhaps he'll tell us his name then."

"What are we going to do now, Miss Cantrell?"

"I'm headed for the loft to sort through some more of David's belongings. Your time's your own, but I know there's not much to do here."

"There's some Hawthorne Miller dime novels over on that far wall. If I promise not to smudge the pages, can I read one of them?"

"By all means. Do you have one selected already?"

"Thought I'd read *Stuart Brannon and the Renegade Apache War*."

"Don't get too carried away with fictional characters."

"But Stuart Brannon's a real man. He's down in Arizona. I met a man who knew a fella whose brother's best friend was at Paradise Meadow when Brannon cleaned 'em out."

Carolina, lantern in hand, hiked up the stairs at the back of the room. *I should have some of my books shipped out. July should read Dickens or Melville. My word, he really believes that those tall tales about Stuart Brannon are true. Perhaps July should attend school somewhere.*

For the next four hours, Carolina Cantrell sorted through the personal possessions of her brother. With her window still half-open, she felt the loft begin to cool, while her heart warmed.

She found David's folding knife that she had given him when he was eighteen and she was fourteen. There were suspenders they had purchased in Edinburgh, pearl buttons from Amsterdam, an ivory-handled antique dagger from Seville, clothes, bills of lading, books, maps, ledgers, and souvenirs.

Carolina found a stack of letters she had sent to him over the years. She cried her way though most of them. In the bottom of the dusty leather valise was a sealed letter addressed to Miss Carolina Katherine Cantrell.

He never mailed this one!

She tried to take a deep breath and relax before she opened it. Tears puddled up again in the corners of her eyes.

I really miss him, Lord. He hadn't been home in years, but I always counted on him coming back. It's not fair. He was so young!

She ripped open the stiff brown paper envelope and read the date out loud, "'November 6, 1879.' That was four years ago!"

Dearest Sweet Carolina,
Happy Birthday!

I'm not sure when this will get to you, but I wanted you to know that you are on my mind on your birthday. I wish I could be there. I'd take you to supper at the Magnolia Hotel. We'd have their seven-course French cuisine, minus the champagne, of course. Then I'd hand you a small purple velvet bag that contained a sparkling pair of diamond earrings. You deserve them.

I can't believe you haven't married one of those rich Eastern industrialists yet. But I'm glad you're choosey. The man who marries you gains one of the most intelligent, witty, and beautiful women in the western hemisphere, and he'd better take good care of you, or he'll have to answer to me!

I wish I could tell you that I'm excited about your friendship with Jacob Hardisty. Yes, we did attend Princeton at the same time, but he's . . . it's my opinion that he . . . Ah, Sweet Carolina, please keep your eyes open with Hardisty. He troubles me. Enough said. Maybe I shouldn't have said anything. He's probably changed. I trust your judgment.

Please report to Mother that I am well. I presume Mr. Franklin still bosses her around and recklessly spends her (our?) money. I just can't bear to think about it.

I wish I could recite great success in the goldfields. At the moment I am in the Big Horn Mountains of Wyoming, huddled around a small fire in near freezing temperature. We've found enough gold to keep us from starving to death, but that's all.

It is an interesting feeling to be hundreds of miles from any signs of civilization—nothing around for as far as one can see except unoccupied wilderness and occasional savages (both red and white). It reminds me of being in the middle of the Atlantic. Remember that time we lay out on the deck and tried to count the stars? How far did we get?

I'm cold.

I'm tired.

I'm hungry.

I'm broke.

(Don't send money. You know I'll send it back. We both said we could make it without Father's money. I'm determined to do just that.)

I love it out here, Sweet Carolina. It's wild and rugged, but it's fresh and new.

Now it's time to crawl under the blankets. One of the men with me, named Starke, has plans to go to Fort Laramie in a day or two. I'll have him post the letter.

Happy 20th, sweet sister. Oh, how I wish I could see your face tonight.

Your loving big brother always,
David Lee Cantrell

It was a little after midnight when Carolina snuffed out the lantern and crawled into bed. She had no idea when it was that she finally stopped crying and drifted off to sleep.

The room was much too bright for early morning, and Carolina knew she had slept longer than she intended. But the bedding was clean, the cobwebs gone, and the loft fairly well organized. She heard July busy in the store but didn't call down to him.

David Lee, I've shed my last tear for you. "Oh, Lamb of God, who taketh away the sins of the world, have mercy on us."

Her dress was a deep blue with white lace on the high collar and cuffs on the sleeves. The sapphire and silver earrings were no larger than a dime, but they sparkled in the reflection in her hand mirror. Her curls fell in place quickly, but each showed some wear.

I'll need to spiral my hair in a day or two.

She peered around the loft as if checking to make sure no one was watching. Then she brushed some rouge on her cheeks and rubbed it in with a small cloth.

I should go for a walk today and get some sunlight, providing Mr. Starke doesn't steal the store once I walk out the door. At least I could stroll out by the corrals and the shed. The chickens! I could check on the chickens if July hasn't already done so.

She cracked open the two-shot derringer, dropped the bullets out into her hand, and fingered them for a moment. Then she pushed them back into the small handgun and locked the double barrels back to the grip. She slipped it into the right pocket of the blue dress. She tied a clean white apron over her dress.

After she laced up her black high-tops, Carolina stood and brushed down her skirt. She glanced in the only large piece of mirror she was able to find in the entire store.

All right, tall man, I owe you an apology for being judgmental and stingy.

July Johnson glanced up from the woodstove about the time she reached the bottom step. "My, you look so . . . so purdy, Miss Cantrell."

Overdressed is probably the word you searched for. "And you look quite handsome, Mr. Johnson."

"Thank you, ma'am, but this is the same thing I wore yesterday."

"You looked handsome yesterday too."

"Eh . . . eh, you want breakfast now? I fried us up some sweet-bread to go with our eggs." He blushed.

"Oh, you already collected the eggs? I thought I'd do that today just to get some fresh air."

"He already rode off," July announced.

Young man, how do you know what I'm thinking? "Who?"

"The tall man on the tired horse. He pulled out right after he shod your horse and ate breakfast."

"Shod my horse?"

"Those rear horseshoes were loose and pickin' up rock. He had all the tools in his saddlebags. Said he used to do some black-smithin' for your brother from time to time."

"Oh . . . that was nice of him." Carolina looked at July's big blue eyes. "Breakfast? Did he have—"

"I fed him. There was six eggs this mornin', so I figured you wouldn't mind."

"He really has no money?"

"As far as I can tell. He wouldn't take nothin' for shoein' the horse except a handful of coffee."

"Which direction did he go?"

"Said he had to go to Billings, but he was on his way to the Slash-Bar-4 first to see if they were hirin'."

"Did you ever find out his name?"

"No, but you ought to see how strong he is. When he was nailin' down those shoes, he rolled up his sleeves. His arms was as big as my legs."

"Let me guess—he has wide, square shoulders; a relaxed, easy smile; strong chin; two-day beard; big, callused hands; and blue eyes that twinkle when he laughs."

July Johnson stared at her for a minute.

"I don't rightly know what his eyes was like. I surely didn't pay them no mind. But the rest was true. Was you spyin' on him this mornin'?"

Carolina glided over to the teapot and poured her cup full of water. "Oh, no. I never laid eyes on the man. I could just tell from his voice what he looked like."

"You could?"

"Yes."

"If you weren't lookin' at me, what could you tell about me by my voice?" July pressed.

Carolina stared out the open doorway toward the corral as she stirred the perforated spoon into her water. "Well, I could tell that if a fourteen-year-old girl comes through here, you'd trot after her for six miles trying to get her to smile at you."

"You can tell that by my voice?" he groaned.

"Yes, but don't worry. To a fourteen-year-old girl it is a lovely sound."

"It is?"

This lad needs a mother to explain some things to him . . . or a father . . . or both!

She ignored July and pointed out toward the corral. "What are those men doing out there?"

"Oh, Mr. Starke bought a couple of spades this mornin'."

"While I was asleep?"

"I reckon so, Miss Cantrell."

"Are they digging for gold?"

"He hired a couple of bummers to dig post holes."

"In the middle of our corral?"

"He said he was dividing the corral. His side is on the left, and your side is on the right."

"But his part is four times larger than mine. We won't have room for more than a couple of horses."

"He said that's where the line goes."

"Then the shed belongs to us!"

"That's what I told him."

"What did he say?"

"Said it was so rickety that it wasn't worth savin'. Said it wouldn't surprise him if the wind blew it over or it got hit by lightnin' some night and burned to the ground."

"Starke said that?"

"Yes, ma'am. Sort of sounds like he has evil intent, don't it? You ready for some fried sweetbread?"

"In a minute, July." Carolina wandered out onto the front porch and surveyed the men who leaned on their shovels in the corral. *Lord, I can't stand by and allow him to chase me off. This is David's store. It should always be called Cantrell's. It's his memorial. His marker.*

She sauntered back into the store. "It looks like another beautiful day, Mr. Johnson."

"Yes, ma'am, it surely does."

"I think I'll go for a little walk today. I've been stuck in this store for two solid days."

She stared at two wooden crates, each about two feet wide, two feet high, and six feet long.

"What kind of mining gear is in these boxes, July?"

"The top one has the pump and pipes for a water well."

"And the other?"

"I think it's got a long Tom in it."

"A what?"

"A ready-made rocker for separatin' out the gold from the sand."

"If we took the two lids off those boxes, we could use them for a couple of sections of fence."

"What do we want a fence for?"

She grinned, sipped from her tea, and then raised her eyebrows. "I'll show you after breakfast. You finish cooking, and I'll read a Bible passage."

Before breakfast was finished, customers drifted in through the front door of the store. Most wanted directions for Devil's Canyon, and many left with a package or two under their arms.

It was past 1:00 P.M. before the store settled down and July made the run to the river with the buggy for water. It was around 2:00 when Carolina had him remove the lids from the two large crates.

"Now what do we fence?" he asked.

"The porch," she announced.

"How's that?"

"Let's nail them end to end straight across the chalk line."

"Divide up the porch?"

"Yes."

"Mr. Starke ain't goin' to like that."

"No, I don't suppose he will."

She and July Johnson nailed the crate-lid fencing across the porch to the shouts and curses of Horatio Starke. But several customers in the saloon soon occupied his attention. With a big card game of some sort building steam back by the bar, the front of the porch quieted.

Carolina and July hiked around the building. He pointed to the window on the east side of the store. "I figure we should dig a well right here, then put a counter and sink under the window, and pump the water inside. Even if we couldn't rig the pump to work from in there, we could mount a couple barrels above the window and use them like a cistern. Ever' day we could just hand-pump them full."

"Yes, that would work. At least until winter. What would we do when the water freezes up?"

"One time up in the Big Horns, we wrapped our pump in a couple of gunny sacks full of wood shavin's, and it lasted all winter. Them raised cisterns would freeze sure enough, but we don't need much water in the winter, do we? How much tea can two people drink?"

"But we need to clean. Mop. Take baths."

"In the winter?" he gasped.

"All of that is a moot question, isn't it?"

"A what?"

"It's inconsequential if—"

"Miss Cantrell, you have the most beautiful words I ever heard. Did you learn them in school?"

"At the university."

"You graduated from a college?"

"Yes, I did."

"I ain't never knowed a woman who done that."

"I didn't want to get married when I was sixteen, so I went to college. Anyway, there's no reason to talk about winter if neither of us intends to be here."

"You're goin' to sell out before then?"

"I certainly hope so. But I have decided I might spend the summer."

"No foolin'?"

"I want to fix the place up a little more and make the name Cantrell remembered."

"He got to you, didn't he?"

"Who?"

"The tall man on the tired horse. He said you'd pull out after one hoo-rah. As soon as I heard that, I figured it wouldn't set well with Miss Cantrell. You're goin' to prove him wrong, ain't ya?"

He's fourteen, and I've known him for a few days. I'm not really that transparent . . . am I?

"Well, are you?"

"Yes, I am. But don't you start thinking you know everything about me, Mr. July Johnson. One of these days I'll do something out of character and totally surprise you."

His blue eyes grew wide. "Really?"

"Really." *That's the way, Carolina, paint yourself into a corner. Of course, you're predictable. Every man you ever dated has told you that. Especially Jacob Hardisty.* "As predictable as a weed in a garden," *was his exact phrase at that French ambassador's party in Washington.*

I am a steady, self-controlled, reasonable person, that's all.

"I said, Miss Cantrell, do you want me to start diggin' that well now that you reckon to stay the summer?"

"Oh . . . I just haven't decided. I mean, I know we need to dig one, but I think you need someone to help you."

"I sure wish you could have hired that tall man."

"If he comes back through and needs some work, why don't we do that? What should we pay him?"

"Cowboys get a dollar a day, plus room and meals. I hear miners are gettin' three dollars a day in Deadwood."

"Why don't we pay two dollars a day, plus meals, and he can sleep in the shed."

"Yes, ma'am. 'Course, he was headin' west. Ain't likely that he'll be back through."

"Perhaps someone else will come along. But I don't want to hire a man who drinks."

"No, ma'am. Then we'll wait for help before we dig the well?"

"That's my idea." She gazed down toward the river. "You run the store. I think I'll take a little walk."

"By yourself?"

"It's a beautiful day. I need some air. You'll be all right, won't you?"

"Me? I can take care of myself." He patted the hunting knife he wore in a sheath laced to his belt. "How about you?"

She pulled off her apron and handed it to him. "Mr. Johnson, don't ever stop worrying about me. I like that. But I've got to talk a little with the Lord, and I'm quite confident He'll look after both of us. Now, you open up the rest of those mining crates and make us a tally of all we have. That way we'll know what we can sell."

Carolina walked down the incline toward the river without even glancing back at the store. She passed the corral, the shed, and a couple of chickens before she came across the road to the river.

The blue sky contained only occasional high, streaked white clouds. A slightly cool breeze came up from the Yellowstone River and tickled her cheeks and neck.

I should have put on a hat or bonnet. On the other hand, a little real color would be better than rouge. Back East it was a virtue to be lily-white, but out here I'm too pale. . . . This is not exactly a hiking dress. More like a nonchalantly-impress-the-drifting-cowboy-who-left-before-I-got-up dress.

The ground sloped down more than she remembered. She dug each boot heel into the dry, soft dirt.

It's a steep climb back to the store, Carolina.

When she reached the bluff that overlooked the river ten minutes later, she saw several large boulders. She spread her embroidered handkerchief on one about the size of a trunk and then plopped down.

There's the road back to Billings. It seems like three weeks, not three days, since I came down it. This is remote, Lord. No buildings in sight. An empty road and a lonely railroad track. I've never even heard a train on it. Of course, I don't hear customers who come into the store in the mornings either.

She took a deep breath of air and let it out slowly. It tasted like wildflowers and new green grass.

Jacob Hardisty in the West? Lord, I don't know why I needed to hear that. I've shed my tears. Paid my dues. Found strength in You. Dismissed the whole matter. I didn't bring it up. I don't care where he is, what he's doing, or who he's with. Especially, who he's with. Your plan for my life doesn't include him. That's obvious.

I'm domineering? Bullheaded? Too independent? What did you want, Hardisty—just a decoration to wear on your dinner jacket?

Lord, why do I waste my time thinking about him again? I've got too many more important matters at hand.

Carolina, for a woman with friends all over North America and Europe, you surely are alone. A self-imposed exile? But for how long?

If I'm really staying for the summer, I'd better make some plans. The carriage is rented for only a week. I'll need more inventory shipped out. I need to go to Billings. But I can't go to town because Starke will steal everything he can. I can't leave July to guard the store. That wouldn't be fair.

You aren't going to sell the store, C. K. C., if you don't get to town and let someone know it's for sale. "Your stubbornness will get you in big trouble someday, Carolina Katherine." "Yes, Mother."

All my life they called me stubborn. Everyone except Daddy. He knew. "Don't ever let them make you change your mind when you know you're right." "Don't worry, Daddy, I won't."

Even when I'm wrong.

They think I can't run a store in Montana? I not only can run it, I can turn a profit and sell the whole works for a tidy sum.

Lord willing.

You are willing, aren't You?

Maybe I could just put a lock on the door and take July with me to town and . . . I don't think Starke'll shoot me, but that's about all he won't do. I shouldn't even have hiked out here. If he finds out I've left, he'll . . .

"You don't make money sitting on your backside, Sweet Carolina." "Yes, Daddy."

She felt her forehead with the palm of her hand. *Maybe I got a little color. Next time I should sit on the porch.*

Carolina stood up, brushed out her dress, and then began to hike back to the store. Her toes felt warm in the thick leather lace-up boots.

If I cut through that brush, the way back would be about half as far. What kind of animals are around here? Panthers? Snakes?

She reached into the deep pocket of the dress and felt the grip of her little pistol. *Oh, sure, I'm going to shoot accurately enough to hit a snake with this? Only if I hold it up to his ear. Do snakes have ears?*

The dark green brush proved to be thicker than she had thought. After about a hundred yards of picking her way up the gradual incline, she turned east. *This is ridiculous. My dress is filthy. I'll just cut back to the road.*

The sound of hushed voices brought her to a quick stop in a thicket of willows just short of a rocky clearing. She strained to hear each word.

"They say that Andrews and Odessa brought down the whole Yellow Sash outfit."

"Don't mean nothin'. We ain't movin' in permanent. Just cut about fifty head, swim them over here, and drive 'em to Deadwood. That's $2,500 split three ways."

"I heard Andrews was as tough as Brannon and the Earps."

"But we ain't goin' to face him. That's the point. We cut ourselves out fifty and swim 'em at night. A big ol' ranch like that won't miss 'em until roundup time."

"We better cut sixty. We're bound to lose some in the river. It's high and fast right now."

"Okay. Sixty."

"I ain't goin' to die over sixty head."

"No one's goin' to die. They're up there takin' care of those babies and thinkin' they cleared all the rustlers out of the country. I looked it over yesterday when he told me he wasn't hirin' 'til fall. By the time they figure out what we've done, we'll be in the Green Hotel eatin' chops and dancin' with purdy girls."

"I like the purdy-girl part."

"Why don't you go up there and get us a jug from old Starke? I hear he's got a purdy girl workin' for him."

Carolina bit her lip. *Work for him? People think I work for Starke? That's the most insulting . . .*

"We're takin' the beef tonight?"

"Ain't no reason to wait."

"I'll go get the jug."

"Don't tell him we're down here."

"What should I tell him?"

"Tell him you're going to 'see the elephant' down at Devil's Canyon like all those other fools."

"What if that purdy girl wants to . . . dance?"

"Bring us the jug first. Just ride up the road like any other pilgrim. I aim to catch a nap since we got night work."

When Carolina had been nine years old, she had sneaked silently through the woods behind their burned-out Blue Ridge estate to spy on her brother and five of his twelve-year-old friends as they made secret plans to resurrect the Army of Virginia. As far as she could remember, it was the last time she had sneaked through the woods. That time it ended with her capture, and Tommy Wayne DuPree slipped a slimy frog down the back of her dress.

This time she knew the stakes would be higher.

Carolina tiptoed slowly, each step as soft as she could make it. The voices faded behind her, either because the men had dozed off or because they were listening to her footsteps. The distance to the store seemed like miles as the brush caught on her dress. Rocks slipped under her feet. Every strange noise made her freeze in place.

By the time she reached the yard, she carried the small gun in her right hand and had several bleeding scratches on her left. She waited by a thick-trunked cottonwood and surveyed the scene.

The horse must be the rustler's. . . . I don't know who the wagon belongs to. Maybe customers are in the store. I don't see anything suspicious.

She glanced up at the faded sign on the roof of the building.

Starke & Cantrell? I need to repaint the sign. I'll paint half of it, just the part over the store. I think there's some white paint in those crates next to—

She stepped back out of sight when Horatio Starke and another man came out of the saloon. Each carried an amber-colored bottle. Starke pointed to the fence on the porch and the open doorway to the store.

"She's over there!" he announced in a voice too loud to be sober.

"All alone?" the man slurred.

"And a kid."

"She has a kid?"

"Ain't her kid. Shirttail-sized."

"Does she . . . dance?"

"If she don't, maybe you can persuade her."

"Yep. Maybe I can. What's her name?"

"Cantrell."

The dust-covered rustler sauntered down the stairs of the saloon, across the yard, and up the stairs to the store, bottle still grasped in his hand. He staggered a little and climbed the last stair twice. His uneven beard reflected a red tint.

"Miss Cantrell," he hollered, "how about a dance?"

She waited behind the tree to see what kind of reply he would get from July.

"I said, I want to dance, girl!" the medium-built, bearded man with the black hat man blustered.

July Johnson appeared at the door. "This is a store, mister, not a dance hall. You aimin' to buy somethin'?"

The man slid his free hand to the grip of his holstered revolver. "I don't aim to pay nobody for nothin'!" he challenged.

Oh, no! July, don't! Carolina stepped out into the yard, but those on the porch didn't see her.

July raised his hands.

"Now that's a smart boy. Where's the woman?"

"Go look for yourself." July stepped back away from the door.

The man stalked toward the door. As he neared the assistant manager of Cantrell's, July kicked his shin with a heavy boot. The red-bearded man stumbled and fell headlong in the doorway. The amber bottle smashed into the side of the store. Glass and whiskey sprayed through the air.

No sooner had he hit the floor than July jammed a knee in the man's back and swung his hunting knife at the rustler's neck. "You ain't goin' in there, mister. Miss Cantrell don't like your kind in the store!"

Carolina held her breath. *July, where did you learn to do that?*

Hardrock Starke stumbled down the stairs of the saloon porch and over to the store. He had a revolver in one hand and the bottle in the other. "Let him up, boy!" he hollered.

"I cain't do that, Mr. Starke," July shouted.

"Get him off me!" the man on the porch shrieked.

Starke leaned against the edge of the porch and pointed the revolver at July Johnson. "If you don't back off by the time I count to three, I'll put a bullet in your brain."

"Mr. Starke, you're drunk. Go on back to your saloon!"

"I ain't bluffin', kid!" Starke growled.

"Neither am I!" Carolina stood on the first step of the stairs and jammed the barrel of her revolver into Starke's right ear.

"Do somethin', Starke!" the man pinned to the wooden porch hollered.

"You know, my father told me never to point a gun unless I intended to pull the trigger," she proclaimed. "I never have."

"I could kill the boy!" Starke threatened.

"The gun's in your left hand. You're right-handed, and you're ten feet away. You could miss and hit that bummer on the floor. What do you think the chances are for me to miss you?" She shoved the steel barrel deeper into the ear until he winced. *Snakes do have ears—at least some of them.* "Drop the gun, Starke!"

"No woman can get the jump on me!" he grumbled.

"One just did. July, if Starke doesn't drop his gun by the time I count to three, go ahead and finish your business there."

The man on the porch tried to peek around at her, but July kept one hand gripped on the man's hair and the other on the knife to his throat. "Drop the gun, Starke!" the man cried. "I changed my mind. I ain't in a dancin' mood anymore."

"Bah!" Starke took a swig from the bottle in his right hand and then tossed the gun on the porch. "We was jist funnin' you two anyways."

"Let him up, July," Carolina commanded.

Johnson released the man and scooped up Starke's pistol. He pointed it at the rustler, who struggled to his feet.

"You busted my bottle!" he groused.

July stepped back toward the edge of the porch. "You dropped it."

Carolina scooted up the stairs next to her assistant manager. "I'm sure Mr. Starke will sell you another bottle."

"Sell me?"

"You don't expect him to give away free liquor, do you?"

The man lurched down the stairs and reached out for the bottle in Starke's hand. The saloon owner yanked his hand back.

"I done paid once," the man growled. "I ain't payin' again!" He reached for his revolver but stopped when Carolina and July both pointed their guns at him.

"Looks like it's time for you to ride on," July suggested.

"You three is in cahoots, tryin' to do me out of my money."

"No, but we are business owners," Carolina informed him. "And a person must pay for the merchandise—right, Mr. Starke?"

"She's right on that, mister."

Neither Carolina nor July lowered their handguns when the man reached in his vest and pulled out a coin.

"What will this buy me?" He handed the money to Starke, who held the amber bottle in his hand up to the sun. "About this much." He shoved the bottle at the man, who grabbed it and took a swig.

Starke, Cantrell, and Johnson all watched the man mount and ride out of the yard back toward the river.

"He's as dumb as mud," Starke muttered. "Said he wanted to go to Devil's Canyon and then turned around and went back to the river."

Carolina slipped her gun into her pocket. July looked at the revolver in his own hand. "What should I do with this?"

"Give it back to Mr. Starke, of course."

The heavily whiskered and whiskied Horatio Starke stared at her with his bloodshot eyes. "You bushwhacked me and then bailed me out. Why's that?"

"I'm not at all sure, but please keep your customers on your side of the porch. We will try not to interfere with your business and would appreciate the same consideration from you."

A voice rumbled from deep within the saloon, "Barkeep! Do we get any whiskey? The pot's too big to leave the table ourselves!"

Starke hustled up the stairs and into the saloon. Carolina tried to shake the dirt and twigs off her dress. "That was quite a scene."

"Yes, ma'am. I was surely glad you came along."

"Were you scared?"

"Yep. But only until you showed. Once I heard your voice, I

knew it'd be all right. You and the Lord bein' such good friends and all, things like this probably don't scare you at all."

"Are you kidding? I just thought that if a fourteen-year-old boy isn't panicked, I shouldn't be either."

"You mean we both thought the other was courageous?"

She smiled and put her arm around his shoulder. "We make quite a team, don't we, Mr. Assistant Manager?"

"Yes, ma'am, we surely do."

"Come on inside. We've got something to talk about."

He pointed to her left hand. "Like how you got your hand all chewed up in a berry bush?"

"That's part of it."

Carolina cleaned up, doctored her hand, and waited on two male customers who wanted to buy gold pans and groceries. When the men finally left, she poured herself a cup of tea and plopped down at the table.

"You goin' to tell me about your walk?"

"Yes!" she blurted out. "There are some men camped down by the river, including the one we had to chase off."

"People camp along the river all the time."

"That might be, but these men are cattle rustlers."

"How do you know that?"

"I heard them talk."

July stared out the open doorway. "You think they'll come up here and shoot up the store?"

"I don't think so. That would give away their position. They plan to steal cattle tonight."

"Where?"

"From the Slash-Bar-4."

"Is that the big ranch across the river?"

"Yes. There was a man in here the other day named Mr. Odessa who works at the ranch. He helped me straighten up the place before you came along."

"You thinkin' maybe we should warn 'em?"

"Yes. I'd like you to hitch up the buggy and—"

"I could jist ride your horse."

"I don't have a saddle."

"There's an old McClellen out in the hay shed. I'll use it."

"All right, but ride straight west to the hills and then cut north to the river. I don't want those men in the brush to see you."

"How far away is the Slash-Bar-4 headquarters?"

"I have no idea, but I would imagine at least twenty miles."

"I'd better go now if I want to make it before dark. Are you going to be all right, Miss Cantrell? I'd hate to go off and leave you in a tough spot."

She looked at the boy. *If you were twelve years older, Mr. Johnson . . .* "I'll be fine. I don't intend to take any more walks until you return. You go saddle the horse, and I'll write Mr. Odessa a note and tell him all that I overheard."

A few minutes later, Carolina stood out on the porch with a letter in one hand and a lumpy flour sack in the other. July took the letter, folded it in half, and jammed it into his vest pocket. With his hat pulled down, his ears stood out in an awkward way. Then he reached down and grabbed the sack. "What's in here?"

"Something for you to eat on the trail. But those two airtights of pickled peaches are for Mrs. Odessa. Tell her they are a gift. Be careful, Mr. July Johnson."

"Yes, ma'am."

"You stay at the ranch overnight. I know they'll let you bunk there. Don't start back until daylight. I don't want you to get hurt riding at night."

"Yes, Mother."

She put her hand up over her eyes to block the sunlight. "I don't care if I do sound like a mother. I need you here with me, so don't take any chances."

He rode about five feet and then pulled the horse around toward her. "It's okay, Miss Cantrell. I don't mind if ya mother me. I sort of like bein' needed somewhere. You know what I mean?"

She smiled, nodded, and waved to him as he trotted to the distant western hills.

Actually, Mr. July Johnson, it's been a long, long time since anyone really needed me.

She took a deep breath and let it out slowly.

It's been way, way too long. Carolina, it's a tough thing to admit, but no one really needs you.

When she turned to reenter the store, she could see Horatio Starke peer out at her from deep inside the smoky, whiskied stench of the saloon.

The early evening passed quickly, thanks to three different parties of gold seekers who asked directions to Devil's Canyon and added to their meager kits. She didn't have a chance to sit down until she glanced up at the brass clock that read eight o'clock.

Well . . . it's around eight . . . or seven . . . or nine. Out here it doesn't matter much. July will be almost at the Slash-Bar-4. I'm not sure why I feel so intent on warning people I don't really know twenty miles away. It just seems like what ought to be done.

Lord, it's that way out here. So far from town, people, government, lawmen, justice. It makes me feel responsible to see that things are done right.

Of course, others don't get that feeling. They seem to think it gives them license for evil. I suppose lack of constraints either brings out the best or the worst in a person. The trouble is, I'm not sure which it's doing to me. I was ready to shoot a man this afternoon. This land is like a test. Most of the time, life in the East is just practice. Like a rehearsal. Out here it's the actual performance. Lord, please keep me out of situations that are over my head.

She walked to the front door and looked out. The same wagon remained parked in front of the saloon. Muffled voices from the poker game continued to rumble out the saloon door. There was no traffic on the road up from the river.

Carolina returned to the oak straight-back chair and unlaced the high-top black shoes. She tugged them off and peeled off her black silk socks.

Wool might be the rage in the States, but I'll stay with French silk.

The wooden floor felt cool to her size-five bare feet. She strolled to the back of the store, picked up her ledger, and returned to the table.

As long as I don't pick up a splinter. I'll wash my feet later.

She slumped down in one chair and propped up her feet in the other chair. Then she opened the journal and reviewed her entries.

We've made $200 in four days. At that rate, we should take in about $1,500 per month. If I can set aside $250 per month, I'll have $1,000 profit by September. Then I could buy out Starke and make the entire building into a store and paint it before winter.

Leaning her head against the back of the hardwood chair, she stared up at the high ceiling. She ran her fingers through the tight curls of her bangs and then reached up to unfasten the sapphire and silver earrings and tugged at her earlobes.

But why would I want to buy out Starke? Surely, I'm not thinking of spending the winter out here!

Let's face it, Carolina, you have no husband, no children, and with Mr. Franklin running your father's business, you have nothing special to do and nowhere to go. Of course you'll stay here.

"That's not true!" she blurted out loud.

"What isn't true?"

The sound of a male voice in the doorway brought her up out of her chair. The ledger tumbled to the floor.

"What are you doing here?"

"I wanted to buy something."

"Who are you?"

"Does it matter? I've got money."

"You can't come in here!"

"Why not?"

"I don't have on my shoes!"

"I've seen women's feet before."

"You haven't seen mine."

"No, ma'am, I haven't."

"Could you wait out on the porch, please? It will only be a minute."

"Yes, ma'am."

Is this the tall man with the tired horse? His voice sounds different. Maybe he's not tired anymore. He's too well dressed to be a drifter. My, oh my, he is tall!

As she pulled the socks and shoes on, she heard the man talk to someone. She brushed her fingers through her hair and then fluttered toward the door.

The man on the porch looked about six-foot-five, strong, and rugged. He had a scar on the side of his neck under his right ear. He held a crisp, black silk hat in his hand.

"Excuse me for being so ill-prepared," she explained. "Do come in."

"Yes, ma'am. I didn't mean to barge in. I thought the store was still open."

"Oh, it is. You caught me daydreaming. I do believe I was talking to myself. Please accept my apologies. I'm Carolina Cantrell. This is my store."

"Pleased to meet you, ma'am. Most folks just call me Stack."

"What can I do for you?"

"I don't rightly know. I'm goin' callin' on a fine Christian lady, and I'd like to bring her a gift. But here I am, far away from town, and I just now thought of it. Would you have any item that might be appropriate without makin' it look like I'm just a big old, dumb piano player?"

"You play the piano?"

"Yeah, I used to. Don't look much like a musician, do I?"

"What do you do now?"

"Oh, I've kind of got my hand in several different pots, you might say. A business here, a mine there—that sort of thing."

"You wouldn't be interested in buying another enterprise, would you?" she asked. Carolina waved her arms around the room.

"You sellin'?"

"I just came out to settle accounts for my brother's estate."

"To tell the truth, ma'am, and don't think me proud—Lord knows, I don't claim any credit for it—but I've got so many things goin' now I have to hire a lawyer just to keep track of finances." The lines were deep and leather-tough around his big, kind eyes.

"If you hear of someone who wants to buy, you might point them this way."

"I'll do that, Miss Cantrell. But if I was you, I'd stick it out for about a year."

"Why's that?"

"All those stampeders are headin' for Devil's Canyon. This is the perfect spot for a supply town. If they find a bonanza, this little place . . . What's the name of the store?"

"Cantrell's."

"The town of Cantrell will be as big as Helena or Fort Benton."

"And if they don't find gold?"

"Sell out around Christmas, and you will have made yourself a tidy sum."

"Thanks for the financial advice, Mr. Stack."

"No, no, no. My first name's Stack."

"Oh, well, Stack. . . . How much money would you like to spend on this gift?"

"The cost don't matter." He stared around the store. "I reckon I could afford it."

"I did receive a shipment of women's clothing. If you'd like to—"

"No offense, ma'am, but I'd be too embarrassed to buy something like that."

"Yes . . . tell me something about her."

"She's a widow lady about my age with a passel of kids. She's a Quaker, so she dresses plain."

"If she has several children, I think she might like some material for their clothing."

"Yes, ma'am, I reckon she would. What have you got to fit the bill?"

"I've got several new bolts of nice cottons."

"I'll take 'em."

"Which one?"

"All of them."

"Oh . . . all right. Would you like to take the children a gift also?" she prodded.

"What do you have?"

"You might sort through those jars of stick candy."

"I'll take them all."

"Oh, well, if you wouldn't mind, I'd like to keep a jar here for my other customers."

"Yes, ma'am. I didn't mean to be greedy. Whatever you can

spare would be just fine. Is that an apple peeler?" He pointed to a shelf on the back wall.

"Yes, it peels, cores, and slices all at once."

"I'll buy that too."

"Would you like me to bundle them all up?"

"Yes, ma'am."

Carolina gathered the goods, wrapped them in brown paper, and then tied them off with bright red ribbon. The tall man wandered up and down the aisles.

"Are you nervous?" she asked.

"Yes, ma'am. Does it show?"

"A little."

"How does this suit look? I feel like a hog caught between the fence and the gate."

"It's a handsomely cut English suit. It will certainly turn any woman's head."

He tucked the huge bundle under one arm without any effort and tipped his hat. "I sure do appreciate your helpin' me settle down, Miss Cantrell. I'm kind of anxious. I've just never spent much time around a woman like her before."

"You mean, one with several children?"

"No, I mean one that's quiet, sensible, God-fearin', and respectable."

As the tall man stooped to exit the front door, Carolina noticed an old, worn holster strapped low under his long dress coat. She watched from the doorway as he drove his carriage pulled by two beautiful matched black horses down the road toward the river.

I've got a feeling there's a Christian widow lady and some children who'll have a delightful evening.

Carolina had one more customer, a short, bald man who bought so many supplies he had to strap them on a travois behind his huge draft horse. She closed the store around dark. Bracing the front door, she carried a pitcher of water upstairs with her to the loft.

I should really cook myself a little supper, but I don't want to heat up the store. . . . And I really don't like to eat alone. After I wash up,

*I'll read a little more Tolstoy. I must improve my Russian if I go back to
St. Petersburg in the spring.*

The Russian novel read slowly as the noise from the saloon
seemed to increase. She expected to lie awake even after she
turned off her lantern.

She didn't.

They labeled it a peasants' revolt, and the Russian army was quick
to put it down. From the privacy of her third-story hotel balcony,
Carolina could hear the gunshots and see people drop on the cob-
blestone square. There were screams, curses, confusion, noise,
panic, gunfire, and blood. She knew she should run back into the
hotel and hide, but there was something, some force that kept her
glued to the spot. It was as if history was being made, and she was
to witness it.

Her green velvet dress had a scooped neckline, and she could
feel a cool breeze. *Why did I wear this dress? It only makes my neck
look longer!*

As the gunshots got closer, she searched for her pocket pistol
but could not even find a pocket.

Get inside, Carolina! Protect yourself!

Her eyes blinked open to the darkness of the loft, and she pulled
the flannel sheet down off her perspiring head.

A dream?

No more Russian novels before bed.

But I did hear gunshots. Maybe it's those rustlers across the river.

A loud explosion from the saloon coincided with the sound of
wood violently splintered and the gong of a 200-grain bullet cym-
baling into the iron woodstove downstairs. She pulled the blanket
back over her head.

Someone in the saloon is shooting into the store!

Four

THE BULLETS CEASED WITHIN SIXTY SECONDS.

Carolina, blanket over her head, prayed until dawn. At first she prayed for her own survival. Then she petitioned the Lord's help to control her intense anger with Horatio Starke.

By the time she swung her legs out of bed and felt the rough wood floor gouge her bare feet, she had eliminated murder and lynching as alternatives.

I have $500 available now, and I'm sure Mother could send the rest. But I do not now nor in the future need their help. I will go to Billings, borrow another $500 from the bank, and buy out Starke.

It's highly unlikely that they will be eager to loan money to a woman with a wilderness store. On the other hand, a soft voice and a coy smile can do wonders to convince a banker. Or a merchant. Or an attorney. Or even a drifting cowboy.

If I were a manipulative woman.

Which I'm not.

At least, not very often.

Carolina quickly pulled on what she thought of as "that old dress"—a brown medium-weight cotton garment with matching collar and cuffs. In Europe she labeled it her "marketplace" dress. She wore it whenever it would be to her advantage not to stand out in a crowd.

With hair combed, earrings in place, and shoes laced, she descended the stairs into an empty store.

No breakfast on the stove. No tea water boiled. No front door open. No fourteen-year-old with a sheepish grin. I want my July, Lord. Bring him home safely . . . please!

A tinge of acrid gun smoke laced the more pleasing aromas of fresh leather and exotic spices. Her shoe heels struck the floor in a rhythmic tune. Silence greeted her when she stooped to examine the bullet holes in the doorway between the store and the saloon. Five splintered and jagged punctures about the size of two-bit pieces decorated the otherwise thick wooden door. She peeked through one of the holes but managed only to view darkness and smoke.

And just what merchandise of mine did you destroy, Mr. Starke? Bullets ricocheted all over the room. It's a good thing I sleep in the loft!

She discovered a spent lead bullet on the floor in front of the stove. Her teacup lay shattered on the table. Another bullet had lodged tight in the east wall just below the tin sign with two little girls selling seeds. She found no other damage until she strolled by the cot at the back of the room where July normally slept. Carolina snatched up the Hawthorne Miller book propped up on the window sill. A spent 200-grain piece of deformed lead had buried itself just below the *p* in *Apache*.

If July had been asleep here and raised up, that bullet could have hit him!

Her hand shook as she dropped the book on the cot.

"You aren't getting away with this, Mr. Starke!" she muttered.

July needs the iron plate more than I. Of course, it wouldn't be of much help under his bed. He needs it beside his bed.

With a fire built, water in the teapot, and apron in place, she opened the front door and stepped out on the porch. The contrast shocked her senses.

The early morning air felt fresh, with a hopeful taste. The sky reflected a deep blue. The morning sun, barely up, cast long summer shadows across the yard. A distant reflection filtered through the trees from the meandering Yellowstone River, and the rolling hills across the river displayed a light green tint.

But in front of the store, in the dirt yard that served as hitching rail, wagon parking, and roadway, several amber bottles had been shot or smashed. A broken chair decorated the ground. And a dirty bearded man in coveralls sprawled across the buggy seat on the porch in front of the store.

I don't know if he's dead, drunk, or asleep. I think the place got hurrahed.

Carolina hurried back into the store and retrieved a pick handle. The smooth, polished hickory conformed to the grip of her right hand. She hiked back out to the porch and hammered the sole of the man's boots with the handle.

"Excuse me!" she barked. "Mister?"

One bloodshot eye squinted open.

"I don't run a hotel on my porch. Come on, get up!"

The man closed his eye and didn't move. She slammed his boot again. Still no movement. Finally she cracked the handle into his leg, just below his kneecap.

"Ow!" he bellowed.

This time both eyes opened.

"I don't feel well," he mumbled.

"You look worse. Now get a move on! You can't sleep off a drunk on my porch."

He struggled to sit up on the buggy seat. "When I opened my eye and saw you, lady, I figured I was in heaven."

"When I stepped out on my porch this morning and saw you," she replied, "I thought I was in . . . the other place. Now I'm sorry you're ill, but you do reap what you sow. It's just that you'll have to reap it some other place besides my front porch."

The man struggled to his feet. His head clutched in his hands, he staggered toward the saloon side of the porch.

"Watch out for that . . . ," she called out.

The man tripped over the barricade dividing the porch and fell facedown on the saloon porch.

" . . . fence. Are you all right?" Carolina asked.

The man didn't reply.

Or move.

Well, at least he's on that side of the line now.

Carolina toted a trash crate out to the yard and picked up all the broken pieces of glass she could find. Then she carried the pieces of broken chair to the west side of the saloon and tossed them against the building.

Other than a drunk passed out on the porch, everything's back in place. He has to wake up sometime. I think.

Carolina climbed the stairs in front of the saloon and skirted the prone man in coveralls. She rapped her knuckles on the rough-cut wooden door.

"Mr. Starke, I need to talk to you!" she commanded.

She reached into the deep pocket of her dress, felt for the derringer, and then knocked again.

"Mr. Starke!" she shouted.

The door swung open a few inches.

"Mr. Starke?"

I do not want to go into this building, Lord.

She shoved the door completely open and leaned into the dark, smoke-filled room. "Mr. Starke, I really must talk to you about the gunfire last night."

There was no sound. No movement. No sign of life.

"I intend to file reckless endangerment charges with the county sheriff as soon as I get into Billings," she announced and then waited for a reply.

None came.

"Mr. Starke, there is a drunk passed out on your porch. Would you please come here and help him back into the saloon? A scene like this will turn customers away from the store."

Carolina slipped her hand down on the pistol grip and stepped into the saloon. Two tables were turned over. Several chairs looked recently broken. Shattered glass crunched beneath her feet. A tattered twelve-foot picture of a black racehorse decorated the wall behind the rough-cut bar.

I feel like I've jeopardized my health just walking into a place like this. Where is Starke? In his loft, I presume.

She walked to the door between the bar and the store and peeked through the bullet holes. She could see the aisle of dry goods and her woodstove on the far wall. Then she ambled across the broken glass until she stood below the railing of the loft that was a mirror image of hers.

"Mr. Starke . . . are you up there?" she called.

Her eyes adjusted to the darkness of the room. Two legs and a pair of boots peeked out from under a table in the corner of the saloon.

Mr. Starke? I pray he's not dead. At least I think I do.

A loud, obnoxious snore alleviated her hopes, or fears. Sprawled on his back, Hardrock Starke still clutched an empty bottle in his left hand; his revolver dangled from his right. His head was propped up on an overturned brass spittoon.

I need some fresh air! Lord, this is surely not the purpose for which mankind was created. What a horrid way to live.

She stood at the doorway of the saloon and breathed deeply. Carolina looked up at the wide, cloudless Montana sky. "Last night I wanted to kill him, Lord. But this morning I feel nothing but revulsion and pity. Nothing I could wish upon him could possibly make his life worse than it is."

She glanced down at the man lying on the porch.

"Come on, mister. You might as well sleep it off with Starke."

She reached down and awkwardly lifted his feet. With a tight grip on each soiled canvas cuff, she tugged the man toward the saloon's open door. She had to stop and rest in the doorway with his shoulders and head still halfway out on the porch. The sound of horseback riders caught her attention. Two men rode up in front of the store. One carried an extremely long rifle across his lap and had a bullet belt draped across his shoulder. The other looked Mexican. He wore a short jacket with silver trim. Both straddled brown horses.

"Did you do that to him, or are you that hard up for customers?" the one with the rifle laughed.

She dragged the man inside, dropped his legs with a crash, and exited, closing the saloon door behind her. She brushed her hands together and then strolled to the edge of the porch. "I didn't like the tone of his voice. Now what do you two want?" she snapped.

"Eh . . . " The Mexican pulled off his small, round hat and held it in his hands. "Are you open for business?"

"Depends on which side of the building you're headed for. The saloon's closed."

"We wanted to buy some supplies," the other man put in.

"Good. That's my business. The saloon belongs to Starke."

"He the man you drug inside?"

"No, I don't know who that is. He just littered up my view."

"Did you shoot him?" the Mexican quizzed.

"Not yet," she replied. Carolina hiked down the saloon steps, across the dirt yard, and back up the steps to the store. "Well, don't just sit there bug-eyed! Come on in. The store's open for business. I assume you have money."

With hats in hand, both men cautiously entered the store.

In less than fifteen minutes they left with bundles tied behind their cantles and silver deposited in Carolina's cash box.

She stood at a small tin basin full of hot water and washed the grime and whiskey smell from her slightly glass-cut hands.

Lord, I behaved poorly. I was sure grumpy with those men for no reason. I don't know why. I'm not sure life out here has brought out the best in me. At least, Horatio Starke brings out the worst in me. Every time I'm around him, I have to struggle to stay civil. If You sent him into my life as a test, I'm a failure.

I feel dirty. This dress now smells like a saloon. I should change, but I can't. I have a store to operate. And I can run it. I'll prove to them that I can . . .

Prove to whom? To the drunk asleep on the spittoon? Or maybe to the tall man with the tired horse, whom I'll never see again. He didn't think I could stick it out.

She turned and shouted toward the door, "They 'hoo-rahed' the place, and I didn't leave! Do you hear, Tall Man? They didn't chase me away!"

I don't think he heard.

I have to have someone to talk to besides myself. Lord, is there any way You could send a woman along here to be a friend to me?

Carolina began to laugh aloud.

No woman in her right mind would come out here! I'd settle for a woman who isn't in her right mind. This country is so wild and vast, a woman alone would go mad.

At least, this woman would.

A steady stream of pilgrims bound for the promised land of Devil's Canyon kept Carolina occupied most of the morning. Many asked directions and left with a few purchases. Around noon she glanced out a front window and saw the man in coveralls pull himself into his saddle and ride toward the river. She hadn't heard anything from Starke.

With the store finally empty of customers and the road up from the river deserted, she carried her lunch and tea to the table, sat down, and faced the door.

Look at this! I'm eating stewed tomatoes on top of two cold biscuits. What kind of lunch is that? Even on a bad day in Istanbul, I ate better than this. I doubt if this is on the bill of fare at the Racquet Club in Chestertown. Lord, You know I don't like to cook. I like to eat—sometimes.

You've got to get to town, Carolina. You need better food. Fresh fruit and vegetables . . . A garden. I'll have July plant a garden and . . .

Perhaps one of the stores can freight supplies out to us. There must be a wholesaler in a town the size of Billings. Cheyenne has wholesalers. They were customers of Father's.

Even with salt, the tomatoes tasted bitter, the biscuits doughy. The tea was lukewarm.

I'm glad You're here, Lord. You're my friend—the only One I can't get along without. And I'm glad I'm proving something to someone, because if it weren't for those two things, I don't think I could stand being out in the middle of nowhere, all alone, eating this horrid lunch.

"Work is not fun, Sweet Carolina! If it were fun, it would be play. This is work. We do it because it's our responsibility to see that society survives!"

"Yes, Father."

I suppose I could make a list of everything I need to purchase in town.

She retrieved a pencil and piece of paper and strolled over by the door between the store and the saloon.

I'll need some milled lumber to board up those holes. Of course, that will only last until the next hurrah. What I should order is a big flat sheet of iron. That would keep the bullets from . . . If I can keep the flying lead in the saloon, I don't need all that iron under my bed. Maybe July and I can . . . He ought to be back by now.

She glanced at the brass clock. *Two o'clock!*

An explosion in the front yard brought her to her feet and out to the porch. Horatio Starke stood at the water well, near the corrals, barefoot, with his revolver in his hand.

"Is there trouble, Mr. Starke?"

He leaned against the well with one hand, turned back and shaded his eyes with the hand that gripped the gun. "I lost my key. Had to shoot the lock off the well."

"You did a lot of shooting last night!" she complained.

"I think I got a little drunk."

"Someone could have been seriously wounded or killed. I will not tolerate your doing that again. If one more shot is fired into the store from the saloon, I will notify the sheriff. I expect to be reimbursed for the damages."

With shoulders slumped and head hung in pain, Starke stared back at her. "Lady, this ain't New York City."

"No, and it's not Bodie or Tombstone either. I have all the damages itemized," she informed him. Carolina was not sure of the definition of the words Starke used in return, but she knew that she didn't want him to repeat them.

She reentered the store and marched straight up to the loft. *If we're going to move this sheet of iron from under the bed, I'll need to move the bed and all the boxes under it . . . and the boxes against the wall.*

With the room finally organized and David's belongings stacked under the window, Carolina tugged, pushed, pulled and panted, but she couldn't get the massive bed to budge. With her shoulder against the bedpost and her feet braced against the wall, she continued to try to slide the bed. She thought she heard a noise out in the yard and stopped to peek through the gingham curtains. July Johnson led her rented horse into the corral.

July's home! Thank You, Lord. He can help me move this sheet iron. Iron? He can help me move this bed. Come on, Carolina, you weakling. Surely you can slide the bed.

The noise of footsteps coming into the store caused her to halt the effort. *It really does feel good to have him back.*

"Come up and help me with this bed, will you, please?" she called.

Carolina wiped the perspiration from her forehead as she listened to the footsteps. "I should have waited for you to get here, but I thought I could do it myself. I don't know why David built such a heavy bed. Anyway, I decided to take this iron plate and . . . "

Tall.

Broad shoulders.

Dark brown hair with a sprinkling of gray.

Wide nose, slightly crooked as if it had been broken in the distant past.

Easy smile.

Gray eyes.

Two-day beard.

Leather chaps.

Canvas vest.

Road dust from the tips of his extremely worn boots to the top of the uncrowned, wide-brimmed beaver felt hat.

"What . . . what are you doing up here?" she gasped.

"You called me up to help move a bed or something." It was a deep sonorous voice. She had heard it before.

"I most certainly did not! I asked July to come up here, not you!"

"July is out tendin' the horses. I thought you were talkin' to me. Can I help you?"

The tall man with the tired horse. The tall, ruggedly handsome, egotistical, sweet-smiling man with a tired horse.

"No, thank you. I'm sure that July can . . . " She glanced down at the massive bedposts. "Actually, perhaps you can. I want to slide the bed over there and pull up this sheet iron. I have a better use for it."

He reached down and grabbed the far side while she pushed. The bed suddenly lunged across the room with ease. Carolina stumbled and fell headfirst onto the feather bed.

"Miss Cantrell? Hey, where's everyone at?" It was Johnson's voice down in the store.

"We're up here, July!" she called back as she pulled herself to her feet.

"What are you two doin' up there?"

She glanced over at the tall man's eyes and blushed. "Eh, we're moving furniture. Could you come help us?"

Every other step echoed from the stairway, and a panting July Johnson soon stood beside the man in the loft.

"Oh, good, I see you met Ranahan."

"Ranahan?"

The tall man pulled off his hat and held it in his hands. "Ranahan Parks, ma'am. Most folks just call me Ran."

"Is Ranahan Irish?"

"No, ma'am. Just something my mama liked the sound of."

"You know, Miss Cantrell," July blurted out, "a ranahan is what they call the top hand on a ranch."

"Oh . . . well, I'm Carolina Cantrell, and this is my store."

"Yes, ma'am, I was in the other day, but I reckon you were nappin'."

I assure you, I wasn't taking a nap.

"As long as you two are up here, could you haul this sheet iron downstairs?"

"You don't need the protection up here anymore?" Ranahan asked.

"I think it would serve a better purpose fastened over the interior saloon door. Five bullets were fired through it last night."

July's mouth dropped open. "No foolin'?"

"I believe that piece of iron should dissuade the shots, if not the shooter."

July watched Ranahan Parks lift the heavy iron plating. "Mr. Starke really shot at the store?"

"I think it's called hoo-rahing. Isn't that right, Mr. Parks?"

"Yes, ma'am."

"And, contrary to opinion, I am not running away!"

"No, ma'am," he drawled, "I reckon I was wrong about you on that account."

You were wrong about me on every account, Mr. Parks. I certainly

*hope you stick around long enough to find out how really wrong you
were!*

"July, this is goin' to be too heavy for you to lift. Must weigh
300 pounds," Ranahan declared. "Don't know how David ever got
it up here in the first place."

He suddenly turned and tipped his hat at Carolina. "Please
accept my condolences over your brother, ma'am. David was a good
man who deserved better than he got."

"Thank you, Mr. Parks. Your kind words are truly a comfort.
I've not known many of David's friends over the last few years. I
will miss him. 'The Lord giveth and the Lord taketh away—'"

"'Blessed be the name of the Lord,'" Parks completed.

"That's in the Bible, ain't it?" July piped up. "We been readin'
the Bible, you know."

Ranahan Parks gazed at Carolina. "That don't surprise me."

*Well, Mr. Ranahan Parks, if you know some more Scripture, that
would surprise me.* "Are you saying that iron is too heavy to move?"
she asked.

"No, ma'am, just too heavy to carry. I'll hike up this end, and
July can guide the other. Have you got an old gunny sack or something we can poke under that corner so we don't gouge your stairs?"

It took all three of them half an hour to drag the iron downstairs and over to the interior door. While Ranahan and July bolted
the iron across the door, Carolina waited on several patrons.

All men.

All headed for Devil's Canyon.

"That ought to hold back the bullets, Miss Cantrell," July
reported when the last customer left.

"It could ring like an alarm bell," Ranahan chuckled. It was a
deep, teasing laugh.

"Mr. Parks, I want to thank you for your help. You'll stay for
supper, won't you?"

He pulled off his hat and scratched his head.

"He's goin' to stay a lot longer than that!" July blurted out. "I
hired him to help me dig the new well."

Ranahan jammed his charcoal gray hat on the back of his head.
"Miss Cantrell, if you'd rather not hire me, I can just ride on."

"If Mr. Johnson hired you, you're hired. That's what I have an assistant manager for. Did he tell you about the arrangements?"

"I told him two dollars a day, meals, and he could use the shed to sleep in."

"You do understand it might only be for a couple of days."

"Yes, ma'am. Would you like for us to get to diggin' now?"

"Oh, my heavens, no—not this late in the day."

"Well, in that case I promised July I'd stick some new shoes on that paint horse of his. Do you mind if I use some of these #2s?" He pointed to a wooden barrel full of horseshoes.

"That's fine. What do you mean, paint horse?"

"July earned himself a horse."

She turned around to look at the beaming fourteen-year-old. "You did?"

"You fill Miss Cantrell in on your adventure, and I'll go tend the horse." Ranahan replaced his hat and strolled across the store.

She watched him stoop to exit. "Well, Mr. Johnson, what's this about you earning a horse?"

"Can I cook us some supper as I talk? We ain't had nothin' but sweetbread and jerky since breakfast."

"By all means. Your trip to the Slash-Bar-4 was peaceful?"

"Didn't have no trouble at all. Got there just before dark." He pried open the flour barrel. "Think I'll bake up a pan of biscuits. We're gettin' low on baking soda, you know."

She pointed to some papers on the table. "It's on my list. Did you find Mr. Odessa at the ranch?"

"Yes, ma'am, and he took me straight over to the big house to talk to the ol' man. Hand me the salt, please."

She handed him a blue enameled tin shaker from the table. "Old man?"

"He ain't old, but the boss is always called the old man. Anyway, Mr. Andrews had us eat in the cookhouse and get ready to ride."

"Us? Don't tell me he allowed you to go with his crew to capture the rustlers!"

"It wasn't exactly a big crew. Just Mr. Andrews, Mr. Odessa, Mr. Parks, and me."

"Mr. Parks? He was at the ranch?"

"They weren't hirin' until fall, but they had him trim hooves and shoe horses for a day or two."

"So the three of them went after the rustlers?"

July opened the woodstove door and let the fire burst into flames. "There was four of us."

Carolina retreated from the heat of the stove. "I thought a big ranch would have a big crew."

"Only keeps four or five through the summer, and they were makin' wood up on the mountain. Besides, Mr. Andrews said three rustlers wasn't hardly worth saddlin' four horses over." July wiped the sweat off his forehead onto his cotton shirt sleeve. "Anyway, he picks out that paint for me to ride and tells me to give your horse a rest. Mr. Andrews was a gunfighter down in Arizona years ago. Ranahan told me that."

"Oh, my! Well, did you meet up with the rustlers?"

"We cut across them within a mile or two of the river about midnight. They had a gather of about seventy-five head of Slash-Bar-4 beef."

"Did you have any trouble apprehending them?"

"No, ma'am, we shot 'em all dead."

Carolina's mouth dropped open.

"Actually, I didn't have no gun, so I didn't shoot." Sweat dripped from his smooth-skinned chin.

"You—you mean they murdered all three rustlers?"

July turned from the stove to stare at her. "Murdered? No, ma'am. They started shootin' at us the moment we halted them."

"They shot at you?"

"Yes, ma'am. Ol' Tap, Lorenzo, and Ranahan shot 'em dead."

"My goodness . . . that's horrible!"

July carried the blue pottery mixing bowl to the table. "They was stealin' cattle. You can hang a man for that even in the States."

"Were any of the Slash-Bar-4 men injured?"

"No, ma'am."

"Three rustlers killed—no injuries to the others? How do you account for that?" she pressed.

"They was lousy shots. We weren't. It was just like I was livin' out a Hawthorne Miller dime novel!"

"But that doesn't explain the paint horse."

"Ol' man Andrews said he was grateful for my long ride to warn him. Said a man was 'worthy of his hire.' That's in the Bible, you know. Ranahan told me that. He knows all about the Bible. So Mr. Andrews just up and gave me the horse and saddle and everythin'!"

"Well, that was quite generous of him."

"Mr. Andrews sure does know a lot about shootin'. Ranahan said if he were to find out that Tap Andrews was on the other side of a gunfight, he'd ride away right then and there! We had those three surrounded before they ever knew we were in the neighborhood. He called to them to throw down their guns, but I guess they figured to make a fight out of it."

"I hope they didn't allow you to be in the line of fire."

"Nah. Mr. Andrews made me promise to hide behind the rocks."

"Did you?"

"Sort of."

"Oh."

"I peeked around the rocks a little. But I couldn't see much but flames shootin' out of gun barrels. There wasn't much moonlight last night. Anyway, when it was all over and they was loadin' up the bodies, Mr. Andrews—"

"Loading bodies?" Carolina gasped.

"Mr. Andrews tied 'em to their horses and was goin' to take 'em into Billings. He said even cattle rustlers ought to have their kin notified and be given a decent burial."

"How considerate," she said primly.

"Oh, that's the way he is. He had prayer over those rustlers right out there in the night. Then we pushed the cattle back up on the range and went back to the ranch. By the time we got in, it was breakin' daylight. He fed us at the bunkhouse. He offered to pay Ran for ridin' with 'em, but Ran refused. Ranahan said he knowed what it was like to lose cattle to rustlers and wouldn't take pay for doing what any decent man ought to do for free."

"Mr. Andrews sounds a lot like Mr. Odessa."

"They've been friends a long time. You should've heard the story about the time they was down in Mexico and . . . " July paused and glanced over at Carolina.

"Are you blushing?" she asked.

"Maybe I shouldn't tell that story."

"Maybe you shouldn't."

"Anyway, that's when Mr. Andrews said a young man is 'worthy of his hire' and gave me the paint. I'm going to call him Blaze. What do you think? I ain't never named a horse before. Shoot, I ain't never had a horse of my very own neither."

"I think Blaze is a good name for such a fancy-colored horse." Carolina walked over to the doorway and stared out at the tall man with a horse hoof on his knee.

"You know, Ranahan's goin' to work for the Slash-Bar-4 in the fall if he don't land somethin' better before that. Maybe he could come visit us at the store from time to time."

"July . . . what do you know about this Mr. Parks?"

"I think he's had some hard times lately, but things used to be better." July rolled out the dough on a flour-covered cutting board.

"How's that?"

"We had lots of time to visit ridin' back to the store today. I think he had his own spread and lost it . . . or somethin' like that. He can ride, shoot, and work cows with the likes of Andrews and Odessa."

Carolina still stared out across the yard. Her fingers twisted the tight curls of her bangs. In a soft voice she asked, "Does he . . . you know . . . have a family?"

"You mean, like a wife and kids?" July dropped lumps of dough into the iron skillet of sizzling pork fat.

"Yes."

"Now don't that beat all? It's strange that you should ask."

Carolina stepped back inside the store and retreated toward the table. "Why's that?"

"'Cause it's the exact same question he asked about you."

"Oh." Her face burned as she turned down an aisle of harness leathers.

With the money he earned from work on the Slash-Bar-4 horses, Ranahan Parks purchased a new shirt and a pair of copper-riveted blue jeans. He wore the new clothes when he joined July and Carolina at the small table next to the woodstove for supper.

"Oh my . . . I forgot that we only have two chairs!" she apologized.

He plucked up a 100-pound wooden keg of nails and banged it down beside the table. "No problem, Miss Cantrell. This suits me just fine."

Both Parks and Johnson busied themselves with biscuits, beans, pork, peaches, and fried red onions. Carolina picked at the peaches and onions.

He sits straight.

No elbows on the table.

Doesn't use his knife for a spoon.

Doesn't wipe his mouth on his sleeve.

Doesn't belch.

He had to learn that from a mother or a wife or a lady friend.

"That's good cookin', July." Ranahan nodded. "Thanks for boilin' some coffee."

I wonder how he'd look if he shaved? I always said I would never marry a man with a beard. It makes them look old. Besides that, it scratches. At least, it looks like it would scratch. I mean, if I were to kiss such a man. For some reason.

"I cain't stand coffee myself," July announced. "It's too bitter."

"I can't stand coffee," she corrected.

"Yes, ma'am. Can't instead of cain't." He turned to Ranahan and smiled. "Miss Cantrell is goin' to make a store manager out of me."

The tall man let his natural smile widen. "I'll bet she's mighty good at that."

What do you mean? That I'm good at nagging men? That I'm too pushy? I have never in my life nagged at a man who didn't need nagging. Where would this world be if men didn't have women's . . . eh, influence? Carolina chased a fried onion across her plate with her fork.

When he finished eating, Ranahan stood and stretched his arms. "Gettin' a little stuffy in here. Think I'll sit outside a spell."

"We've been doin' that most ever' evenin', haven't we, Miss Cantrell?" July remarked.

"Yes, we have. You men go on out there and get some fresh air. July, bring me in a bucket of clean water, and I'll do dishes."

"I can do that, Miss Cantrell," July insisted. "You can go visit with Ran."

We would exhaust topics in about two minutes. He could tell me the price of cattle in Chicago, and I'll tell him the price of silk in Rome. After that we'd just sit around counting cobwebs on the rafters. "No, go on. You two have to discuss that well-digging project."

With pale, thin hands shriveled in the hot, soapy water, Carolina finished the dishes and listened to the talk on the porch. After a long discussion about water wells, the subject turned to cattle.

"Ran, did you ever have your own place?" July asked.

"Never owned property. But I grazed 600 head of my own on some government land. I worked five years for room and board to build up that herd."

"Did you make a lot of money when you sold them?"

Ranahan was quiet for a long time. Carolina stood motionless with her hands in the water until he started to speak.

"Me and a few friends pushed them up across the border into the British Possessions. Some rich Englishman started a ranch on the slope and offered to pay me thirty dollars a head."

"He didn't pay you?"

"We were about three days' journey past the border when we got jumped by a dozen men."

"What happened?"

"My friends were killed, and I took a bullet in the shoulder and two more in the leg. When I saw my compadres were fumed, I rode a horse into the ground and then limped to the first house I found. Turned out to be a preacher's. He and his wife looked after me for a few weeks until I healed enough to ride. They gave me a horse and a saddle and sent me out with prayers. They were good folks. Real good Christian folks."

"What happened to your cattle?"

"The rustlers got off with them."

"Did the Mounties find out who stole them?"

"They traced them back down to North Dakota. After that no one knows what happened to them. I figure they sold the cows and shipped 'em off to Chicago. But I've been ridin' up and down ever' trail tryin' to find them."

"Do you know their names?"

"It was dark when they bushwhacked us. I don't know what they look like. And the only name I have is Cigar."

"Cigar?"

"One of 'em's called Cigar."

"Maybe them three that got blasted last night were part of the gang that wiped you out."

"No way of knowin', I suppose."

"I moved out here from Nebraska," July offered. "What part of the States did you come from?"

"Oregon."

"I ain't never met no one who was actually born in Oregon. Ever'one wants to go there. How come you decided to leave?"

"The homestead was just big enough for my older brother, so when I was about your age, I signed on to drive cattle to Idaho. After doin' that awhile, I started workin' for Conrad Khors. Was plannin' on sellin' those bovines and then buyin' me a place of my own. But I reckon the good Lord has other plans."

"You mean, God rustled your cattle?"

"Nope . . . but He didn't stop those hombres from doin' it either. Some things we just have to accept, Mr. Assistant Manager."

"Like my mama and daddy gettin' killed by stray bullets in that gold heist?" July questioned.

Carolina stood very still so she could hear Ranahan's reply.

"Well, son . . . I don't know about your folks. That's a mighty rough ride for any boy . . . or man. But I reckon you do have to accept it and go on. I got a feelin' that's what they would tell you."

"My mama was a pretty woman," July blurted out. "She was almost as pretty as Miss Cantrell—in a Nebraska sort of way. You know what I mean?"

"I know what you're sayin', and you're right." His voice softened to a whisper. Carolina leaned toward the doorway, afraid to step closer and reveal her eavesdropping. "Miss Cantrell is one of those gals that makes you mighty glad that you're a man."

What is that supposed to mean? Is that a compliment?

"'Course, if I knew her better, I might find other things, but there's only one thing wrong with her that I can spot at first glance."

Wrong with me? What's wrong with me?

"What's that?" July asked.

"Her ears."

Carolina instantly lifted dripping hands to her ears. *You can't even see my ears.*

"What's wrong with her ears?" July pressed.

"Too big."

Too big! How dare you? Oh, my neck might look a little long, but . . .

"They don't look big to me," July argued.

"Don't be fooled. I bet they're listenin' to every word we are sayin' right now."

Of all the . . . You knew I was listening! Mr. Parks, you are a despicable and conniving man! I absolutely refuse to acknowledge that I heard you. You think you know me? You think you can predict what I'm doing? Mister, you are in a sinking ship.

After Carolina cleaned up the supper dishes, she hollered out, "I'm going up to my room, July. You close the store."

"Ain't you comin' out and sit with us on the porch?" he called back.

"What did you say?"

"Aren't you coming out tonight?"

"No, I have things to do upstairs." *Pout . . . for one.*

Once in the loft, she pulled off her apron and heavy dress and sat on the bed in her petticoats.

Well, Carolina, it's hot and stuffy up here. You ought to be out on the porch with the others. No, I ought to be out on the porch with July. Mr. Parks enjoys playing too many games. I suppose I'll have to put up with humiliations until that well is dug. Perhaps this would be a good time for me to go to town for a couple of days.

Of course, he was right. I strained to listen to every word, especially those about me. But the point is, he didn't have to draw attention to it. Big ears? How about you, Mr. Parks? You've certainly got big . . . big . . . and your . . . You need a shave, haircut, and some new boots!

She woke up in a dark loft still in her petticoats on top of the comforter. The lamp had gone out, and church bells were ringing.

Church bells?

Those are bullets chiming off the sheet iron!

She opened the gingham curtains and stuck her head over the loft rail into the dark store. A faint glimmer of moonlight reflected through the windows.

"July?" she whispered between chimes. "July, are you all right?"

"Yes, ma'am," came a fourteen-year-old voice right below her.

"How long has this been going on?"

"That's the fourth shot."

The simultaneous sound of an explosion and a chime echo caused Carolina to flinch back inside the curtains.

"That's five."

"Well, at least the iron held."

"As long as he doesn't start shootin' through the walls."

"Stay back behind the counter until the shooting stops," she instructed.

"It's stopped. Sounds like there's a fight in there now," July called up.

"Let's go back to sleep then."

"Yes, ma'am."

There was a steady rap at the front door.

"Someone's at the door, Miss Cantrell."

"Probably just a drunk."

"What do you want me to do?"

The knock persisted.

"Well . . . light a lantern. I'll be right down."

Barefoot and in petticoats, a flannel sheet wrapped completely around her shoulders, she hustled down the stairs and glided toward the door. She reached for her dress pocket.

No pocket! No dress! No handgun!

"July, grab that shotgun off the wall and shove a couple of shells into it. Have you ever used one before?"

"Yes, ma'am, but I ain't never shot nobody."

"Well, don't start tonight. Just point it toward the door to show them we won't take any guff from them."

"Miss Cantrell? July?" the deep voice called from the porch.

"It's Ranahan!" July shouted.

"Mr. Parks?" she called out.

"Yes, ma'am. I was just checkin' . . . "

July unbolted the door before she could protest. Hatless, Ranahan peeked inside the store, lit only by the flickering lantern in Johnson's hand. "Is ever'one safe in here? There's been a ruckus next door."

"We're fine, Mr. Parks. Thank you for checking on us." She held the flannel sheet tightly around her neck.

"You won't have to worry about Starke."

"You didn't kill him, did you?" July blurted out.

"Nope. He's asleep. He'll wake up with a headache and a sore jaw. You all go back to bed."

"Thank you, Mr. Parks."

"You can call me Ran or Ranahan, ma'am."

"Thank you for looking after us . . . Ran."

He nodded his head. "You're welcome, Sweet Carolina."

He hustled back across the yard toward the hay shed and left her staring into the moonlit darkness.

Sweet Carolina? No one out here calls me that! How dare you? He must have heard David mention me by that name. Well, Mr. Ranahan Parks, no one calls me Sweet Carolina unless I give him permission. And I don't care how amiable I sounded. I don't care if it did tickle my throat. I definitely have not given you such permission!

Not yet anyway.

Tucked comfortably into the feather bed, Carolina stared at the pitch-black ceiling until daylight lightened the room. She decided to wear her gray tweed dress with black velvet cuffs and collar. She didn't feel overdressed until she descended the stairs and saw July Johnson's face look up from the woodstove where he was cooking flapjacks.

"You look like you're goin' on a trip," he blurted out.

"Yes, I am. This is a comfortable dress to wear when I travel."

"We aren't pullin' out and givin' up, are we?"

"Oh, no. But I will need you to put the buggy seat back in the carriage and hitch up my horse. If I'm going to stay the summer, I'll have to rent the rig longer than a week. Plus we will need some more inventory. I'm going to Billings to see if any of the wholesalers will deliver out here."

"Clear to Billings? You need me to come along?"

"No, I'll get along just fine, thank you. Let me finish cooking breakfast, and you go hitch up my carriage. Then I'll explain everything to you and Mr. Parks."

"You want me to run the store?"

"That's what assistant managers are for."

"Yes, ma'am." He beamed.

With a wooden spatula in her hand and a long white canvas apron tied around her, she watched the flapjacks bubble and fry.

What makes you think you can trust the impulsive Mr. Parks to help July? Is it the sparkle in his eyes when he said Sweet Carolina? No, that was just the reflection of the lantern. Is it his friendship with July? His helpfulness to the Slash-Bar-4?

Maybe it's because you've wondered what it would be like to have that rough, callused hand in yours. Or maybe those chapped lips brush . . . I can't believe I thought that!

Maybe I want to put him in a position to fail. Maybe I secretly want him to turn out to be a scoundrel. Now there, C. K. C., is a thought to contemplate.

As they were seated around the table with a mound of flapjacks on a platter in the center, Carolina explained the arrangements.

"I'd like you to dig on the well this morning. If we can have the pump right under the window, let's do that. I'll bring some sort of sink with me from town.

"July, you're in charge of the store. When customers come, you'll have to stop and wait on them. I left twenty dollars' worth of change in the cash box. I believe you know most of the prices. If not, whatever you and Mr. Parks agree upon is acceptable. There is an inventory on most of that mining gear."

"What if Mr. Starke tries to give me a tough time?"

"Mr. Parks, can I count on you to assist July if necessary?"

"Yep. A man sticks by his pard. But I have a feelin' that Mr. July Johnson can pretty much take care of himself."

"When will you be back?" July quizzed.

"Tomorrow around noon. If I'm delayed because of business, I'll send word with someone coming this way."

July carried her small leather valise down the stairs and out to the waiting black buggy. She draped a brown cape across the leather buggy seat and felt into the deep pocket for the small derringer. With her money belt hidden well under the folds of her dress and her small handbag beside her, Carolina waved at the two who stood on the porch.

"Take care of my store, Mr. Johnson."

"Yes, ma'am, I will." July beamed.

"I'll drive you down the road a little just to get the kinks out of the horse," Ranahan announced as he swung up beside a startled Carolina Cantrell.

"I'm perfectly capable of—"

"I need to talk to you in private," he whispered. Then he turned back to July. "Find us a couple of sharp-pointed spades, and we'll start diggin' as soon as I get back." He tugged the reins out of her gloved hands and slapped the horse's rump.

"Mr. Parks, I've driven horses since I was a seven-year-old and lived in Austria. I do not need your help. So what is this secret you wanted to talk about?"

"No secret, Miss Cantrell. We just haven't hit it off real well, and I needed to tell you a thing or two without July listenin' in." He stopped the rig at the cottonwoods beyond the dirt yard.

"Well, what is it?" When he sat beside her in the buggy, he seemed to be a full head taller.

"You don't know me, and I don't know you, but I want you to

know I'll look after young Johnson—without bein' a baby-sitter. Your store is safe. You've got my word on that."

"Thank you, Mr. Parks. Was that all you wanted to talk to me about?"

He climbed down off the buggy. She adjusted her straw hat and then laced the reins between her fingers.

It was almost a little boy grin. "Well, Miss Cantrell, I owe you an apology. I embarrassed you and me both last night, and I laid awake stewin' about it 'til mornin'."

"Embarrassed? How's that?"

"I should never have called you Sweet Carolina. I have no idea why I said those words. They were inappropriate and way too famil-iar. Please accept my apology."

"Oh? I assumed you had heard David call me that and—"

"No, ma'am. He did mention he had a sister, but I don't recall ever hearin' your name. I have no good excuse. Miss Cantrell, maybe I've just been on the prowl so long I don't know how to act around a lady such as yourself."

"Thank you, Ran, for the apology."

He reached up and put his strong hand on her arm. "Now you go on, and, Lord willin', we'll have you a well dug before you get back."

The road to town paralleled the Northern Pacific tracks on the south side of the promenading Yellowstone River. The river itself was lined with cottonwoods, elms, and willows. Heavy brush guarded the rocky shoreline and often blocked her view of the water.

Clumps of white clouds drifted across the blue Montana sky. The hills to the south were covered with a light green grass and limestone rimrock. Traffic was light, and she only passed half a dozen rigs headed east. All were driven by men. And each man tipped his hat as he passed.

Her thoughts drifted from store inventory . . . to a drunken saloon keeper . . . to someone called the Marquesa . . . to a tall man with a firm grip. *He called me Sweet Carolina. From a perfect stranger.*

Okay, he's not perfect. But it is strange. It's like a premonition. I have no idea if it's a positive sign from the Lord—or a warning.

The breeze was slightly cool as she started the trip. By mid-morning it was warm. She drove into a grassy area near the river to water the horse. A sign pointed toward a cliff called Pompey's Pillar. A man, woman, and four little children were sitting on a picnic blanket on the grassy meadow.

"Howdy, ma'am," the man greeted her arrival. "Orvy, go lead the woman's horse down to the river for a drink."

"Oh, thank you very much." Carolina stepped down and felt her legs cramp. "I do believe I got a little stiff."

"Well, come join us for some dinner on the ground," the woman in the black dress beckoned. "We have plenty!"

"I must regretfully decline. I have business in Billings and need to press on. But this a delightful place for a picnic." Carolina scooted closer to the woman. "I'm not sure of the history. What's Pompey's Pillar?"

The man was eager to explain. "Back when this country was still wilderness . . ."

It's not exactly settled now, is it?

". . . Captain William Clark—you know, of Lewis and Clark—came right through here in '06. Yes, sir, he carved his name right up there on that pillar."

"That was over seventy-five years ago!" a little blonde-haired girl piped up.

"Yes, it was, honey. Do you folks live nearby?"

"We farm river bottom land down the river a piece," the man explained.

A young boy circled Carolina. "Do you live around here?"

"I operate my brother's store. Cantrell's. Perhaps you've heard of it. It's down near the Crow Reservation."

"I surmised that was just a saloon," the woman stated.

"Half of it's a saloon—a wretched place—but the other half is my store. Please feel welcome to stop and look at our goods. My name is Miss Carolina Cantrell."

"Yes, ma'am, we just might do that sometime. I'll go help Orvy bring up your rig." The man in clean coveralls strolled toward the river.

The little girl stared up at Carolina. "Lady, you sure are pretty. When I grow up, I want to look just like you."

"Katherine, now don't embarrass Miss Cantrell."

Carolina looked down at the little girl. "So your name's Katherine."

"Yes, ma'am."

"That just happens to be my middle name. Isn't it a beautiful name?"

"Yes!"

"You will probably grow up to be much prettier than I. You already have a head start. I was quite a homely young lady."

The little girl's eyes grew wide as she looked over at her mother. "I'm going to grow up to be pretty," she boasted.

Carolina climbed back into the buggy, and the man handed her the reins. "Now, Miss Cantrell, you be sure and stop by our house on the way home. You can water your horse there, and at least we can share a cup of tea."

"That sounds delightful. If I have time, I will certainly do that."

The trail back to the tracks was dusty. Carolina kept the horse at a walk.

That's almost like having neighbors. That's what's missing at the store. Good, solid family neighbors. Lord, I don't think I do very well alone. I like having people around. That's why I need to go to town.

It will be nice to stay at a hotel.

Have a hot bath.

Curl my hair.

Eat at a nice restaurant.

If I knew people in Billings, I'd invite them to supper. Other than the Marquesa, whom I have no intention of . . . On the other hand, perhaps I should . . . I've been out in the brush too long. Even supper with the Marquesa doesn't sound all that bad. She is definitely not the friend I asked You to send me, Lord.

Is she?

The streets of Billings were much more crowded than the week before. Carolina drove straight for the livery. She turned in the rig and made arrangements to rent it the next day, but this time for a full month. A young boy about ten offered to carry her valise to a hotel. He recommended the England House. She wasn't sure if that was because it was the most attractive or the closest.

Both sides of the main street were jammed with stores, shops, hotels, restaurants, and saloons. The raised boardwalks kept her dress from dragging in the dirt, and the covering overhead kept the noonday sun from her face. Her room was orderly and clean, and fresh flowers in a vase on the dresser added a civilized touch.

We'll plant flowers all around the store . . . paint the building . . . at least half the building.

She washed her hands and face, straightened her hair, picked up her purse, and walked back out onto the boardwalk.

The afternoon passed quickly. Mr. McGuire, who had left the wagonload of merchandise on consignment, was pleased to receive a third of his money so quickly. He agreed to deliver another order of hardware for free if she could get a dry goods merchant to share the shipping expenses.

Albert Duvall of Duvall & Sons' Mercantile agreed to sell her the dry goods. But not without a soft voice and a coy smile.

She paused on the boardwalk in front of the mercantile and glanced at her list. *They'll load the sink in the carriage first thing tomorrow. I'll purchase some fresh produce and grocery goods on the way out of town. Now it's time for that hot bath, Carolina . . . Sweet Carolina. Nice!* She sighed and then quickened her pace. *If they can keep the hot water flowing, I'll soak for an hour.*

An eastbound Concord stage pulled up in front of the Imperial Hotel, and she waited on the far side of the street for the dust to settle. When it did, several passengers climbed out of the stage. It was the one in the silk hat, long coat, and black tie that caught her attention.

Jacob!

— Five —

THE DOOR ON ROOM 12 at the England House Hotel slammed behind her before Carolina ever turned around. She stood at the dresser and peered into the silver-plated mirror as she unpinned her hat.

He looked more out of place than I feel. Lord, I don't understand. This country is huge. A great big, wild West with only a few people scattered throughout the territories. How in the world did Jacob Hardisty and I end up on the same dusty street?

I do not want to see him here. I do not want to see him anywhere. This is an intrusion.

For a few moments during the last week, it seemed as if everything in the past was truly behind me. Being out here is like getting a fresh start. A different culture. A different way of looking at things. Ranahan, July . . . even Horatio Starke—it's a different world. A clearer world. Wrong and right are easier to discern. In a land where you have all the time in the world, decisions come much easier. I think I'm beginning to like this world. I believe I'm ready to forget the past and embrace life on the frontier.

But then along comes Jacob March Hardisty. It's as if all of the contamination of life in the East follows him like a cloud. When I see him, I feel hurt, pain, rejection. He's not to blame for it all. He just represents all in my life that I'd like to escape. For the past twelve months, we've lived only forty miles apart, and I've not seen him once!

Now here he is.

Is this a joke?

I'm not amused. The Marquesa can have him.

Anyone can have him.

She said she wanted to kill him.

She wasn't serious.

Was she?

Carolina Cantrell slipped out of her dress and hung it on a hanger that dangled from a peg on the flower-papered wall. Her bare feet padded across the polished hardwood floor where she retrieved a clothes brush from her valise. The room had a stale, unused smell that she had not previously noticed. She wore only her white petticoats as she brushed down the dress and jacket.

I wanted to dine at the Imperial Hotel, but obviously that's out of the question. I do not want to run into Jacob, especially if I'm alone. He would just think I followed him. This is too wild to believe it's merely a coincidence. This is stupid! I come to town, and I have to hide in my room. I might as well be out at the store.

Carolina, you will not let Jacob Hardisty dictate what you do and don't do. You may do whatever you like. Hardisty be hanged.

But I'm not going over to the Imperial Hotel. I'll take a long bath, and I'll eat here at the England House. Jacob won't dine here. It's much too boring for him.

All of Montana is much too boring for Jacob Hardisty.

Of course, if the Marquesa makes good her threat to kill him, it would put a little excitement in his life.

I wonder if I should warn him?

She laid down her brush and stepped back over in front of the mirror.

"Mr. Hardisty, I'm sorry to inconvenience you. I'm really tied up with business matters myself, but I just wanted you to know about a woman in Billings who will try to kill you on sight. No, it's not me. But thank you for asking. Now if you'll excuse me, dinner guests wait."

Dark curly hair, skinny face, pale complexion, long neck, small . . . body, thin arms—you're a real beauty, all right. Maybe you ought to stay out in the wilderness, Carolina . . . Sweet Carolina. Cowboys who've stared at the south end of northbound cattle for months think you're quite the attraction. But those rich Eastern gentlemen think you're about as dull as old snow.

She took a sulfur match and lit the cream-colored candle in the center of a hand-painted porcelain flower arrangement. Soon the room began to smell like vanilla.

That's what we need in the store—scented candles. Actually, it's the saloon that needs them. One on every table. No, four on every table. The place would smell like a Jerusalem shrine.

She found an ink pen in the top drawer and searched for a bottle of ink, which she ferreted out from the floor under the dresser.

Maybe I should just send him a letter: "Dear Mr. Hardisty, this is to inform you that a woman who goes by the name of the Marquesa has stated that she intends to kill you. Have a nice stay in Billings. Sincerely, a former acquaintance."

Carolina had just written the note when she heard a knock at her door.

"Yes?" She observed her dress, which still hung on the hanger.

"It's Yvonne. I have the hot water for your bath."

Carolina scooted over to the closed door. "Are you alone?"

"Yes, just me and Darnell."

Darnell? That's what you call alone?

"Just a minute." Carolina scurried to the green velvet chair by the bed and pulled her cape around her like a robe. Then she dashed over and unlocked the door.

The upstairs housekeeper, Yvonne, and a young man about eighteen stood at the doorway. Both carried wooden buckets of steaming water in each hand. They marched across the room and filled the glazed iron tub that stood tucked in the corner near the window.

"Will you need some cold water?" Yvonne asked.

"No, I'll just let this cool until I can slip in. Thank you very much."

"Is there anything else?"

Carolina dug through her handbag and pulled out a two-bit piece. Then she picked up the folded letter on her dresser. "Your name is Darnell?"

"Yes, ma'am." The round-faced young man answered with his blue eyes focused on Carolina's bare toes.

"Here's twenty-five cents. Could you deliver this note to a gentleman at the Imperial Hotel?"

Yvonne raised her eyebrows. Carolina looked at the housekeeper. "I heard some distressing news that Mr. Hardisty should be made aware of, but I'm not interested in having him know it came from me." She looked right at the top of Darnell's neatly combed and oiled brown hair. "Please keep this anonymous."

"Yes, ma'am. I'll do it right now."

"Thank you very much!" She closed the door and locked it. She heard someone whistle in the hallway but couldn't tell if it was Yvonne or Darnell.

I don't remember humor in my private note.

Her third attempt to stand the heat of the water and ease herself into the small tub finally proved successful. Even when she sat perfectly upright, she couldn't stretch out her legs. But the water level came within inches of her shoulders. And it was hot. The aroma of lilac bath salts steamed around her face. Carolina felt as if the pores of her skin released several weeks of accumulated grime. The hotel room soon filled with vapors of lilac and vanilla.

If the water would stay warm, I could stay here for hours. I haven't been this relaxed in days.

Weeks.

Months.

I should buy more bath salts. I wonder how long it will be until my next hot bath?

By the time Carolina finally pulled herself out and dried off, the room felt stuffy. Towel-wrapped and squeaky clean, she folded back the white linen curtains just far enough to unlock the second-story room window and push it open a few inches. The soft summer breeze felt faintly cool on her bare arms. The curtains fluttered just enough to allow the aromas of sage, street dirt, and restaurants to enter the room.

Actually, it smells like early summer. Lord, every season has its own texture. Its own feel. Its own smell. There's always a sense of joy at the first taste of spring and a sense of sadness at the first hint of autumn. And summer, sweet summer—it has a promise of hard work and of reward. I'm ready for the hard work. I've never minded that. But I'd like to know the reward. A successful store? A vigorous, healthy body? Christian influence in a pagan land? A strong, yet tender cowboy?

I can't believe I'm thinking of him . . . again.

Through the crack in the curtains no wider than her palm, she continued to stand and stare down at the street. She had no idea what transpired on the boardwalk beneath her, since all she could view was the top of the shingled porch. Several rigs creaked slowly by as if they strained to make sure they didn't arrive at their destination too soon. People on the far side of the street seemed more intent on visiting with each other than on any commercial enterprise.

Twenty-two men and three women. Seven to one. It must be difficult for a lady to have a close woman friend. Each would be quite busy with husband or suitors. Of course, Sweet Carolina, you've never done well in your attempts to make friends with women. Except for DeLisa.

She doesn't count.

She was like a sister, only closer.

Until she married Paul Luke Magadan, III.

We always promised we'd be married on the same day. But somehow I knew DeLisa was bound to find the right man before I did. All she wanted was a man who was crazy about her.

Me? I needed much more than that. The reason why seems to be growing more faint with each year.

She spied on two women who stood in front of a millinery shop. She could not hear their voices nor read their lips. They laughed and spoke in rapid turns. One waved her arms wildly about and explained something that delighted the other. Finally, the yellow-haired one nodded enthusiastically, hugged her friend, and departed with a wave.

Carolina Katherine Cantrell felt extremely lonely.

Well, you did it, Sweet Carolina. You set out to prove that you can run any business as well as your father. A successful businesswoman has little time for social visits. No time for inconsequential relationships.

At least Father had his family to come home to. How about you, C. K. C.? Do you plan to spend your life proving something to someone and eat all your suppers alone in some hotel?

It's a beautiful country out here. The drive to town from the store would be a wonderful memory for most of those who live along the Eastern seaboard. It's wild, unpredictable, and filled with expectancy. The senses come alive. I can hear, see, touch, smell, and taste the day.

But I will eat supper alone.

"No, Mother, I don't need to get married. I just want some friends
to enjoy each day with."

Sort of like the first day at the university. Everyone else knew the routine. Everyone had someone to talk to. Everyone had someone to eat with.

Except me.

As she mused, she was startled to see Jacob Hardisty step out
of the tall front doors of the Imperial Hotel. Carolina dropped the
curtains. She peeked back to the distant boardwalk, but Hardisty
stared across at the England House. Then he whirled around and
reentered the hotel.

Carolina retreated from the window and began to dress. In no
hurry, she flopped on her back on the brass-framed bed and decided
it was nearly as soft as the one in the loft back at the store.

"Lord, is it possible to be in a crowd of people and feel lonely?"
she asked aloud. "I think I'll go have an early supper and visit with
all the people in the restaurant."

She bounced out of bed and began to tug on her dress.

"Hello, I'm Carolina Cantrell. Do you mind if I join you for supper? This old dress? Oh, why, thank you. I bought it in London last year.
You have? Oh, aren't the Isles delightful? I went there to buy Scottish
wool for a mill down in Georgia. Oh, yes, I get to Europe almost every
year. And you?"

Sure.

I'll probably eat alone.

Again.

The large dining room at the England House held sixteen tables.
Each one was covered with white linen, fresh flowers, silverware,
gleaming china, and crystal goblets. Starched waitresses and wait-
ers stood almost at attention. Only four tables were occupied. It was
still early when Carolina peered in.

I should go for a walk. Enjoy the summer evening. Look for a light
dress. There is no Chesapeake chill in a Montana summer. Maybe I
should buy a gift for July.

"Would you like to be seated now, or are you waiting for
someone?"

With a stiff boiled white shirt and crisp black tie and vest, the middle-aged man held a bill of fare in his hand and tilted his head at her. There was a gap between his upper front teeth and singsong in his voice. The hair on the top of his head was extremely thin, and he sported a generous double chin.

"Excuse me?"

"I said, would you like to wait for others, or would you like to be seated now?"

"Oh, yes, I'm sorry. I was thinking of something else. May I have that table by the window? I'd like to view the street."

"When our supper guests arrive, I'll need that table for a party of four. Perhaps the madam would enjoy one of the smaller tables under the crystal chandelier?"

Carolina could feel the heat rise in the back of her neck. She narrowed her brown eyes at the man and flashed him her classic poker-faced smile. "If you feel unable to seat me by the window, would you please call the manager?"

"Wha . . . you want me to—"

"What I want," she motioned with a sweep of her ungloved hand, "is to sit by the window. I was under the impression that the tables were not reserved. Would you please call your manager?"

"He does not like to be disturbed while—"

"Oh, in that case I'll just seat myself!" She waltzed across the room toward the table by the window. The man trailed after her and, with the wave of a hand, summoned a waiter. "When every chair in this room is filled with hotel guests, then by all means, you may seat some others with me," she threw over her shoulder.

From her position she could glance to her left out the white lace curtains at the street and across at the steps leading up to the Imperial Hotel. If she looked straight ahead, she could see each person who entered the restaurant.

She sipped Chinese tea and studied the bill of fare in her hand.

Raw Oysters. Mock Turtle Soup.
Baked Filet of Trout, larded with Madeira Sauce.
Parisian Potatoes. Spinach, with Cream.
Boiled Leg of Mutton, Caper Sauce.
Sweetbreads Glazed. French Peas.

Tenderloin of Beef Braised, with Mushrooms.
Stewed tomatoes.
Roast Beef, with Yorkshire Pudding. Corn.
Roast Young Turkey Stuffed, Giblet Sauce.
Green Peas. Browned Mashed Potatoes.
Roast Quail, larded with Jelly. Boiled Potatoes.
Celery. Lettuce. Queen Olives.
English Plum Pudding. Rum Sauce. Mince Pie. Assorted Cakes.
Lemon Meringue Pie. Confectionery.
Port Wine Jelly. Seasonal Fruit. Cheeses. Tea. Coffee.

The rattle of a westbound stagecoach caught her eye, and she glanced out only to see a cloud of dust. She was still staring out when she realized someone stood near her table.

She pointed at her bill of fare. "Yes, I'd like to order . . . Oh!"

Both men stood square-shouldered, hats in hand, guns on hips, with relaxed easy smiles in their eyes.

"Mr. Odessa!"

"Miss Cantrell." He nodded. "I saw you sittin' here and wanted to introduce you to my boss, Tap Andrews. Tap, this is David Cantrell's sister."

"Pleased to meet you, ma'am. I'm obliged for you warnin' me about those rustlers. We just brought them into town."

"Oh? July told me all about it."

"He's a good kid," Odessa remarked.

"That Ranahan will do to ride the river with too," Andrews added. "Sure wish I could have hired him on, but you beat me to it. Said he'd promised to work for you."

Work for me? He said Andrews couldn't give him a job until fall.

"Don't want to take up your time, Miss Cantrell." Odessa glanced down at the large oak table. "You're probably waitin' for someone."

"Actually, I just came in for a few supplies for the store. I thought I would have to sit here and dine alone. Would it seem improper to invite two married gentlemen to join me?"

"For me it would be considerably more enjoyable than havin' to stare at Lorenzo all evenin'," Andrews replied. "You'll have to

let me buy your supper." He and Odessa seated themselves opposite of Carolina.

"That is something I'm afraid I can't do," she protested. "I have
a certain sense of independence when I pay my own way."

Andrews lifted his eyebrows and glanced over at Odessa. "You
know, too bad more folks don't have that same conviction."

"Oh, no you don't, Tapadera. You're buyin' my supper, and I
don't feel one bit guilty!" Odessa laughed.

It was not the last laughter of the evening.

For the next two hours Carolina watched the restaurant fill up,
listened to the cowmen talk about babies, cattle, wives, horses,
and wild times on the Western frontier.

Carolina wiped her mouth on the linen napkin and returned
it to her lap. She studied the two men across from her. *Maybe I do
belong out here. These are my type of people. They work hard. They
fear God. They talk honestly. They have a fierce commitment to do what
is right. Men of honor. That's all I ever wanted, Lord.*

*They can dress any way they like, be covered with dust from boot
to hat, and destroy the king's English, but I can relate to what they say
and feel a kinship to how they think.*

*There is a regalness on the plains. These men are princes. And they
have treated me like a princess. I like that. I like their wives already. I do
believe I have found some future friends. Of course, friendship with an
unmarried woman may be awkward. But I have no intention of staying
unmarried forever.*

Do I?

*This has been a good evening after all. Lord, no matter what hap-
pens next, this has been a very good evening.*

They had just turned up the kerosene lamps, and the waiter
had brought a large tray of assorted cakes, fruit, and cheeses when
the swish of a full silk skirt caught Carolina's attention. She peered
toward the double doors that led from the hotel lobby into the
restaurant.

*The Marquesa! That dress is off the shoulders and way too tight.
It's definitely cut too low. She's not really going to eat here, is she?*

The dark-haired woman with the purple silk dress swooped over toward Carolina. "Well, I can hardly believe this," the Marquesa purred. "If it isn't my good friend, Miss Cantrell!"

Both Andrews and Odessa stood and nodded.

"Gentlemen," Carolina offered, "this is the Marquesa. I'm sure she has a name, but I'm unaware of what it is. Marquesa, this is Mr. Tapadera Andrews and Mr. Lorenzo Odessa."

"You know, I said to myself at the door, 'There's Carolina with two handsome gentlemen.' That hardly seems fair, does it? I do hope you don't mind if I join you. I'm a little pressed for time. I have a nine o'clock performance."

Odessa pointed to the empty chair next to Carolina. "We're just scrapin' our plates, but please join us. What kind of performance do you have to go to?"

"Oh, I'm an actress. We've staged *The Pirate King* at the Tripoli Theater. I play Ashley Vane, of course."

Carolina glanced away from the others and looked out the window at a stooped man lighting street lights. *That's spelled V-a-i-n, no doubt.*

"Are you and Miss Cantrell old friends?" Odessa probed.

"Actually," Carolina interjected, "I only met the Marquesa a couple of days ago. I really know very little about her except that we had a mutual former acquaintance."

The Marquesa dropped her chin and batted her heavy eyelashes. "I'm afraid we were both loved and jilted by the same man."

Andrews and Odessa looked somewhat embarrassed. "Obviously, a man with extremely poor judgment," Lorenzo inserted.

"He is not just a dolt but a lunatic as well. But that was in the past. Now what subject were you three so engrossed in when I arrived at the table?" The tone of the Marquesa's voice blanketed every conversation in the room.

"Probably babies," Carolina replied.

"Babies? Oh, my dear innocent Carolina, don't tell me you've transgressed!"

"Mr. Andrews and Mr. Odessa are married men and—"

"Is that a boast or a complaint, dear?"

"I am stating why it is that we discussed children. Mr. and Mrs.

Andrews have twins, and Mr. Odessa's wife is with child. Do you have any children, Marquesa?" Carolina prodded.

"Raising a family is one thing that can't be done on the move like I am. Oh, heaven knows, I want a family, but my career never seems to give me a break."

Carolina's expression was completely without feeling. *I'd be happy to give you a break? Your arm? Your leg? Your neck? Just how great a career is it when you have to bum a ride with a drummer and end up in Billings, Montana?*

"Do you men live here in town?" the Marquesa asked as she leaned far over the table toward the men. Carolina noticed that both turned their eyes to the ceiling.

Andrews stared at the chandelier and answered, "I run a ranch about four hours down the road. Lorenzo ramrods it for me. In fact, we better be hittin' the trail pretty soon."

"You mean you don't intend to linger in town tonight? What a shame!"

"We need to push on, ma'am," Lorenzo maintained. "I don't like leavin' Selena—that's my wife—alone too much. We just came to town to deliver some rustlers."

"You captured cattle rustlers? What excitement! You rode into town with a string of bound prisoners trailing behind," the Marquesa cooed. "I wish I could have seen that. It reminds me of one time in Philadelphia when I starred in a Victor Hugo play."

"Actually, they shot the rustlers," Carolina informed her. "They brought in the bodies."

The Marquesa sat straight up and put her hand over her mouth. She fixed her eyes on the far end of the room. "Oh! . . . . Oh!"

Carolina studied the woman's pale face. *Talk about dead bodies does that to you?*

The Marquesa clutched her leather purse and pushed her chair back. "If you'll excuse me, I've decided not to eat."

Carolina watched the two men stand as the Marquesa did. *She does look ill!*

A voice called out, "Carolina, what a surprise! I got your mystery note and recognized the handwriting."

Jacob!

Suddenly, the Marquesa whirled toward the newcomer and yanked something out of her purse. "You villainous blackguard!" she snarled.

"No!" Carolina lunged at the woman's arm.

"Isabel, what are you—," Jacob blubbered.

The blast from the pocket pistol went off at the same instant that Carolina's hand shoved the Marquesa's bare shoulder.

People screamed and dove under tables.

Jacob Hardisty dropped to the floor.

Andrews grabbed the pocket pistol.

Odessa restrained the Marquesa.

Carolina gasped for air and then burst into tears. *She killed him! Right in front of me. Control, C.K.C. I can't faint. Breathe deeply.*

"Get a doc!" Andrews hollered.

"He deserves to die!" the Marquesa shrieked. "Give me my gun. I'll shoot him again!"

Tears.

Cries.

Groans.

Confusion.

Odessa carried a kicking and screaming Marquesa toward the sheriff's office.

Andrews and a stout, dark-skinned man toted the bleeding and groaning Jacob Hardisty to his room at the Imperial Hotel. Carolina trailed along. She turned her head toward the open door as the doctor began to probe in Hardisty's shoulder with a scalpel.

"Give him a whiff of that chloroform," the doctor instructed.

She peeked back to see Tapadera Andrews rummage through the doctor's bag and pull out a green glass bottle and a cotton wad. Fresh red blood on Hardisty's suit coat caused her to turn away again.

"Are you his wife?" the doctor asked.

She gave him a puzzled look and then realized he was addressing her. "Oh, no . . . We used to be . . . Well, I knew him back east, but I haven't seen him in a year."

"Does he have a wife?"

"Why? Is he going to die?"

"I don't think so, but if he has family, someone needs to find them and tell them he's been shot."

"He's not married. At least I don't think so. I saw him get off the stage alone."

"I'll patch him up, but someone ought to sit with him through the night. If the wound festers and he runs a high fever, someone needs to come get me. There it is!"

"Sure looks like a .41 caliber," Andrews observed.

"Yeah. You're right about that, Tap."

She glanced back to see Andrews examine a small lump of deformed lead. "You can tell the caliber by looking at that?"

"It isn't the first bullet I've ever dug out," the doctor mumbled. "Four inches lower and to the left, and this man would have been dead."

"Miss Cantrell pushed the woman with the gun just in time."

"You saved his life," the doctor announced.

"If I had been faster, perhaps he wouldn't have been shot in the first place."

The doctor glanced up at Andrews. "How many times have you been shot, Tap?"

"Seriously or just clipped?"

What? There are non-serious ways of being shot?

"How many bullets stuck in you?"

"I lost count, doc," Andrews replied. "Maybe five, maybe six."

Have they grown immune to pain out here? They speak of bullets like we mention a chill or fever. You've got to get tough, Sweet Carolina.

Lorenzo Odessa sauntered through the hotel door. Blood trickled down his tanned cheek and neck.

"What happened to you?" Carolina asked.

"That Miss Leon—the Marquesa's name is Isabel Leon—is a rip-roarin' wildcat. Holdin' her back is like being trapped in a hole with a badger."

"Selena will pitch a fit when she sees you with fingernail scratches," Andrews laughed.

"I reckon you'll have to bail me out." Lorenzo grinned.

"I'll just say when we hit the railroad track, you headed for the dance hall, and I didn't see you for hours."

"Your breathin' days would be over, Andrews. You do want to live long enough to see those twins grow up, don't you?"

"Well, you could tell her you got scratched when you rescued a cat out of a tree for a little girl, but maybe we should just stick with the truth."

"And maybe we should hit the trail. We could be home by midnight," Odessa suggested.

"Are you all through, doc?" Andrews asked.

"Yep. I'll sew him up, and we'll see what happens. He should pull through fine, but he does seem to have a low pain threshold."

"In that case, Mr. Scratched Face and me will be ridin' on down the trail. I promised Pepper we wouldn't get into trouble. Miss Cantrell," he tipped his hat toward Carolina, "pleased to meet you. You come up to the ranch and visit with the ladies one of these days. I'm afraid those twin babies keep my wife pretty close to the headquarters."

"Thank you, Mr. Andrews, I appreciate the invitation. I'm not sure I know where you are located, but July said it was easy to find."

"Can't miss it if you stay on the north side of the Yellowstone River. And tell that Ranahan he's got a job any time he wants it."

"Yes, I'll tell him." *And I'll ask him why he fed me a line about how he couldn't get a ranch job until autumn. I have a feeling someone's trying to manipulate me, and I do not like it!*

Unless, of course, I'm the one doing it.

She watched both men exit the room.

Ranch folks. I like them. But the Slash-Bar-4 is half a day's ride from the store. Lord, I like my neighbors, but why do they have to live so far away?

She glanced over at the doctor wrapping Jacob Hardisty's shoulder with a linen bandage. Carolina stepped over next to him and looked down at Hardisty's sleeping face.

You're still an attractive man, Jacob March Hardisty. Not a sturdy man, but a handsome one. Why are you so far away from your world?

"Will you stay with him the night, ma'am?" the doctor asked.

"Stay with him? I'm not . . . "

"No offense, ma'am. Didn't mean anything improper. You can leave the door to the hall open. Someone should sit with him."

"Don't you have a nurse to do that?" she asked.

"Ma'am, this is Billings, Montana Territory—not Boston."

"Mr. Hardisty is a man of wealth. I'm sure he has the money to pay someone. Do you know anyone who could be hired?"

The doctor pulled off his gold wire-framed glasses and wiped them on a clean place on the sheet. "If he comes to, it might be best if he saw a familiar face."

"I really don't feel right about sitting in this man's room tonight." Carolina hadn't worn a hat or gloves to supper and now suddenly felt improperly attired.

"Well, that does present a problem. Perhaps I could . . . There might be . . . " He pulled out his pocket watch and opened it.

"Might be what?"

The doctor closed the watch and slipped it back into his black silk vest pocket. "I do know a lady who takes care of an older woman here in town. She might be able to slip away."

Carolina paced the braided throw rug on the polished wooden floor. "That would be good. There is really no way I can stay with him."

"Could you do me a favor? If you'd just stay here until I can locate someone, I'd appreciate it. It shouldn't be too long."

"What time is it?" She laced her fingers in front of her and turned her palms toward the doctor.

"About nine." He reached over and felt Hardisty's forehead.

"I suppose I could stay here half an hour or so."

"Thank you. Say, do you know if this man has friends here in Billings? Perhaps they could look after him."

"As far as I know, only the lady who shot him and I have met him before."

"Okay. I'll go see what I can arrange. I don't think he'll come to for an hour or so. But if he does, he might want a drink of water. Give him just a swallow or two. He may take a spoonful of this if he wakes up pained." He pointed to a small blue glass bottle. "He can chew on a wet towel if his lips are dry. You might wipe his brow as well."

I do not even want to be here! Why would I want to wipe his brow?

"Yes, well, I do have my own plans, so I'd appreciate it if you hurried," she informed him.

"Quite right. Thank you, Miss . . . Miss . . . "

"Cantrell. Carolina Cantrell."

"Oh, are you an actress also? I understand the young woman who shot him was a actress."

An actress? You mistook me for an actress?

"No, I operate a store out near the Crow Agency. It's a long trip back, and I need to rest up for it. I need to return home first thing in the morning."

"Thank you for your help." The doctor hefted his black leather valise and walked to the open door.

She pulled a padded straight-back chair over to the side of the bed.

Sweet Carolina, how did you get yourself into this? I want to be in my large, comfortable, clean hotel room. How can you lie unconscious, Jacob Hardisty, and still control my life? That's what you always wanted. Total control of everything I do, everyone I meet, and every thought I think.

I have no idea why I'm here.

Unlike Isabel Leon, I did not seek you out nor follow you to the West. I had no intention of ever seeing you again. I no longer grieve over the way you dealt with me.

At least I haven't in a long, long time.

Carolina reclined in the chair for about an hour before she finally stood and ambled to the open door. She stood in the doorway and glanced down the lamp-lit hallway. A door slammed. A woman giggled.

The doctor said he'd send someone soon. It's late. I really need to get to my room.

She paced the hall and looked down the expansive mahogany stairway to the lobby. A roar from the parlor rolled up the stairs.

I could just go on. I should leave. I owe nothing to Jacob. The last time we spoke, he said I was the most unfeeling, insensitive, and cold woman he had ever met.

What he meant, of course, was that my biblical view of moral purity did not fit his present needs. He meant that I was fine as a companion but not of wife caliber. Not for the only son of Atlantic Starboard

Railroad. I'm just a Confederate merchant's daughter. A trinket to be fondled like a toy and eventually discarded.

Mr. Hardisty, I am not an embellishment. There are actually men in this world who enjoy my intelligence, my wit, my strong, independent spirit. Of course, I haven't found one of those yet. But I will!

She gulped down a sigh, walked back into the hotel room, and stood by his bed. "I wish you well, Mr. Jacob Hardisty, but I do not need you in my life anymore. And obviously you do not need me." Her voice faded with the flicker of his eyelid and a groan from his lips.

She retrieved a wet washrag from an enameled bowl and wiped his forehead. Suddenly, she gazed at two pained deep blue eyes.

"Carolina?" he groaned. "Oh . . . oh, my shoulder. It's like there's a hot knife stuck in my shoulder."

"You've been shot, Jacob."

"Isabel did it? She shot me?"

"I'm afraid so. Don't you remember?"

"Not too well. Where is she now?"

"In jail."

"Where's a doctor? I've got to get this bullet out of me! I need something for this pain!"

She plucked the spent bullet off the nightstand. "The doctor's already taken this out of your shoulder. He's gone to hire a nurse to stay with you. He said you can take some of this." She held a spoon-ful of the white syrupy liquid in her right hand and lifted his heavy head with her left. "He should be back shortly."

Hardisty's left arm lay laced to his side with linen wraps. His right hand was on top of the covers, fist clenched.

"Isabel was the one you warned me about in the note, wasn't she? How did you know she wanted to kill me?"

"She told me."

Hardisty took a deep breath and shook his head.

"I paid the boy two dollars to tell me who had sent the note. I just couldn't believe you were in Montana."

I can't remember when Jacob looked so pale and weak. I used to think of him as muscular.

He stared at the shadowy ceiling. His brown mustache seemed to underline the pain in his face. His blue eyes dulled with the effect of the medicine. They now looked sunken, hollow. He turned his head toward her.

"I still can't believe that I strolled into a hotel in Montana Territory, and my Carolina was sitting there."

"I'm really not your Carolina, am I?"

"Darling, you'll always be my Carolina. My only mistake, if I made one . . . "

You made plenty, Mr. Hardisty.

" . . . was being too crazy about you. Self-control has never been a virtue of mine. We needed to separate before I succumbed to temptation."

We didn't separate. You abandoned me at Rosalini's and disappeared with a mysterious, dark-haired lady. Self-control is not an optional virtue. Your lack of it only accents your problem—no moral foundation.

"I . . . I don't think I've ever been through such an emotional situation. Suddenly, there you were—an answer to my prayers. Why, I can't begin to count the nights I've drifted to sleep with you on my mind. Then there she was with a gun. My worst nightmare unfolded."

How many women have you sweet-talked in your life, Jacob Hardisty? Crazy about me? I was never the center of your attention. You told me I was hopeless, a shrew, and left me for a promiscuous actress. I don't need to hear this.

"Why did she shoot me, Carolina?"

"I thought maybe you'd know."

"She didn't say anything to you or the authorities?"

"What did you expect her to say?"

He turned his head away. "Nothing. I merely hoped to understand why a woman would do that."

"I presume you jilted her for someone else."

"Jilted? Of course I didn't. I was so depressed and despondent after I lost you that I turned to the first beautiful, willing woman I could find. But you spoiled me, Carolina. I kept looking for your qualities in others. Isabel was only a dim shadow."

There is nothing about that woman that is dim.

"Of course, there was another woman after her. You left a void, a heartache that just wouldn't stop. Now you know how excited I was to see you! Even if someone threatened my life, I had to come to your hotel and find you."

Hardisty, do you really believe this garbage? This is incredible. Why are you saying these things? Is your wound affecting your mind? You have rewritten our past lives! You deserted me for a woman with more curves and a willingness to use them. It's the isolation of the West that makes you say such things. If you were surrounded by your Baltimore friends, you wouldn't think of me at all.

"Carolina." He reached out his right hand.

She hesitated.

"Please!" he begged.

After a moment she slipped her hand into his. It felt limp, soft, foreign. *Is this really the same hand that used to make my heart jump when he touched me?*

"Carolina, please . . . would you stay with me tonight?"

Without expression, she stared right through him without a word.

"I'm scared. I'm out of my element out here. You know that. I need you to spend the night with me."

I turned down the same request a year ago when you were healthy. Why should I do differently now?

"Talk to me . . . say something! I hurt, Carolina. I really, really need you!"

She pulled her hand out of his and glanced around the room. "I'll sit here in this chair until the doctor can send someone."

At first the laudanum made him talkative. Between groans and sighs he blabbed on and on about how destiny had brought them back together. He had acted poorly, he confessed, and asked her forgiveness.

She said nothing.

Then Jacob Hardisty dozed in and out of sleep.

Carolina Katherine Cantrell didn't.

When he woke up, he talked and talked and talked.

"Do you remember the time we were at the French ambassador's party in Washington? You had to translate for the president's wife. That prince from French West Africa repeatedly told off-color jokes, and you told her he quoted Scripture. I can't believe how you pulled that off. I didn't know until then how much of the Bible you had memorized."

"I can't believe I had to endure those horrid stories. I should have walked out, only I didn't know my way out of the White House."

His deep blue eyes began to tear up.

"I need you, Carolina. I've always needed you." He held his hand out to where she sat.

She didn't reach back.

"Jacob, let's change the subject. Tell me why in the world you are out here in Montana. This is not your kind of place."

"How about you, Carolina Katherine Cantrell?"

"That's easy to explain. David was murdered."

"Oh, I hadn't heard. I'm sorry, Carolina. How's your dear mother doing with this?"

My "dear mother" despises you as always.

"Mother seems to be handling it well. Mr. Franklin allows her to supervise the construction of a new home on the bay. Anyway, David owned a store about thirty miles east of here. I came out to settle his estate, ran across the Marquesa, and she—"

"Marquesa?"

"That's the name Isabel Leon goes by now. Anyway, she recognized who I was and told me laughingly that she planned to kill you on sight. I didn't know whether to believe her or not."

"But you warned me. Could it be my Carolina still cares about me a little?"

"I would have warned the prince from French North Africa if someone threatened his life. Don't take it personally. But you still haven't told me what you are doing here."

"Attempting to make a fortune," he admitted.

"You already have several fortunes."

"That's true, but I've never made one on my own. You know that. It's not for money. I just want to think that I could make the right decisions on my own."

"So how do you intend to make this fortune?"

"In mining."

"That's what everyone thinks. Most go broke."

"There is a difference. I'm looking for claims that have already been made but need capital to develop."

"But what do you know about mining claims?"

"Not much. But I've hired some experts to do the groundwork for me. That's why I'm in Billings. My men have made a find near here that could be just what I've been looking for. They think it could be as big as the Comstock."

"Where is it?"

He motioned her closer. She rose from the chair and walked to his bedside.

"I don't want anyone to hear."

His whispered mumble caused her to lean nearer. "What did you say?" Her ear hovered just inches above his mouth.

Suddenly, the parched, full lips reached up and kissed her cheek.

Carolina pulled back. "That was uncalled for!"

"That was for old times, darling."

She picked up her skirts and stomped back to the chair. "I've really got to leave. I think you'll do all right tonight. I'll check on you in the morning."

"Could you wait until I fall asleep? I've never been shot before. I ramble on and on because I really am scared. What if I don't wake up?"

"In that case, I suggest you settle up with the Lord right now."

"You can still turn every subject into a religious discussion."

"Death is a religious subject!"

He looked away from her. "I realize I have no right to ask this," he mumbled. "But will you stay until the nurse arrives?"

"You're correct. You have no right to ask. But I'll stay for a little while if you close your eyes and stop talking. Maybe you'll get to sleep."

Hardisty nodded and closed his eyes.

Carolina turned the lamp completely off in the room and slumped down in the chair. The light from the hall beamed through the open door, leaving flickering shadows in the room.

She scooted the chair around to enable her to view anyone who came into the room and Jacob Hardisty at the same time. She leaned her head against the back of the chair and closed her eyes.

Her eyelids ached.

Her head felt heavy.

Her shoulders slumped.

Her feet felt cramped in her boots.

It's been a long day, like a whole week of days. This is not the way I had it planned. I hope this is the way You had it planned, Lord. What started as a relaxed, delightful evening turned into a tar pit. I feel stuck. I was so looking forward to coming to town. Now I want to hurry home.

To my store.

To my July.

To my . . .

May the doctor return quickly!

The knock at the door brought Carolina to her feet. The room seemed lit by a lantern outside the window.

The door's closed?

"Who's there?"

"Dr. Hersmann."

"Come in."

"The door's locked."

"It is?" Every bone in her body felt stiff. She turned the key and opened the door.

The doctor strolled in and proceeded straight to the bed. "How's the patient? Looks like he's as well as can be expected. So glad you changed your mind and decided to spend the night. Mrs. Barber told me all about it."

"Spend the night?" Carolina glanced out the window. "It's morning already?"

"Yes, I'm glad he's asleep. I couldn't believe it when she came back and said he sat up."

"Sat up? When did he sit up?"

"Mrs. Barber came to relieve you about midnight, but Mr. Hardisty said he didn't want to bother her. Said you were taking excellent care of him. He asked her to shut the door on the way out."

"He said that?"

"Shhh . . . don't disturb him."

"Who locked the door?" Carolina glanced at the row of neatly fastened small buttons down the front of her dress. "He knew I was waiting for her. I did not intend to spend the night in his hotel room sitting in a chair!" She reached over and spanked his cheek. Hardisty's eyes shot open.

"Wha . . ."

"You have manipulated me for the last time, Jacob Hardisty. Why didn't you wake me when Mrs. Barber came to the room?"

"I didn't want you to walk back to your hotel room alone at that hour. I tried to sit up and see if I was strong enough to go with you, but I just couldn't make it. Your safety was first and foremost on my mind."

"Is that why you locked me in your room?"

"Certainly. It was for your own safety. An open hotel room door is an invitation to trouble."

She spun on her heels and stalked out of the room.

The early morning air felt cool. The dust had compacted on a nearly abandoned street. Carolina could hear several roosters crow, a mule bray, and the heels of her boots as they slammed into the boardwalk in front of the England House.

The man at the lobby desk cleared his throat to get her attention. "Excuse me, Miss Cantrell, but the hotel is not used to female guests coming in at daylight!"

She stared at the weak-eyed man with large ears and mustache hanging like a limp brush beneath a very skinny nose. "And I am not used to having my honor questioned! Please draw up my statement. I'll depart within the hour."

"Oh, your account is paid up in full."

"Who paid it?"

"You don't know?" He raised uneven eyebrows.

"I said, who paid it?" she demanded.

"A Mr. Jacob Hardisty. He sent over the funds just after midnight. Most unusual, don't you think?"

"I assure you, I pay for my own room whether I use it or not!" she insisted.

"But . . . but . . . what will I do with Mr. Hardisty's money?"

"My Christian character restrains me from answering that question." She stormed up the stairs, slammed the door behind her, and plopped down on the unused bed.

Now my virtue has been compromised. My, what rumors will circu-

late on the streets today! "Did you hear the one about the Eastern woman who tried to keep her lover from being shot and ended up spending the night with the wounded man?" "Yes, and I heard he paid all her expenses. They should keep women like that on the other side of the tracks!" "I should say!"

I didn't do anything, Lord.

You know that.

I know that.

I'm glad I'm responsible to a higher authority than rumor.

Now get up, Sweet Carolina. You've got a store waiting for you. And wear some clean clothes today.

She pulled herself off the bed and stopped in front of the mirror. "You can make me angry faster than any man on earth, Jacob Hardisty. But you can't make me cry. Never again."

Carolina felt like a peddler as she left Billings. Boxes of produce, groceries, and an enameled tin sink were all awkwardly lashed to the black buggy.

I look like I've been run out of town. Well, maybe I have. I'm certainly not coming back as long as Jacob is here. I can't believe I got sucked back into his scheming ways.

I am in control of my life, not you, Jacob Hardisty!

That's the heart of my problem, isn't it, Lord? I have to be in control. I have such a difficult time allowing You to control things. Are You in control here? It wouldn't be so tough to take if I knew that for sure.

The constant bumps, rattles, and dust of the carriage produced almost a hypnotic rhythm. Her mind floated from formal receptions in Baltimore, to planning a party for the Andrewses and the Odessas, to a wounded man in Billings.

"I've always been crazy about you, Carolina!"

"All you've ever been crazy about is yourself, Jacob Hardisty. If the roles had been reversed, and I'd been the one to shoot you, you'd be chasing after Miss Isabel Leon right now. But if I had been the one to shoot you, you'd be dead."

With the faint summer breeze behind her and the bright morning sun in her eyes, Carolina warmed quickly as she drove toward the store. Several times she nodded off to sleep, but the well-trained black gelding kept a steady gait, no matter how inattentive the driver. She stopped to rest at Pompey's Pillar and found she had the area to herself. After she gave the horse ample time to drink from the river, she climbed up the dirt embankment at the northeast side of the limestone cliff.

Carolina shaded her eyes and strained to read the autograph. "Wm. Clark, July 25, 1806" *What would it be like to be the first . . . the first person to see a sight, to write about it, to try to describe something none of your readers has ever seen—to capture the smells, sounds, texture of a location? How can anyone describe how grand it is and the feelings they must have experienced, being so alone, removed, remote?*

In comparison, this land is crowded now. Days of exploration are past. I would like to write, Lord. Vast, expansive adventurous dramas. But it's so utterly impractical. You gave me a romantic heart and an analytical mind. Why is that?

She hiked back down off the ramp of dirt that surrounded the pillar, her boots caked with yellow dust.

A grand novel that describes the entire journey of Lewis and Clark from Sacajawea's point of view. Not some sugary prose or dime novel, but straight from the heart of a woman. I could use my journal, jot down notes during the day, and then write in the evenings. Perhaps in a few months I could send a sampling to . . .

She held the hem of her dress above her ankles and climbed up into the buggy.

"*Sweet Carolina, don't waste your time with such thoughts. Writing, literature, the arts are all a waste of time. Where is the profit in that? The good Lord has blessed you with a business mind. It would be ungrateful to waste it on daydreams.*"

"Yes, Father."

Her mind, as well as her body, was totally exhausted by the time she turned off the river road and began the gradual climb toward the store. A bright white canvas tent top caught her eye as she approached.

Someone's camped near the store? Next to the saloon? It's huge.

The tent turned out to be only the top of the building. The side walls and flooring of the structure were made of rough-cut cedar.

I left yesterday morning, and they built that in little over twenty-four hours?

"Miss Cantrell!"

She stopped the rig in the middle of the yard and waited as July Johnson ran to greet her.

"Isn't this something? We've got a new business in town!"

"Town? What town? It's just a store and a saloon out here in the wilderness."

"And the Assay Office."

"A what?"

"A couple of San Francisco mineral engineers, or something like that, rolled in yesterday in a big freight wagon and a ready-made building. Them walls was all nailed together and ever'thin'. They just leaned the pieces together, drove a few nails, and stretched the canvas."

"But we own . . . I mean, the 160 acres is in the name of Starke and Cantrell."

"Mr. Starke sold them a lot."

"A lot?"

With sleeves rolled up above his elbows and sweat dripping off his chin, Ranahan Parks moseyed over to the carriage. He tipped his hat. "Miss Carolina, welcome home."

"Ranahan, what's going on here?"

"Starke had a plat map that he and your brother had filed with the county. He said half the lots were his, and he sold one of his to the geologists."

"Why did they want a building here?"

"It's close to the Billings road and at the edge of reservation land. They can't put up any building on Crow ground yet."

"They said whenever things open up for official settlement in Devil's Canyon, they'll just fold up their building and move it down there. Ain't that somethin'?" July chimed in. "They might even turn it into a bank."

"Yes, well, I'm shocked."

"Wait until you hear the name of the town." July grinned.

"It has a name? I've been gone twenty-four hours, and we now have a town with a name?"

"Starkeville!" July boomed.

"This has to be a joke."

"No, ma'am, that's what Mr. Starke calls it."

"I refuse to live in a place named after a drunken saloon keeper. Where is Horatio Starke?"

"He's in the saloon." July pointed to the open door at the back of the roofless raised wooden porch.

"You two put away these things I brought from town and put up the horse. I'm going to see Mr. Starke."

Ranahan didn't move.

"Well, Mr. Parks," she asked, "aren't you going to help July?"

"Nope. You hired me to dig a well, not tote groceries," he replied.

She stared into his unflinching piercing gray eyes. "Yes. I'm sorry, Ran. You're right." She climbed down off the rig and handed the reins to July. "How is the well digging coming?"

"We struck water at twelve feet but dug her on down four feet deeper."

"How did you do that?"

"It was a muddy mess. Me and July looked like a couple of hogs wallowin' last night. But we took a swim in the river. That cleaned us right up."

She glanced at the dirt caked on his arms and smeared across his forehead. *This is clean?*

Carolina carried her purse and hiked toward the saloon.

"You goin' to talk to Starke?" Ranahan asked.

"Yes. I don't know what this town business is all about."

"I'll tag along with you," he offered.

Carolina untied her hat ribbon and lifted the straw hat off her head. "I am quite capable of—"

"He's already drunk, Miss Carolina." Ranahan rested his hand on the walnut handle of his holstered revolver. "There are others in the saloon. I'd surely appreciate it if you'd allow me to walk in there with you."

Okay, Sweet Carolina, just how stubborn are you?

"Ma'am?" he prodded.

"Mr. Parks, I would very much appreciate it if you would escort me into that horrible saloon."

"I'd be cheerful to oblige, Miss Carolina." His dirt-smudged grin made a teasing tickle in her throat.

You are not getting to me with a silly grin, Mr. Ranahan Parks.
Jacob could not succeed with manipulation, and you can't use your
rugged good looks. For safety's sake, I need an escort. You just happened
to be available. It means absolutely nothing more than that.

She took a big deep breath and let the air out slowly.

I just happen to like having you with me. Don't take it personal.
Well, not right at this exact moment anyway.

Horatio Starke sat at a table with his back to the west wall. In
his right hand was a pencil. Maps covered the table. In Starke's left
hand was an open amber bottle of rye whiskey. He wore the exact
same clothes she had seen on him for nearly a week.

"You wantin' to buy somethin'?" he slurred.

"We need to talk, Mr. Starke," she announced in a voice that
stopped all conversation in the saloon.

The two other men at the table stood as she approached. She
held out her hand to them. "I'm Carolina Cantrell. I own the store
next door."

Both hats came off their heads. "Pleased to meet you." The older
one nodded. "I'm Isaac Milton, and this is my associate, Ted Ostine."

The younger man shook her hand. "I'm afraid we're a little surprised. You don't exactly fit Mr. Starke's description."

"Oh?"

Ostine glanced over at Starke, who took a deep swig from the bottle. "He said you looked like a woman raised on prunes and Proverbs."

"Don't be fooled by them good looks, boys!" Starke bellowed.
"I was talkin' about her heart."

"Miss Cantrell, please join us. We're mining engineers but also
have some general experience in this sort of thing. We were discussing some future developments for Starkeville, and I'm sure
you'll be interested."

She walked over to the empty chair. Before she reached it,
Ranahan pulled it back for her to sit.

"Oh," Isaac Milton stammered, "I . . . it's Mr., eh, Ranahan, right?"

"My first name's Ranahan."

Carolina sat down. Parks lifted the entire chair off the floor and
placed it closer to the table.

"And you are Miss Cantrell's, eh, friend . . . eh, associate?"

"I'm her hired gun."

"Her what?" Ostine gulped.

"If anyone starts to hassle Miss Carolina, I shoot 'em."

"But—but we aren't even armed!" Ostine whined.

"Makes my job a whole lot easier, don't it?"

Carolina saw a twinkle in the steel gray eyes.

"Actually," she continued, "it's a very rare case indeed when Mr. Parks has to actually kill anyone."

This time the sparkle was in Carolina's narrow brown eyes.

"Now what is this utterly ridiculous proposal to call this place Starkeville?"

July Johnson unloaded the goods, parked the buggy by the porch, and led the horse into the corral. He had waited on two customers by the time Cantrell and Parks entered the store.

"We got the well all dug, Miss Cantrell."

"I refuse to live in a place called Starkeville!" she fumed.

"You should have seen Ranahan dig! I couldn't carry out buckets fast enough."

"That drunken churl now sells lots to who knows whom. And calls the entire place Starkeville."

"Ran's as strong as an ox. He used to be a blacksmith. Did you know that?"

"A town! We can't have a town out here. We have to have people to have a town."

"We figure we'll have the pump mounted and workin' by sundown. Won't that be something?"

"This isn't even a good location for a town. If you want a town, you'd build it down by the railroad tracks. It's a little swampy down there, but with some fill and a good land plane, it could be passable."

"I sold $83.12 worth of goods while you was gone."

"I just don't understand why there has to be a Horatio Starke in my life. What did I ever do to deserve the likes of him?"

"A couple prospectors came in and wanted to buy that long tom. I didn't know what to sell it for. They might be back today."

"This store is not in Starkeville, do you understand? The city limits end at that wall."

She glanced at Ranahan Parks. "Well, are you just going to stand there and gawk?"

"I only got two ears. I can only listen to two conversations at once. You two remind me of a couple of pups in a pen—a lot of yappin' but not much listenin'. Think I'll go mount that sink under the window."

Carolina stared at July's bushy brown hair and his blue eyes. She reached out and laid her hand on his shoulder. "I'm glad to be home, July."

He reached out to put his hand on her shoulder but blushed and pulled it back. "I'm really glad you're back too, Miss Cantrell. We missed you."

"We?"

"Didn't we, Ranahan?" he shouted.

"Didn't we what?" came the reply from across the store.

"I said we really missed Miss Cantrell, didn't we?"

"Yep. It's a mighty grimy place without a purdy dress and some sweet perfume."

Dress and perfume? That's real personal, Ranahan Parks. Next time I leave I'll mail you a skirt and a bottle of cologne. How about my charming personality? How about my warmth and wit? How about my irresistible beauty? What a sweet-talker you are!

She stalked toward the loft.

On the other hand, I've spent most of my life around sweet-talking men. They aren't all that great either.

Six

THE CRUDELY PAINTED "Welcome to Starkeville" sign hung from the crate lid fence that divided the porch. A newly installed sink and water pump perched under the east window of the store. One half of the rough-cut wood-frame building now sported two coats of white paint.

Some of the paint remained on Ranahan Parks's shirt and two-week stubble of beard as he descended the ladder with a bucket of paint in his right hand and a paintbrush handle clamped in his teeth.

For almost a week after she returned from Billings, traffic to Devil's Canyon had increased. The delivery of the dry goods and hardware freight wagon had come none too soon. Carolina sent an order into both stores for the following week's delivery.

"How's that look now, Miss Carolina?" Ranahan asked.

"It looks great, Mr. Parks. The second coat really makes the building stand out, doesn't it?"

"It surely makes the saloon look pitiful," he drawled.

"Precisely!" she triumphed. Her new red gingham dress felt thin compared to the more formal dresses she had been wearing. But it was cool and comfortable.

She shaded her eyes from the hot summer sun and stared up at the roof of the building. "Mr. Ranahan, is there some way to build scaffolding so that I can stand up there and paint the sign?"

"I reckon so. Are you really going to letter it yourself?" Each word drawled out slower than the one that preceded it.

"Yes, I've done it before. My father employed a full-time sign

painter. I used to pester him until he taught me a few things."
When she stood close to him, he seemed a whole foot taller.

"I never heard of a woman sign painter," Ranahan remarked.

For some reason she could not recall later, she reached out and
laid her hand on his arm. "The times have changed, Mr. Parks."

"Yes, ma'am. I reckon they have. Are you goin' to want that
black paint?"

"Yes." She thought for a moment that he planned to lay his
hand on top of hers.

He didn't.

"I'll mix it up for you."

July Johnson followed two customers out the front door of the
store and stood on the porch next to Carolina and Ranahan. A
noisy poker game raucused out of the open saloon door. "That's our
last two gold pans, Miss Cantrell. It must be a crazy scene down at
Devil's Canyon. For over a year there was only six or seven of us
there." July studied the paint job. "You all done, Ran?"

"Providin' we don't get some showers out of these afternoon
clouds. That would make the whole building look like a zebra.
Only the signboard is dry."

"You ain't goin' to move on now, are ya?"

"I need to build some scaffolding for Miss Carolina, but after
that . . . I reckon—"

"Mr. Parks, I thought of a way to expand the hay shed,"
Carolina blurted out in what she thought was a much too loud and
eager voice. "Right now it looks like a tumbledown cabin. Is there
a chance we could build something more substantial?"

"You thinkin' about a log buildin' or sawed lumber?" Ranahan
jammed the paintbrush into a glass jar half filled with kerosene.

She stepped over to the front of the store and gently touched
the paint with her finger. "I thought about construction similar to
the store." *Cute, Sweet Carolina, you just painted your finger white.*

"We can frame and rafter it with cut logs from around here, but
we'd need a load of lumber from town."

"Make me a list and I'll order some next week. It will be delivered the week after. Could you please stay until then and oversee
the construction?"

"I suppose I could stick around and do some blacksmithin' until the lumber gets here. Seems like every one of these gold seekers needs a little work done before they head into the hills."

"Thank you, Mr. Parks. Your assistance around here has been invaluable."

Okay, back off. That was a little too obvious. You invented work to keep him around. It just feels a little safer with a strong man who wears a gun on his hip nearby. Of course, the fact that he is handsome and chivalrous might have something to do with it. As does the distressing fact that he seems quite content to ignore me, which presents an interesting challenge, if I were so inclined.

Which I'm not.

Of course, he won't stay all summer.

Unless I can think of a lot more things for him to do.

Evening.

It was Carolina Katherine Cantrell's favorite time of the day.

The store was officially closed.

Chores done.

Supper over.

Sign painted.

She, July, and Ranahan engaged in the daily ritual of sitting on the front porch to enjoy the stillness of a warm, muggy, overcast summer evening. At least nature was peaceful even if the saloon next door was not. Half a dozen horses and rigs were scattered around the yard in front of it.

She sat on the east side of the door on a newly constructed bench. Ranahan sat on the west side, also on a new bench. July flopped down on the porch out by the stairs with his legs hung over the edge.

"The more traffic that rolls through here, the more this looks like a street," she remarked.

"You'd better up and name it before it's called Starke Street," Ranahan laughed.

"Has Mr. Starke seen your sign, Miss Cantrell?" July asked.

"I don't think so. I'm sure he'd have some comment."

Ranahan pulled his charcoal gray hat with peaked crown over his eyes and leaned his head against the now dry siding of the store. "He can't complain about calling it Cantrell's Store."

She could feel the perspiration soak through the back of the high collar on her dress. She tried to fan herself with her hand but soon gave up. "It's the second line he'll be upset over, I imagine."

"The 'Cantrell, Montana Territory' part?" July asked.

The air smelled like rain and seemed to drift west. "Yes." For a moment she could smell neither smoke nor alcohol.

July pulled his hunting knife out of his scabbard and began to whittle on a twig. "I think Cantrell's a mighty fine name for a town. Someone will ask, 'Where are you from, Mr. Johnson?' And I'll say, 'I'm from Cantrell, Montana.' Don't that sound fine?"

Carolina unfastened the buttons on her sleeves and rolled them halfway up to her elbows. "I suppose some might complain that the two towns are a little close to each other."

"Why?" Ranahan laughed. "They have a whole wall separatin' them."

She thought she saw a wide, easy grin under his hat. *I like the way this man laughs.*

"And a fence on the porch," July added.

"Don't forget the line drawn in the dirt!" Carolina brushed some white powder off the skirt of her dress. This time all three chuckled.

"I figure we did a whole mess of business today, Miss Cantrell." July tossed his whittled stick out into the middle of the yard.

"For a store in the middle of nowhere, we do all right, don't we? I'll be able to pay off Mr. McGuire for all that mining freight by next week. After that, there will be some profits, I hope. Anyway, as long as the rush to Devil's Canyon continues."

July jumped off the porch into the dirt yard. "Miss Cantrell, I've been thinkin' I'd saddle up Blaze and ride down to the river."

"You wouldn't be going down to see if that family with the teenage girl is still camped near the tracks, would you?" she teased.

July winced. His Adam's apple wiggled as he swallowed hard. "Eh, yes, ma'am, I am. I ain't doing nothin' improper, am I?"

"I certainly hope not!" Carolina flashed a poker face at July and then broke into a wide grin.

"What's her name?" Ranahan asked without looking out from under his hat.

"I don't know, but she sure is purdy," July gulped.

"Let me give you some advice," Ranahan interjected. "When you go visitin', you ought to take a gift."

"What kind of gift?" July slipped his knife back into his leather scabbard.

"What would you suggest, Miss Carolina?" Parks asked.

She laced her thin, pale fingers and let them drop to her lap. "There's a limited number of choices in the store, but I would suggest you take her a piece of stick candy."

"I'll go get her one! I'll buy it with my own money."

"One?" Carolina called out as July scampered up the stairs toward the door. "You'll have to buy one for each member of the family."

"She has six brothers and sisters!"

"Miss Carolina's right," Ranahan added. "You've got to take one for everybody. You don't want any of her kin riled at you."

July raced into the store and then, a few minutes later, rushed to the corrals.

"There's one enthusiastic young man," Carolina commented.

"He's fourteen . . . and it's summer. Life is awful excitin' at that age. When I was fourteen, I drove my first herd to Fort Boise. How about you? What were you doing at fourteen, Miss Cantrell?"

"Father was in Europe when the war ended. We stayed there for several years. By the time I was fourteen, we had moved to Chestertown, Maryland. Father couldn't bear to view his cherished Virginia under a Union flag. But we did sail to Europe that summer. Father bought denim cloth in France for trousers like those you wear."

"You surely have traveled a lot, Miss Carolina."

"Always on business. Mother, David, and I got to tag along. I think Father was afraid of something happening to him on one of his trips, and he would never get to see us again. So off we went with him."

"With all those exotic destinations, this Montana life must seem mighty tame."

"Oh, sure, that's why I carry this." She pulled out the small gun from her deep pocket.

Ranahan sat up and pushed his hat back. "Miss Carolina carries a sneak gun? Now that does surprise me!"

"There are rogues and ruffians all over the globe, Mr. Parks."

"Yes, ma'am. I believe you're right about that. You probably had those European boys fetchin' stick candy for you when you were fourteen."

Carolina rocked back and forth on the bench. *Fourteen? They brought me presents when I was six.*

She looked over at the chiseled profile of his face. "Mr. Parks, would you think me forward if I asked how old you are?"

"No, ma'am. I don't mind telling you Mr. Parks is sixty-one years old."

"What?"

"You were askin' the age of my daddy, weren't you?"

She glanced over at him. He didn't look her direction, but she knew his eyes danced. His long legs were stretched out in front of him, legs crossed, chin on his chest.

"Okay, I get the message." She pulled her embroidered handkerchief from her sleeve and wiped her neck. "Ran, how old are you?"

"Don't let the gray in my hair fool you. I'm only thirty-four." It was the teasing, throat-tickling voice that made Carolina wish she had looked in a mirror before she came out to the porch.

"My father was solid gray before he was thirty," she consoled him. "I wonder why gray hair on a man looks so distinguished and on a woman just looks old?"

"Do you have any more questions for me?" he probed.

Have you been married? Do you have children? Is there a woman who waits for you somewhere? Are you able to keep a lifetime commitment? Are you threatened by an independent woman? Do you ever get drunk? Have you ever hit a woman? How many children would you like to have? Just where does Jesus Christ fit in your life? Do you like curtains with flowers? Do you like to sit on a porch swing just to hug, kiss, and count stars? When your wife wakes up ugly and grouchy, will you still be crazy about her? Do you ever sit alone in the dark of the night and wonder what it would be like to be married to a woman like me? Do you think people should know each other for a long time before they commit themselves to marriage? Can you promise you won't move me somewhere I don't want to go? Are you a man of honor?

Carolina clamped her lips shut and smiled toward his boots. Then she glanced into his steel gray eyes. "Oh, no . . . no more questions."

"Miss Cantrell, I have a question to ask you."

"I hope you don't plan to ask me how old I am."

"No, ma'am," he chuckled. "I know better than that."

"A very wise decision."

"I've just been doin' some thinkin' . . . " Ranahan's voice sounded hesitant.

Carolina felt her chest tighten in anticipation. "Oh?"

"Just how long do you really aim to stay out here and operate this store?" he blurted out.

"With business like it is, I think I'll spend the summer."

"Then will you sell the store?"

"That's always been my intention. Why do you ask?"

"Oh, it's nothin', I guess."

Ranahan, what are you holding back? Don't beat around the bush. Speak right up. What is it you wanted to say? "How about you, Ran? What are your intentions?"

He sat straight up. "What do you mean, my intentions?"

"What do you intend to do this summer and this fall?" *What kind of intentions did you think I was talking about, Mr. Ranahan Parks? Come to think about it, what intentions am I talking about?*

"I'll tell you the truth, Miss Carolina. The last week or so have been mighty relaxin' for me. I've been tired for a long, long time. I've been on the go for over a year tryin' to locate those rustlers who gunned down my partners."

"The man called Cigar and the others?"

"Yep." He licked his chapped lips and glanced over at her. "The hopelessness of ever findin' justice, or revenge, wears a man out. Then I rode in here, and it's been like an oasis in the desert."

"You can't have rested much. You've worked very hard every day you've been here."

"Oh, it's not a man's body that wears out first. It's his spirit. I might be doin' physical work, but my spirit is gettin' refreshed. Does that make sense?"

Cowboy, you are definitely saying all the right words. Either you're the slickest man I ever met or one sent straight from heaven. "Yes, it makes sense to me. In a way, coming out to Montana has been a needed break for me as well. But you still didn't tell me what you plan to do for the rest of the summer," she prompted him.

"In the fall gather, I'll work for Andrews at the Slash-Bar-4, but before then . . . "

"That reminds me. When I told you all about what happened to me in town, did I mention that I had supper with Lorenzo Odessa and Tapadera Andrews?" She raised her dark sweeping eyebrows and could feel the dangling silver earrings bounce against her neck.

"I think you stated that," he acknowledged.

"Well, I had a very curious conversation with Mr. Andrews. He seems to think you will make a good cowhand."

"That's mighty generous of him."

"In fact, he was so impressed with your qualifications, he said he offered you a job immediately, but you turned him down."

"He said that?" Ranahan sat up, but he talked to the porch out in front of him.

"Yes, he said you told him you had promised to work for me. Now, Ran, Mr. Andrews seems like an honest man to me. I have a tendency to believe him." She stared out at the corrals and watched as July Johnson galloped off toward the river. "Just exactly why did you tell Mr. Andrews that when I hadn't indicated any intention of hiring you yet?"

His voice was slow and deep. "Two reasons."

"Oh?"

"First off, he wanted to hire me as a way of sayin' thanks for helpin' him with the rustlers. But a man don't need thanks for that. It's what any honorable man would do. Besides, there isn't much to do around a ranch in the summertime that the crew he already has can't do."

"And second?"

"Shoot, Miss Carolina . . . everybody can see I lost my heart to you the first time I heard your sweet voice and saw your face."

Carolina's heart stopped.

She couldn't move.

Not even blink.

It was like every part of her body froze solid at the exact same moment.

Total shock.

Like being struck with a bullet.

What? Did he just say what I think he just said? Everybody can see he lost his heart to me? Who's everybody? You mean July? You mean Starke? You mean some stranger who rides up from the river?

I didn't know that's the way you felt. You don't even know me. You don't say things like that if you don't mean them, Mr. Parks. Are you stringing me along? You don't say things like that to a woman you've only known a week or two.

Unless, of course, you're absolutely crazy about her and can't live without her and think that it's God's will that has led you together.

What am I supposed to say? "Oh, that's nice." Or, "I would prefer this conversation wouldn't turn personal." Or, "Control yourself, cowboy." Say something, Sweet Carolina, you have to say something!

"Oh, my, isn't that interesting?" she mumbled, staring up at the sky. "It certainly is a . . . a pleasant evening, isn't it?"

I can't believe I said that! That's the most stupid reply I've ever given in my life. Tell him how you really feel. Tell him how much time you've spent thinking of him. Tell him those are the sweetest words you've heard in a long time. Tell him you'd love to talk to him about that some more.

"Yes, ma'am, it is. If you don't have any more questions for me, I think I'll mosey out and check on the horses. I might just put some markers down to show where to build the new hay shed."

"That would be nice."

Good work, Sweet Carolina. Another suitor wanders off in frustration. Maybe I am "totally inept at developing any significant relationship"—to quote a certain East Coast capitalist.

He sauntered across the porch and down the stairs and then turned back. "Thanks for not laughin' at what I said. I'm not too polished talkin' to purdy gals, as you can tell. I just got a crazy streak of honesty that makes me blurt out exactly what's on my mind and heart. Gets me into trouble from time to time, as you can imagine. I apologize for bein' so forward. In some ways, I reckon I still act a lot similar to a certain fourteen-year-old."

"Oh, your apology is accepted, I assure you."

"Thank you, ma'am." He tipped his hat. "I reckon you get fellas who tell you silly things like that all the time."

Yes, but they don't usually make my throat dry, my fingers tremble, my neck burn, and my heart jump.

He ambled on out to the corral. He didn't look back or seek a reply.

"It certainly is a pleasant evening?" I didn't really say that, did I? What a sweet-talking woman you are, Carolina Katherine Cantrell!

The man said he lost his heart to you! I wonder if that's cowboy for "I love you"?

You wanted him to say that, Sweet Carolina.

"Why, Mr. Parks, I'm flattered by your feelings for me. I must admit I have some feelings for you as well. I'm still trying to have the Lord help me understand them. Please don't consider me cold. . . . This is just a sudden development, and we hardly know each other. I am curious, though, as to where the Lord will lead in this matter."

Oh, no, Sweet Carolina, you just said, "Oh, my . . . isn't that interesting. It certainly is a pleasant evening, isn't it?"

For weeks you've hoped for some indication from him. You've daydreamed about what it would be like for him to be interested in you. You probably sounded reserved, uninterested. The truth is, you're just insecure and scared to death! Is it any wonder you end up chasing off every man who has shown a real interest in you?

Now what?

Carolina had the urge to run up to her loft and throw herself onto the bed.

She wasn't sure what to do after that.

Maybe laugh.

Or cry.

She nodded as Isaac Milton and Ted Ostine sauntered up the stairs to the saloon. She was still sitting on the bench pondering her next move when Horatio Starke boiled out on the porch, followed by the two mining engineers.

"Mr. Starke, you've changed shirts and shaved!" she exclaimed. "I'm impressed."

"Well, I ain't. You cain't put that sign up there!" He pointed to the roof.

"Mr. Starke, I won't tell you what sign to put on your saloon, and you don't tell me what I can do with my store," she bristled.

"This ain't Cantrell; it's Starkeville, Montana Territory."

"No," she corrected. "Over there is Starkeville. This is Cantrell."

"You cain't do that. This location is platted for only one town, and I named it first."

She jumped to her feet and crossed her arms. "You named it illegally."

"There ain't nothin' illegal about it," he bellowed.

Carolina paced her side of the porch. "Normally, the citizens of a town get to vote on its name, isn't that true, Mr. Milton?"

The gray-haired man loosened his bow tie. "I suppose if there's a dispute, that would be the fair way to handle it."

"Vote?" Starke hollered. "We ain't goin' to vote. I've already decided on its name. I've been here a lot longer than you. I ain't naming it after some newcomer."

"I named my town after my brother," she countered. "I believe his roots here go back as far as yours."

"Oh," he snorted. "Don't matter. It's all settled. You have to take the sign down."

Ranahan Parks meandered back to the porch. "You got trouble, Miss Carolina?"

"You stay out of this! This ain't none of your business, Ranahan!" Starke growled.

"Certainly, it is," Carolina corrected him. "You denied Mr. Parks the right to vote."

Ranahan tipped his hat forward and scratched the back of his neck. "Vote on what?"

"On what the name of the town should be," she replied. "Mr. Starke thinks he alone should decide."

Ranahan glanced at the three men over on the saloon porch. "You're right, Miss Carolina. I think we should hold an election."

"An election? There ain't enough people around here for an election!" Starke protested.

"An election would settle the matter once and for all in a civilized manner," Mr. Milton, the older geologist, observed.

"An election is always the fair way," Ostine added.

Starke glanced around slowly at the two men on the porch, then over at Carolina and Ranahan. Finally, he spat a wad of tobacco off the edge of the porch. "You might be right. We'll have us an election!"

"Good," Ranahan nodded. "I vote for the name Cantrell."

"You cain't vote. You're just a transient passin' through. You ain't got no vote. Now Milton and Ostine, on the other hand—"

"They're transient too," Carolina insisted. "They both said that as soon as Devil's Canyon is officially opened up, they plan to move their business up there."

"They can too vote. They have a business in town. They are votin' citizens!"

Carolina hiked to the crate lid barrier and leaned toward Starke. "Mr. Ranahan has a blacksmith business."

"He don't have no real business," Starke countered.

"Of course I do," Ranahan argued. "I operate right out of that building over there." He pointed across the yard.

"That's just a hay shed," Starke fumed.

"And blacksmith shop."

"You ain't even got a sign up. That ain't no business."

"Mr. Milton and Ostine," Carolina inquired, "what does it take to have a business?"

"Eh, doin' work for hire or havin' goods or services for sale from a specific location, I would assume," Isaac Milton responded.

"Then no sign is actually needed?"

"Nobody has to put out a sign. That's just good business."

"All right, then Mr. Parks can vote," Carolina affirmed.

"Don't matter," Starke snorted. "There's three of us. We win the vote. The case is settled. Pull down the sign before I do."

"You touch that sign, and you're liable to get shot," Ranahan threatened.

"You cain't bluff me."

"I'm not."

"Besides, we have three also. Don't forget July," Carolina reminded him.

"The kid? He cain't vote. He's underaged."

"He's a citizen of this community," she maintained.

"He cain't vote," Starke insisted. "In fact, you cain't vote."

Carolina felt her neck stiffen and her eyes narrow. Her hands shook with anger. "What do you mean, I can't vote?"

"Women ain't got no right to vote! They cain't vote for president. They cain't vote for Congress."

"They've had the vote in Wyoming since '69," Ostine informed him.

"This ain't Wyoming."

"On a local election, I reckon folks can decide for themselves who can vote," Ranahan suggested. "On a cattle drive, they let ever'one vote, even the twelve-year-old hoodlums."

"What do you vote for on a cattle drive?" Isaac Milton asked.

"Oh," Ranahan shrugged, "you know, which saloon to hurrah or dance hall to visit. Things like that."

Carolina looked over at Parks, who rested his right hand on the walnut grip of his revolver. *I'm certainly glad you allowed twelve-year-olds to vote on that.* "There is no way on earth you can keep me from having a say about what to call this place," she insisted.

"And I say there are six voters," Ranahan maintained.

"I will not be intimidated by a gun," Starke blustered.

"Would you rather be intimidated by a knife?" Ranahan threatened. "Or maybe just fists?"

Isaac Milton tugged on Starke's grimy sleeve. "Let me see if I can talk some sense into Hardrock." He, Ostine, and Horatio Starke stepped back into the saloon.

Ranahan climbed up the stairs and stood next to Carolina.

"What do you suppose that's all about?" she asked.

"Free drinks for votes maybe."

A hatless Isaac Milton stuck his head out of the saloon. "He's agreed. Everyone can vote."

"Not everyone—just the permanent residents," Carolina maintained.

"Yes, yes. That's what I meant. Why don't we have the election on Saturday?"

"Why not have it as soon as July returns tonight?" Carolina asked.

"I considered that, but the vote would probably end in a three-to-three tie. I thought by Saturday maybe one side would convince the other. For instance, Ostine and I feel a loyalty to Starke only because he consented to sell us a lot. Perhaps we could be convinced otherwise."

Carolina studied Ranahan's steel gray, unblinking eyes. They gave no indication of intent. "It's your decision, Miss Carolina."

"All right," she agreed. "We will have the election right here on the porch on Saturday at noon. Is that acceptable?"

"Let me check with Starke." Milton disappeared into the saloon's shadows. Within a moment his mostly gray head emerged from the doorway. "All set. We will vote Saturday at noon. Each voter must be here—no proxies."

"Good." Carolina returned to her bench. This time Ranahan plopped down beside her.

Perhaps I didn't completely chase him away. Be smart, Sweet Carolina. Say something meaningful.

"How about that? An election out in the wilderness," Ranahan chuckled. "Next thing you know, we'll be votin' for mayor."

"Mayor? We don't need a mayor for three businesses, one of which is very temporary."

"Four businesses. Remember the blacksmith shop."

"Four businesses," she concurred.

"I've been thinkin' about that. I like how that sounds. Would you consider sellin' me the lot the hay shed and corrals are on? I'd have to work off the debt. I wouldn't mind havin' a little business. I could run it until the fall gather. If it's doin' well, I could sell it for a profit, or maybe just stick around through the winter. I figure there's enough business during the summer months anyway. I'll have to wait and see about the rest."

Winter in Montana? I suppose I could give one winter a try. As long as I keep the fires burning. In the woodstove—and elsewhere!

"How about that load of lumber I ordered? You would still need a new building, wouldn't you?"

"Yep. But I'll need you to back me on that. I'm good for it."

"Yes, I believe you are. Will you need some more blacksmith tools?"

"Looks like they aimed to set up a forge of some sort in Devil's Canyon. That load of mining gear has about everythin' to get started."

"Ranahan, is this really the way towns in the West get their start?"

"Yep. But I reckon about seven out of ten fizzle out."

She crossed her ankles and then fidgeted with her fingers. "Cantrell, Montana Territory, will not fizzle out."

"No, ma'am, not with the likes of Carolina Cantrell camped out here."

Carolina knew he surveyed her face, but she didn't return his gaze. "What exactly do you mean by that?"

"I've got a feelin', Carolina, when you make up your mind, heaven and earth couldn't change it."

"Heaven could, Ran," she replied.

She stood in front of the loft dresser at daybreak and gazed into the mirror.

He almost called you Sweet Carolina again. Sometimes his voice is as soft as a pillow. Comfortable. Inviting. Other times it's like a rock.

You look tired, Carolina. You have to get more sleep. You went to bed at ten and stared at the ceiling until two. You acted liked a schoolgirl yesterday. Mr. Ranahan Parks is not the first man to tell you things like that. Come on, it's what you've wanted him to say since the day he first sauntered up these stairs.

Okay. He's said it. Now what do you propose to do about it? Please, please don't just talk about the weather.

"Mr. Ranahan Parks, just how serious are you about this relationship? Are you willing to put the effort into it to make it work? If you have any motive other than a lifetime marriage commitment, I'm not interested."

Well, okay . . . I am still interested.

But I shouldn't be.

Her curling iron warmed on top of the coal bucket. With the precision of a lifetime of use, she recurled her hair and then reheated the iron.

I'm a little overdressed. I realize any old dress will do out here. All right, I'm a lot overdressed! Yes, these sapphire earrings are a little too fancy. But there's no reason a woman can't look her best. Like it or not, cowboy, this is my best.

Three more curls were set. Then again she heated the curling iron. With the ivory comb, she fiddled with the back of her hair, which spiraled several inches below the collar of her sky blue dress.

Do you want to impress him or seduce him, Sweet Carolina?

Lord, do I have to answer that question?

I don't really know him. A cowman without a herd. A man with a vengeful heart. I don't know how many other women there have been in his life. I don't even know if he's been married.

Maybe he's still married. How do I know there's not a Mrs. Parks back in Oregon? Maybe I'd better change dresses.

But what if he's not married? What if he is just what he appears to be?

Should I still return to Maryland as soon as I sell the store? There's no real hurry. It wouldn't hurt me to winter it out here. I don't suppose you go outside much in a Montana winter. Now there's an intriguing thought. We'll probably have to huddle by the woodstove every day.

Carolina made the final ringlets on her forehead.

What then? Maybe you and Ranahan will be madly in love. Maybe you'll hate him. Maybe you'll run off with him to Devil's Canyon and dig for gold. Maybe you'll convince him to relocate to Maryland.

What is it you want, Sweet Carolina? What do You want, Lord? That's what I've got to figure out.

That, and what to say to Ran the next time I see him.

By noon she and July had waited on twelve customers, and still she had time to paint a sign on a barrel lid. July's stew was bubbling on the cookstove when Ranahan made his first appearance of the day.

The bang of boot heels on bare wood and the tinkle of spurs announced his entrance. "Is dinner about ready?"

July Johnson, with face scrubbed clean and center-parted hair freshly oiled, looked up with a wide grin. "Yep. Anytime you want to eat. I got white flour biscuits and stew. Coffee's fresh."

Carolina walked over to the table. "Good day, Mr. Parks."

He tipped his hat. "Howdy, Miss Carolina. I mean to tell you that's just about the purdiest dress I've ever seen. July, did you ever see a more handsome woman?"

The fourteen-year-old began to blush. "No, sir. I don't reckon I ever did in all my born days. 'Course, I ain't all that old. Miss Cantrell, do all women in the East look as winsome as you?"

"Oh, no," she laughed. "All the rest are quite ugly. Gentlemen, you are both a couple of wonderful flatterers. And quite honestly, I love it!"

"We ain't lyin', Miss Cantrell," July assured her. "It's just that I never did see any woman dress so nice. I did go to Denver once, but even the girls in the houses don't look as polished as you do."

"The girls where?" she gasped.

"The opera houses, up on the stage . . . them actresses," July explained.

"Oh, yes, well . . ." She looked across the table at Parks. "We missed you at breakfast."

"I had an old boy from Utah knock on my door at daylight and ask me to repair a wheel rim. It's just been one customer after another."

"We had a mighty good Bible readin' this mornin', Ranahan," July bubbled. "It was about an ol' boy named Nicodemus. I knew a man up in Devil's Canyon named Nicodemus Van Bruno. Did you know him?"

"Nope. I'm sure I'd remember a name like that." Ranahan grinned. "But I do know about the Nicodemus in the Bible."

"What do you think about that born-again business?" July asked. "We read that Jesus told Nicodemus he needed to be born again."

"If Jesus said it, I reckon he needed it."

"I was thinkin' the same thing. In fact, I been thinkin' about doin' that myself."

"Being born again?"

"Yep. How about you, Ranahan? You ever done it?" July asked.

"July!" Carolina cautioned. "You can't ask questions like that! It's personal. Some people are quiet about their faith."

"Yes, ma'am. Sorry, Ran. Talkin' about religion is all new to me."

"That's all right, July. I grew up with very devout Methodist parents. And I assure you, 'I am not ashamed of the gospel of Christ; for it is the power of God unto salvation to every one that believes, to the Jew first, and also to the Greek.'"

"That's in the Bible, ain't it, Miss Cantrell?" July beamed.

"I believe it is in Romans 1."

"Verse 16," Ranahan added. "Does my quoting Scripture surprise you, Miss Carolina?"

"No. But perhaps we should say a blessing and eat the assistant manager's stew before it cools."

July bowed his head. "Yes, ma'am."

Ask him. Here's your chance. "Mr. Parks, would you offer thanks for us?"

"Lord, You've been feedin' us for a long time, and we want to thank You for that . . . and ask Your continued blessing. You know we got a lot of things that need sortin' out in our minds, and I reckon You're the only one that knows how it all fits together. We'd be obliged for Your help. In Jesus' name. Amen."

"Amen!" July echoed.

That man can pray for me anytime.

Ranahan broke a piece of bread and dipped it in his bowl. "You look surprised, Miss Carolina."

"No, I'm not surprised. But you can tell a lot about a person when you listen to him pray."

"What could you tell about me?"

"That wasn't the first time you have prayed. And it was from the heart. But *I* have a surprise for you," she offered. "July, bring that sign over."

"Look at this, Ran," July exulted. "'Ranahan Parks— Blacksmith Shop.' 'Course, the paint's still wet."

"That's mighty fancy, Miss Carolina." Ranahan shoved his

charcoal gray hat off the back of his head and let it hang by the stampede string. "I don't reckon I've ever had my own sign before."

"We got four businesses in town," July boasted. "Four businesses and not one house. It's a funny town, ain't it? If we had houses, I bet the Quincys would move here."

"Who are the Quincys?"

"You know, Molly Mae's folks."

Ranahan winked at Carolina. "Is Molly Mae the young lady camped down by the river?"

"Yeah, she's the one with the purdy yella hair, bright blue eyes, and the sweetest smile this side of heaven. Have you seen her?" July pressed.

"Nope. I'm afraid I missed her. But you're right, July. The next thing we need around here is a house or two."

Perhaps a wedding and then a house? Or perhaps you've been in the wilderness too long, Sweet Carolina. Maybe it's time to run. You could be back in Maryland in four days.

When they finished their noon meal, Ranahan pushed back from the table and stood up. "Miss Carolina, I need to do some more work out there, but I'm lookin' forward to us talkin' some more tonight after supper. You don't have any other plans, do you?"

"Plans? Here? Mr. Parks, I assure you there is nothing else to do."

"Maybe we can send July down to the river to check up on the Quincys' daughter."

"I don't think he'll need any encouragement."

"Good. Because I've been thinkin' about what I said last night, and I figure I need to do some explainin'." He stared down at his boots.

"I've thought about it some too. I need to tell you a few things. I'll look forward to your explanation."

"Yeah, I'll bet you will." He laughed deeply. Then he turned and left the store.

Ranahan, what did you mean by that? Why did you laugh? What did I say that was funny? Did I completely misunderstand what you said? Is this all just a humorous mistake? Were you making a joke, and I thought you were serious?

It was midafternoon when July ran into the store and shouted, "There's a big black carriage with two men in it comin'!"

"That doesn't sound like prospectors."

July looked back out the open doorway. "No, ma'am, and they ain't stoppin' here."

With feather duster in hand, she walked to the front of the store. "I suppose they're headed for the saloon."

"No, ma'am . . . looks like they're goin' to the Assay Office."

"What a strange country. You open a business one day, and customers show up from out of nowhere the next. I think I'll go for a little walk. You can take care of things here, can't you?"

"Yes, ma'am, but those aren't exactly walkin' clothes you're wearin'."

"It will be a short walk."

"Like to the Blacksmith Shop?"

"You like to ride to the river. I like to walk to the Blacksmith Shop."

"Yes, ma'am. I understand that. I surely do."

I believe you. If I had a younger brother, I'd like one just like you, Mr. July Johnson.

The eighty-pound anvil was strapped down to a tree stump. A hot bed of coals blazed in a river-rock fire pit. Ran's shirt sleeves were rolled up above his elbows. A well-used leather apron hung over his shirt and down to his knees. His hat was pushed back. Sweat rolled down his face.

His spurs still forked the heels of his battered boots, but his revolver and holster hung from a peg in the front of the hay shed. The flat piece of iron clamped in the tongs was red hot. The ten-pound sledge hammer in Ranahan's right hand slammed the malleable metal with explosive force.

He ignored Carolina as she watched him, concentrating solely on the work in his hand. Finally, he turned and shoved the red hot metal into a wooden bucket of water. The metal popped like a string of firecrackers. Steam spewed like a geyser at Yellowstone.

He left the metal in the bucket and tossed the hammer and tongs to the dirt. "Miss Carolina! I didn't see you sneak up."

"I didn't sneak."

"Yes, ma'am. Not in that dress anyway. July's right. He said it was the purdiest dress west of St. Louis."

"He's never been to San Francisco."

"No, ma'am, I don't reckon he has."

"I only brought a few dresses out from Maryland. And I couldn't think of any event coming up in the next few weeks to save this dress for, so I just decided I'd wear it today."

"I'm glad you did." Ranahan wiped his forehead on his shirt sleeve and strolled over next to her.

"Ran, how did you learn to be a blacksmith?"

"Sort of out of necessity. I worked at a ranch where the blacksmith busted his arm and was laid up for six months. The ol' man wanted me to do the work if the blacksmith told me what to do. I guess you might say I apprenticed. I'm not the best in the world, but I can get a rig back on down the trail. I reckon that's what's most important."

She scooted over and glanced down into the bucket of water and then returned within inches of where he stood. "It must be a handy occupation to have. Something you can always do to make a living."

"I suppose. But all I ever wanted was my own spread. One of these days I'll get it. After I settle up with the rustlers."

"Just how is that vengeance crusade going to help you acquire a ranch?"

"Not vengeance but justice. All I want is for them to get what they deserve. That's all. I buried three good, honest, honorable men across the border." He pointed to a downed cottonwood near the corrals. "Would you like to join me for a break? Thought I'd sit on that log bench in the shade."

"That would be nice. It seems especially warm today."

"Just a minute, I'll be right back," he insisted, then sprinted into the hay shed. He emerged with a shirt in his hand. When they reached the log bench, he spread the shirt across the rough wood. "You sit here, Miss Carolina. I don't want you to get that dress dirty."

"Thank you, Ran. But really this dress isn't that delicate."

She sat on the shirt. Ranahan plopped down a couple of feet from her. He leaned forward, rested his elbows on his knees, and stared down at the dirt. "You know, Carolina, these past couple of weeks sure have been peaceful."

Ma'am, Miss Cantrell, Miss Carolina—now just Carolina. I like that. I wonder how Sweetheart would sound?

"Yep," he continued, "I don't reckon I've spent two nights in the same spot in over a year."

"It sounds terribly tiresome."

"I wore out three horses."

"Your buckskin was not too hearty the day you rode in here."

"You're right about that. A couple more days like that, and he would have dropped. Now he's gettin' fat and lazy."

"I've wanted to ask you, Ran, what made you ride that hard to get here?"

"I was up at Fort Union and heard that a man named Cigar was on his way to Billings."

"So you rode all this way and never went into Billings to see if he was there?"

He glanced over at her. His two-week-old dark brown beard was peppered with a little gray. "I decided to see where all of this would lead."

"All of what?"

"This deal with the store and Starke and now maybe a town. Then there's the deal about you and me, Miss Carolina."

Miss Carolina? What happened to just plain Carolina? You're losing ground, cowboy. "Deal? What kind of deal is there between us, Mr. Parks?" *Why did I call him Mr. Parks?*

"I just want you to hear me out. I'm no good at talkin' to women. Ain't much better at talkin' to men. I've been on my own so long I have a tough time talkin' to folks.

"Anyway, you probably need to know a little about me. I always had it in my mind to start my own ranch. That was when I decided it would be a good time to find a gal to marry and start raisin' a family. Over the past dozen years whenever I ran across a good-lookin' Christian lady that I wanted to get to know better, I'd say to myself, 'Ranahan, you don't have time now. You come back and visit her when you get your place built.'

"'Course, I never came close to gettin' my place. Would you

believe that I haven't had a regular girlfriend since I was sixteen? I just haven't had time."

No, I really don't believe that, but it's a cinch I'm not going to say so. How many nonregular girls have there been? I can't remember how many boyfriends I've had since Toby back in the second grade. "You've really been on the run, haven't you?"

"Yep. Then I pulled in here, and July gave me a report on what a handsome and smart sister David Cantrell had. And after seein' you, I figured I'd . . . "

"How did you know what I looked like back then? I believe I was in the loft the first time you stopped by."

"I saw you up there later that evenin' through the window. You were combin' your hair." He pointed toward the east end of the store.

"Did you spy on me?"

"I was walkin' back from the privy. Here's the thing, Carolina—I still can't believe I called you Sweet Carolina that night—anyway, I just wanted one time where I actually did get to know a gal better. But then I began to realize that I have no idea what to talk about with a woman after a time or two."

"You're doing just fine, cowboy," she assured him.

"You make it easy. You spent your life visitin' with folks all over the world. I bet you even visited with Queen Vic."

"Just once."

"See? You know how to talk to anybody. Even tired and lonesome cowboys. Anyway, I just figured it was time for me to slow down and get to know someone better. You're just the unlucky gal who has to put up with it. You've probably never heard of anything so foolish."

Foolish? Ran, that's about the sweetest and nicest and certainly the most sincere conversation I've had in years. "Mr. Parks, I've enjoyed our conversations too. I think the past couple of weeks have been exceedingly peaceful for me as well. Now I want to be honest with you . . . " She paused and looked down at the dirt.

Breathe deeply, Sweet Carolina. You can do it. Don't say anything really dumb. "I'm used to playing oblique games in conversations,

never saying clearly what I mean. I don't want to do that with you."
Tell him you like him too. Don't cry. Don't giggle. Just be honest.

Ranahan stood to his feet. "Look, Miss Carolina, it was not my intention to put you in a bind. You don't need to answer me."

"But I want to answer you . . . "

"Looks like you got a customer." He pointed to a man who had left the Assay Office and was stalking to the store. "He must be one of those men who came in that big carriage and wagon."

"July can handle it." *Don't change the subject now, cowboy. We've just reached the good part.*

"He looks like a rough character."

No . . . no. I want to talk about . . . "How can you tell?"

"The position of the holster, the swagger when he walks, the tilt of the hat. He'll draw on you in a barroom fight."

"You can tell all of that from way over here?" *This isn't fair! Please turn the man around, Lord, and send him back to the saloon or something.*

"Yep. And it looks like July's sent him this way. Think I'll strap on my Colt just in case."

Ranahan sauntered back to the hay shed and buckled on his gun. Carolina noticed that the man with the blue bib-front shirt kept his eye fixed on Ranahan but walked straight toward her.

His brown wide-brimmed hat tilted to the right. Narrow eyes peered out of his clean-shaven face. An ivory toothpick was clamped between his teeth. Jingle-bobs sang on his spurs. Leather oil from the holster had stained the ducking trousers below the suspender buttons.

"Excuse me, ma'am." He tipped his hat and revealed oiled hair parted in the middle. "Are you Miss Cantrell?"

"Yes, may I help you?" She sensed Ranahan ease up behind her.

"Mr. Hardisty asked me to give you his greetings."

"That's nice. I hope he's recovering."

"Yes, ma'am. He's healin' up real good. 'Course the trip out here from town was a bit tirin'. That's why he didn't come to see you yet himself."

"Here? Jacob's here?"

"Yes, ma'am. He's right here in Starkeville. That's his carriage."

"This is Cantrell. That's Starkeville over there," Ranahan corrected in a combative tone.

The man glared at Parks.

"Why is Jacob out here?" Carolina asked.

"Two reasons. First, that's his office." The man pointed to the assay tent building.

"It is?"

"Didn't you know he's the one who hired those two mining engineers? I figured you two had talked about that."

"No, he didn't mention it."

"What's the second reason?" Ranahan butted in.

"Now that's a delicate subject between Miss Cantrell and Mr. Hardisty. I reckon it's a private conversation."

Carolina suddenly felt very uncomfortable in the fancy blue dress. *A delicate subject? I have nothing in the world I want to say to Jacob Hardisty.*

"The point bein' that he asked me if you would be so kind as to call on him this afternoon."

"At the Assay Office?"

"Yeah, they set up some cots in the back. He needs to gain a little strength. He wants to go down to Devil's Canyon in a day or two."

"Why didn't he recuperate in Billings?" she asked.

"Because you are here, I reckon. Can I tell him you'll stop for a visit?"

Tell him to go back to Baltimore. Tell him to get out of town by nightfall. Tell him I do not want to see him today or ever. "Yes, tell him I'll stop by after a while."

Nice work, Sweet Carolina. You're nothing but a puff.

The man turned to Ranahan. "And you can go hang your holster back on a nail, Blacksmith."

"I think I'll keep it on," Ranahan replied. "Never know when I might want to shoot someone."

Carolina watched the two men's eyes lock. Neither blinked. Both right hands rested on pistol grips. Finally, she stood up.

"If fact, I need to head back to the store. So why don't I go over and see Mr. Hardisty now?"

The man with the blue bib-front shirt strolled along about a step behind her to the left. She assumed that Ranahan stayed at the blacksmith shop.

She wasn't sure.

Carolina's first visit inside the Assay Office revealed an extremely neat but spartan quarters. A counter across the front of the building held two sets of scales and racks of weights. On a simple shelf on the west side of the building were various containers of chemicals. On the east wall hung surveyor's transients and other equipment.

The half-wood, half-canvas building was divided in the middle by a canvas tarp hanging straight down like a wall from a rope stretched across the room. Behind the counter were two desks made from wooden doors laid across shipping crates. On top of the desks were oceans of maps, most held flat by chunks of ore. Behind the desks sat Isaac Milton and Ted Ostine.

Both stood as she and the blue-shirted man entered. The older spoke first. "Afternoon, Miss Cantrell. It's a humid day today, isn't it?"

"Yes, it is, Mr. Milton. Hello, Mr. Ostine."

"You want to see Mr. Hardisty, I reckon."

"I understood he wanted to see me."

"That he did. Quite exciting, isn't it? Imagine you two being such, well, such good friends in the East and then winding up in the same location in the West. I find that an amazing coincidence." Milton beamed.

I find it a cruel joke. "Yes. It certainly is. May I go back and check on Mr. Hardisty?"

"Yes, ma'am. Come right around through here." Ostine motioned. "I sure was surprised to learn you knew each other."

Not nearly as surprised as I was to learn you two work for him.

She followed the younger man behind the canvas divider to find four cots neatly lined up against the far wall, with individual trunks placed with precision at the foot of each.

It's like a Prussian army barrack. And the general is injured.

The man in the blue shirt came with her, and the geologists stayed in the front office. Carolina casually slipped her hand into her dress pocket and found the handle of the small two-shot pistol. *Maybe I should have had Ranahan come with me. Mr. Blue Shirt gives me the slithers.*

Jacob Hardisty was propped up on top of the blankets, his head leaning against a pillow. Freshly shaved. Long-sleeved white shirt. Tie. Black trousers. Polished boots positioned nearby. A hand-written journal in his hand.

"My Sweet Carolina, what a lovely sight. Your opera dress is a heart-stopper. I'd like to think you wore it just for me. I do appreciate your coming to visit. I must apologize for not calling on you, my injury being what it is. I just had to lie down."

"You shouldn't be out, Jacob. Why didn't you stay in Billings and recuperate?"

"All I need is rest. I can do that quite well out here."

"You plan to stay here then?"

"Perhaps for a few weeks. Until we check out the claims at Devil's Canyon."

A few weeks! Jacob Hardisty two doors away for a few weeks. Why didn't I let the Marquesa kill him?

"Mr. DuBois, I believe you wanted to step next door and wash down a little trail dust."

"You goin' to be okay, Mr. Hardisty?" DuBois's deep voice rasped.

"Yes, yes. Carolina won't shoot m, will you?."

I have considered it on more than one occasion. "Shoot you?"

"I decided to hire Mr. DuBois as a bodyguard after that incident with Isabel Leon. I don't intend to be shot again. After all, I might not always have you around to save me. Did I tell you, DuBois, how Miss Cantrell saved my life?"

"Yes, sir, you did. Now if you'll excuse me, I think I'll hunt up a bottle of rye."

She watched the black-haired man amble out of the back room.

"Sit down, Carolina. Sit on that cot. You know, I had to come see you. When I found out you were here, I couldn't sleep, I couldn't eat. I believe it was divine restlessness."

"Oh?"

"The more I think about it, the more I'm convinced that it was God Almighty who sent you out to Montana just to save my life."

How do you manage to look so neatly turned out even in this wilderness, Jacob Hardisty? "I think you might be overstating it. Anyone who sat next to the Marquesa probably would have done the same thing."

"But it wasn't just anyone. It was you. I believe God has led us back together, don't you?" His round, dark brown eyes fastened on hers.

Carolina took a deep breath and laced her hands together at her waist. "Jacob, don't do this to me. Don't give me the old 'the Lord wants us together' routine. Too much has happened, and you know it!"

"But you loved me once."

"Yes, I did. But I discovered you weren't the man I thought you were. And I certainly wasn't the woman you thought I was." *Lord, why is he here? I don't need this confusion. Do I? Jacob is out of his element. Just a needless ornament like me!*

Hardisty's voice changed from pleading to preaching. "But forgiveness is a Christian virtue."

"Yes, and so is honesty, integrity, gentleness, and moral purity—to say nothing of honor."

"What do you mean by that?" he demanded.

"What I mean is, I don't love you anymore, Jacob Hardisty." *Speak slowly, Sweet Carolina . . . relax . . . stay calm.* "I haven't loved you for a long, long time. I don't intend to start up again. But I wish you a speedy recovery so you can be on your way. Good day, Jacob."

"Carolina . . . wait! You misunderstood my intentions! I'm not the same man I was a year ago. Please, wait. Let me explain. I acted a bit roguish then, I'll admit. Wait, I really need to talk to you!"

Both Milton and Ostine scurried to look busy as she stormed through the Assay Office and out into the yard.

Why isn't anything simple? I just came out here to pack up David's things. Ship them east. Sell the store. Stop by Chicago and visit Aunt Rebecca on the way home. No more than two weeks. That's all I wanted. I didn't come here to look for confusion.

I didn't want to own a store.

I didn't want to find Jacob Hardisty.

I didn't want to share a building with a foul-mouthed drunk like Horatio Starke.

"Miss Carolina?" Ranahan called out from across the dirt yard. "Everything go all right?"

"And I certainly didn't look for a broad-shouldered, sweet-voiced, handsome cowboy to ride into my life either!" she huffed.

Carolina climbed the stairs to her loft before she realized that she had spoken the last words aloud. She pulled off the fancy dress and hung it on a hanger and then threw herself down on the bed.

I've lost control, Lord. I say things I don't even want to say. At least, I didn't want to say that out loud. Why did You bring me out here? If You wanted to make me feel foolish and out of place, You could have done that in Baltimore or Philadelphia . . . or New York.

You didn't bring me out here to save Jacob Hardisty's life.

Did You?

Well, perhaps to save his life, but that's all. I will not think seriously about someone who is not a man of honor. You know that. Since I was six, I have searched for a man of honor. Jacob Hardisty is a man of convenience, ruled by whatever is convenient at the moment.

How do I know if Ranahan is truly a man of honor?

Did I really blurt out those things? These have been the most humbling days of my life.

Eh, is that Your point, Lord?

Carolina prowled the loft as she pulled on her plain gingham dress. She stopped long enough to peer into the mirror as she fastened the top buttons.

"Always wear a high collar, Carolina. It hides that long neck of yours."

"Yes, Mother."

She tied a white canvas apron over her dress as she descended the stairs and greeted two customers who rushed through the front door.

"Miss Cantrell! Miss Cantrell," the blond one shouted, "we did it!"

She studied the duo from worn-out boots to tattered hats. They looked like they had been painted with dried mud. It was the large one she recognized first.

"One-shot? Bud?"

"Yes, ma'am. It's us. Ain't we a sight?"

July scooted over toward them. "You look like you've been buried in the dirt and left fer dead."

"Almost. We hit pay dirt at Devil's Canyon!" Bud shouted.

"That's wonderful, boys!" she replied. *Boys? I called them boys? What will I do next—start dropping my g's?*

"Yes, ma'am, and it's just the beginnin'. They're runnin' a test on the ore over at the Assay Office. But it looks rich. Meanwhile, we want to buy us some new duds. Nothin' nobby, mind ya. We've still got a lot of work to do up at The Carolina."

"The Carolina?"

Bud grinned. "We named our claim after you. Hope you ain't offended."

"Of course not. I have never in my life had anything named after me. That's quite an honor."

"Could you outfit us? We can pay you in gold. You take gold, don't you?"

Carolina glanced over at July.

"Yep." He motioned toward the back of the store. "We fixed the scale on the counter. We'll give you twenty dollars an ounce. Right, Miss Cantrell?"

"Eh, yes. Is that the proper rate?"

"Yep. 'Course, we'll run a magnet through it before it's weighed," July added.

"That assistant manager of yours is a careful man!" Bud laughed.

"A magnet?" Carolina asked.

"We don't want anyone to slip some iron shavin's in there to pad the weight," July explained.

"Oh." *Lord, are You sure this kid's only fourteen?* "Boys, take a look around and pick out what you'd like. Say, where's Mr. Diggs?"

"Guardin' the claim. You wouldn't believe the scene at the Canyon. Must be 300 men up there already. We had two Indian raids and some flash floods. But we ain't goin' to leave, no, sir.

We've got to get right back. Sure was glad to see the Assay Office here. We figured we had to ride clear to Billings."

Carolina glanced at both men's dancing eyes. "Sorry we don't have a bathhouse in town," she said.

"All we need is a couple cakes of soap. We'll head for the river before we change."

Carolina stood at the back of the store and watched the men saunter up and down every row. *They're like children in a room full of toys. A few weeks ago they counted their pennies. Now they don't bother to ask the price. Two weeks from now they might be broke again, but today . . . today they celebrate. Lord, we all need some days so good we forget about everything else.*

With the purchases made and the merchandise bundled, both men hovered by the back counter. Bud lifted one package to his shoulder. "Miss Cantrell, you ought to build yourself a hotel. When we come to town, we'd surely stay there."

"A hotel? That's an ambitious idea, Bud. However, I'm not sure a hotel would do well out here."

One-shot McColister glanced at the other two. "Shoot, Bud, when we start diggin' out the high-grade ore, we ought to just build a hotel here and give it to Miss Carolina. We could have free rooms for life."

"I do believe you two have gold fever," she laughed.

"Yes, ma'am. It's an illness all right. But I ain't felt this good in years." Bud grinned. "Say, do you have any of them Cuban cigars left?"

"They're over here." July pointed to a glass case. "There's about ten left in this box."

"We'll take 'em all!"

She and July walked them out to the front of the store.

"Do you mind if after we clean up, we come back and camp near the store?"

"Be my guests, boys."

The two men rode north toward the river. Carolina watched them until they were out of sight.

"Hey! You got any of them cigars left?"

Horatio Starke leered out the doorway of the saloon.

"Nope," July called out. "We just sold our last ones."

"To those bummers? What was they trying to do—pinch you for credit?"

"Actually," Carolina informed him, "they paid for everything in gold."

"Gold?"

"Yes, it seems they have a fairly rich claim."

"And they didn't want nothin' to drink?"

"They didn't mention it."

"Are you sure you ain't got cigars? I got a customer that's gettin' desperate."

"All we have are some plugs of tobacco," July reported.

Starke turned in the doorway and went back into the saloon. "Hey, Cigar! They ain't got nothin' but plug tobacco!"

Carolina looked over at July.

"There's a man in there called Cigar?" she asked Starke.

"Yep. Cigar DuBois. But don't cross him. He's a professional shootist. I hear tell he was plumb run out of the British Possessions. But he cain't vote in Saturday's election."

"That's right. There are only six voters in Saturday's election," she agreed.

"Seven," Starke corrected her.

"What do you mean, seven?"

"Mr. Hardisty can vote. He's taken up permanent residence here."

"He most certainly cannot. He came in after voter registration was closed."

"It don't matter when he came in. The Assay Office belongs to him. He was just a little slow gettin' here. A permanent business owner. Yes, sir, he gets to vote."

"Mr. Starke, you are not allowed to change the rules."

"I ain't. We agreed on permanent residents, and Hardisty has had a business here for almost a week. How much more permanent do you want?"

Isaac Milton stepped out of the Assay Office and hiked toward the front porch of the store. "Are those two prospectors still in the store?"

"No, they went to the river to wash up," July called out.

"They brought in some mighty fine ore."

"It proved to be rich?" July asked.

"Yes, son, it all depends on how long it holds out, but they ought to make themselves a little money on that one. If they come back, send them over for a look at my report. I think maybe Mr. Hardisty just might want to buy them out." The older man reached into his vest pocket and pulled out a folded piece of paper. "Oh, I almost forgot, Miss Cantrell. Jacob Hardisty wanted me to deliver this note."

She unfolded the white paper and read the words.

Carolina,
I must talk to you tonight. In private. Could you call on me later?
Love, Jacob.

She folded the note. *"Love, Jacob"? What's your game, Hardisty? Why don't you go back to town and find another actress?*

"You want to give him a reply?"

"My answer is an unequivocal no! I will not go see him."

"That's your final word?"

"Yes, it is."

Milton jammed the paper back into his vest. "Well, will you send those two prospectors over if they show up again?"

"Yes, I'll do that."

Starke disappeared into the saloon.

Isaac Milton meandered back to the Assay Office.

Carolina stared out at Ranahan as he heated another barrel strap in the fire.

"July, would you mind the store? I'm going to talk to Mr. Parks."

"You goin' to tell him about the man named Cigar?"

"I think so," she sighed. "I think so."

— Seven —

"YOU DIDN'T TELL HIM YET, DID YOU?" July prodded from his position over the woodstove.

Carolina flitted along a shelf of clamp-top glass jars and kerosene lamps. "No. I decided to wait and tell him when he comes in for supper."

July's white canvas apron hung at an angle from his hips. "*If* he comes in for supper."

"What do you mean?" She reached up to adjust the heavy silver earrings that dangled down to her collar.

"I saw Ran ride off toward town about half an hour ago."

She restacked coffee tins. "What town?"

July waved a large wooden spoon like a pointing stick. "He saddled his buckskin and rode toward the river."

"That doesn't mean he went to town." Carolina scurried along the shelf where she rearranged everything absentmindedly.

"He came in here and picked out new trousers and a new boiled shirt and I—"

She turned back to the cookstove. "When did he do that?"

"You was up in your room."

"And I didn't hear him come in?"

"Maybe you were asleep. It was the same time that big Mexican family bought flour, salt, beans, and lard."

"I didn't nap. I reviewed David's papers and ledgers. I heard the family, but I didn't know Ran was here at the same time."

July stuck the spoon back into the pot on the stove. "He did it kind of on the quiet."

Carolina plucked up a cheap cherry-red oriental fan and began to cool herself. "Why?"

"Miss Cantrell, I'm just a kid. But when a man buys new clothes, it usually means he plannin' on a big night in town. So when he rides off toward Billings with a new outfit tied to his cantle, I figure he plans on gettin' feathered out and struttin' a little bit, if you catch my drift."

"But he didn't say anything to us about going to town."

"I don't reckon he surmises he has to tell us about his doin's. Does he?" His blue eyes studied her response.

"Well, it's just polite to . . . I mean, we're all in this together. I wouldn't think of going to town without telling him." She stopped by a shelf of spice bins, and suddenly cinnamon replaced fried beef-steak as the dominant aroma.

July stared down at the iron skillet. "Ever'body knows you cain't catch love with a rope."

"What?"

"Well," he mumbled, "it's purdy obvious you're sweet on Ran. But it ain't fair to try and corral him if he ain't wearin' your brand."

"I'm sweet on him! What are you talking about?" she fumed as she stalked toward the open doorway. "I don't need lectures on romance from a fourteen-year-old!"

His normally strong shoulders slumped as his eyes focused on his boots, his voice shaky. "No, ma'am."

"You stick to the role of assistant manager of this store and keep your youthful opinions to yourself. Is that understood?"

"Yes, ma'am."

Carolina stalked out the front door to the porch, put her hands on her narrow hips, and took a deep breath.

He went to town to live it up? Two hours ago he sweet-talked me, and now he's run off to Billings to some dance hall! That's it. I'll sell the store. It's all been a game, and I didn't even know the rules. At least, in the East I know how to play the game.

Of course, Sweet Carolina, you didn't exactly encourage him to stick around. But I was going to. I was just getting ready to tell him how I felt. He should have known that.

Carolina tramped out to the hay shed and watched the coals die in the fire pit.

Ranahan, are you a cur just like the others? But you're smoother. I didn't even know you were stringing me along.

Lord, I didn't need this. Not another failed relationship. Why did You do this to me?

She opened the faded, battered door of the shed and strolled into the shadowed darkness. The room smelled of dirt and hay. Several planks lay across two crates. Loose straw covered the planks. Parks's bedroll was stretched out on top of the straw. An old canvas coat was rolled up as a pillow.

Everything he owns rolls up in this tarp. It's a different kind of life. He's never had any permanent commitments. Why did I expect him to be able to make one? I've lived in a fantasy world.

She noticed a lump in the blanket. *Don't invade his privacy. You would be incensed if he invaded yours.*

She walked back to the door of the dirt-floored building and then spun around and returned to the bunk. She grabbed the dark gray wool blanket, pulled it back, and found a small black leather Bible.

Forgive me, Lord. I have to look.

She picked up the worn book and opened it to the front page.

Presented to:

*Our beloved son
Ranahan R. Parks
upon baptism after
his confession of faith*

*October 3, 1867
Oregon City, Oregon*

*Morgan V. Parks, father
Leena O'Day Parks, mother*

"Our beloved son." I guess I've never considered that Ranahan had parents who think of him as their beloved son. She reached up and wiped tears back from the corners of her eyes. *I have no idea why I cried when I read that. That's what's in the front of every Bible. He said he had devout Methodist parents. He would have been about twelve or thirteen at the time. I should put it back. I shouldn't read this.*

Instead, she flipped the pages of the small Bible until it fell open where a letter had been folded tight and used as a bookmark. She glanced back at the open doorway and then slowly unfolded the letter.

A bill of sale? Six hundred head of Texas longhorn steers, purchased "in exchange for services rendered" from Conrad Khors, May 30, 1881. Those must be the ones he lost in Alberta.

She folded the letter and stuck it back into the Bible. As she did, she noticed a verse that was underlined and some words penciled in the margin. The dim light of the shed forced her to the open door where she squinted to read the words: "Sweet Carolina Cantrell."

He wrote my name in his Bible?

Her eyes raced to the underlined portion of the verse. "Sweet is thy voice, and thy countenance is comely."

Immediately she closed the Bible and hurried back to the bunk. *I shouldn't have looked at his things. It's not right! You're horrible, Sweet Carolina. I can't believe I did that.*

I'm really, really glad I did it.

Lord, I'm despicable, aren't I?

What in the world do You ever see in me?

She jammed the Bible back into the bedroll and pulled the blanket over it. Then she jogged out of the shed into the evening light of a setting sun. Her heart sprinted. She was out of breath when she reached the front steps of the store porch.

July stood at the door with his thumbs in his waistband. His straw hat was pushed back and his apron, awkwardly wadded behind his belted knife sheath, hung almost to his side. "Is somethin' wrong, Miss Cantrell?"

"No . . . no, I was just . . . "

"You were lookin' for him?"

"No. I . . . well, perhaps."

"Supper's ready. Shall I serve it up?"

"I'm not hungry."

"You mean I have to eat alone?"

"I really don't care what you do. I'm going up to my room for a while." She dashed into the store.

"I'm sorry, Miss Cantrell, I didn't mean to rile you with them things I said about you and Ranahan."

She didn't answer him but started up the stairs.

"I'm only a kid. I say dumb things sometimes, but don't give up on me," he pleaded as he trotted behind her.

Halfway up the stairs she stopped and turned back to the eager face that stared up at her. "Oh, July, what did you say?"

"You didn't hear me?"

"My mind was on something else."

"I hope you ain't mad at me for spoutin' off like someone too dumb to drive nails into a snowbank."

"Mad at you? Why would I be angry with you?"

"I talk too much."

"Nonsense. I'll be down for supper a little later."

"Then you ain't mad at me?"

"Of course not. July, I've been terribly crabby today. Women are that way sometimes. I'm sorry. I have no excuse for it."

"I'd rather have a crabby friend than no friend at all," July mumbled.

"And I appreciate an honest friend," she replied.

Carolina continued up the stairs only faintly aware of the tune he whistled.

"Sweet is thy voice, and thy countenance is comely." If my countenance is so appealing, cowboy, why did you run off to a dance hall? This is crazy, Lord. I don't know if it was good to read those things or not. That man needs help in conversation.

He's not the only one who needs help, Sweet Carolina. So far the only thing you've said is that you "enjoyed talking to him" and "isn't it a lovely evening?"

Well, I'll sit him down and tell him a thing or two. But he went to town. Oh, sure, now you're ready to tell him how you feel.

How do I feel?

I feel as if I arrived at the depot half an hour after the train departed! As if I'm standing at the dock, and my ship is out to sea. As if I arrived at the theater after the last curtain has come down.

Lord, this is exactly the confusion that I have spent my life trying to avoid!

She flopped on her back on the bed and stared up at the log rafters and underside of the shake roofing.

Okay, Sweet Carolina, you've got to get that man by himself and have a real open talk. It will either scare him off or . . . or what? Just what do I want out of this?

Lord, this is a puzzle. No wonder I don't know what to say. I still don't know where I want this to lead. I mean, I want to have a happy marriage, a healthy family, a meaningful existence, and accomplish God's purpose for my life. And the sooner I get started achieving those goals, the better.

But how do I know it's Ranahan?

That's the problem, Lord. I don't know how to be any man's wife, let alone some drifting cowboy's. I am scared to death to even try. The more I think about it, the more petrified I am.

I'll probably be a miserable failure as a wife. I'm too headstrong. Too stubborn. Too driving. I'd nag a man right back out into the wilderness, won't I.

I shouldn't be thinking about this. Sometimes I think too much.

I learned to ride a bicycle by getting on it and riding it the first time I saw one. If I had thought about it much, I would have been too scared to try.

This is much more important than riding a bike.

"Miss Cantrell?"

She swung off the bed and stuck her head through the folds of the gingham curtains. "Yes, July?"

"You sure you aren't mad at me?"

"Are you angry with me?" she asked.

"No, ma'am."

"Well, neither am I angry with you. I'm just sorry I've been so preoccupied."

"It's all right, Miss Cantrell. I don't know when to keep my mouth shut."

"None of us do, July. You were right in what you said about me."

"I was? You mean, you really do like Ranahan?"

"Yes. But I didn't want it to be so obvious. Now don't you tell him I told you this."

"No, ma'am. I won't." July motioned to the table. "Do you want to eat now?"

"I think I will a little later. I have a few more of David's papers to look through. You go ahead and eat."

"I already did."

"That's fine."

July waved his arm toward the open front door. "Do you think we'll have many more customers tonight?"

"Probably not."

"I was thinkin' about, well, I'd like to—"

"Visit Miss Molly Mae Quincy?"

His eyes brightened, and his thin chest swelled. "Yes, ma'am."

"So why wait? Go on. But, tell me, when do I get to meet this young lady? Why don't you invite her up to supper one of these nights?"

"You mean it?"

"Yes, I do."

"But . . . but what will I say?" he mumbled. "I don't know how to ask a girl to supper."

"Just say, 'Miss Molly Mae, Miss Cantrell and I would enjoy having you come to supper. I'll bring the carriage by at about 7:00 P.M. if that is acceptable with you and your parents.'"

"I cain't remember all of that. I get sort of lightheaded when I'm around her. You know what I mean?"

"Oh, I know what you mean all right. But you'll do fine. Put your heart into it. She'll get the message."

"Yes, ma'am. I'll surely ask her. Eh, I think I'll go now. I'll scrub them dishes later."

"I'll scrub those dishes," she replied.

"That's what I meant."

"No, what I meant was, I'll do the dishes tonight, July. You deserve a night off. Now be nice to Molly Mae, and don't do anything you'll be ashamed to tell me about."

"Okay, Mama, you can trust me. I'm a good boy." July Johnson whistled a tune as he jogged out the door.

She pulled her head back inside the loft.

Now there is one eager young man. At what age do they lose that enthusiasm?

Carolina was sitting on the edge of the bed reviewing her accounts receivable when she heard boot heels signal a customer downstairs. With the ledger still in hand, she descended the stairs.

Jacob Hardisty stood at the doorway, dressed in white shirt, tie, and black velvet vest. His slacks were neatly creased and his black boots polished. His left shoulder was wrapped, and his arm rested in a linen sling. Below his neatly combed hair, his dark brown eyes seemed to dance. He turned back to speak to someone on the porch.

"It's fine, Mr. DuBois. She's alone. Just wait in the saloon."

Carolina tried to look out at the man called Cigar but saw no one.

"Carolina, we need to talk," Hardisty said.

"Jacob, I have a lot of things to do."

"I'll visit while you work."

"What I meant was, my life is quite full right now without you. I really don't think we have anything to talk about. I thought I made that clear to Mr. Milton."

"I know you don't mean that."

Suddenly she remembered the time he took her to dinner at the Ostrich Club in New York City and everyone asked him if she was European royalty. "Jacob, this is not a good time. I want to eat my supper."

"Go right ahead." He strolled to the table and pulled back a chair for her. "If you have some coffee, perhaps you could spare me a cup."

She ignored his chivalry and stalked straight to the cookstove. "I drink tea. You know that."

"I also know that's a coffeepot on the stove. I presume your clerk drinks coffee." Hardisty surveyed the room. "I saw him ride off, didn't I?"

"Why do you ask?" she snapped.

"I had hoped this conversation could be in private."

"And I hoped we would not have a conversation at all."

He reached up and adjusted the sling on his arm. "Carolina, rudeness is not terribly becoming in you."

"Jacob, forgive my impertinence, but I don't want to waste your time or mine. In plain language, we don't have anything to talk about."

A wry smile broke across his face. "Let's talk about the name of this town."

She stiffened. "It's called Cantrell."

"I hear there's a vote on Saturday."

Carolina folded her arms against her ribs. "Yes, well, I don't know if—"

"And I understand I get to vote." He rubbed his temples with his right hand. "Perhaps we could talk about why I should vote for the name Cantrell."

Carolina's dark eyebrows accented her piercing stare. "Mr. Hardisty, are you trying to get me to buy your vote? Just exactly what are you saying?"

"I'm merely suggesting that we do have things to talk about."

She marched past him to the open doorway and glanced down the road toward the river.

"You expecting a visitor?"

"Maybe," she murmured. *Lord, this is not the man I want to talk to. Mr. Ranahan Parks, this would be a wonderful time for you to walk up. I would love to hear those spurs jingle. And that deep voice call out "Sweet Carolina."*

Hardisty scooted over to the woodstove. "May I have a cup of coffee?"

"Help yourself." Her words flew out like discarded watermelon seeds.

He motioned toward the east wall of the store. "Could we sit at the table?"

"Why?" Carolina opened the wooden lid of a pickle barrel, glanced inside, and then replaced the lid.

"It seems more civilized."

She walked over and sat with her back to the wall, facing both Jacob Hardisty and the open doorway.

"Well, now, what are we really discussing, Mr. Hardisty?"

"Carolina, I only ask for a chance to show you I still care deeply for you. I know I've acted the knave, and you have no reason to believe that I've changed. But give me some time. This is not by accident that we've met again. You have to believe that."

"Jacob, listen to me because I don't want to repeat this.

Whatever happened between us in the past is over. Whether you acted like a rogue or I—as you so graphically pointed out with a loud voice in that Baltimore restaurant—acted like a flirt and a shrew just doesn't matter. Perhaps we are both at fault, but it's over. That's it. I'm not interested in beginning again. You go your way and find a gold mine. I'll go my way and find a . . . "

"I presume there is another man in your life."

"Why do you presume that?" she bristled. "There has been no one in my life for over a year, and I've survived quite well, thank you."

"I don't want to talk about the past year. I speak of right now."

"What are you insinuating? That I have acted improperly?"

His voice tightened. "Carolina, Sweet Carolina—"

"Jacob, I find it distasteful and terribly annoying for you to call me Sweet Carolina. Please do not use that term anymore."

He stared at her for several moments as she fidgeted with her supper.

"Carolina, there was a time when you were full of joy, a time when I never heard a bitter word from your mouth. What happened? Surely it's not all my fault. Yes, I acted horribly, but I wasn't the first scoundrel you ever dealt with. There must be more to it than that."

She reached up and rubbed the back of her neck, then sighed, and shook her head. "Jacob, your presence here complicates my life. I just don't want to deal with it. The manner in which you broke off our relationship hurt me beyond description. I only want to forget it. As long as you are within sight, it just stirs up pain."

"That's my point, Carolina. Your discomfort proves that you still care."

She stood up and walked to the woodstove. "It proves only the extent of my pain. When I was a child and lived in Vienna, I once played tag with a neighbor boy whom I detested. He pushed me off a fence, and I broke my ankle. Sometimes in cold weather, the ankle still aches. I can assure you, it has nothing to do with my affection for the Austrian boy. So it is with us. Go on with your life, Jacob. I'm sure there are plenty of women who have and will tell you yes."

He stood up and walked over to her. "But the only one I respect is the one who told me no."

She stepped away from him. *You have not shown me one ounce of respect in well over a year! Jacob, your words bore me to tears. There is nothing to them. You never back them up with actions. They are like a sales pitch from a patent medicine drummer.*

"Carolina, this is no way to end a relationship."

"We do not have a relationship! Mr. Hardisty, you chose the time and place to end our association last year."

"Isn't there anything I can do to convince you to forgive me?"

"I assure you, before the Lord, you are forgiven. We are just incompatible. Let it rest."

"Carolina, I can still remember all the good times."

"That's wonderful for you. I trust you enjoy the memories. Mine contain only hurt and pain."

"Can't I say anything to make you change your mind?"

"Not that I can think of."

"I know what I can do. What if I voted to name the town Cantrell? Would that help our relationship?"

"I doubt it. It sounds like you're trying to bribe me."

"What if I change the topic of conversation?"

She backed away from him even farther.

He followed.

"What do you mean?" she asked.

"Let me be honest. I am here in Montana to buy gold claims. I understand your brother was in the same business, and I had hoped to learn from him."

"My brother ran a store. He didn't speculate in mining claims."

"Yes, but according to Mr. Starke, David took in as payment for goods some partial interests in gold claims in Devil's Canyon. I would like to review those claims so that I don't purchase any that have already been sold. I would just like my engineers to examine them and make sure there are no conflicts."

She ground her teeth before she spoke. "So you had another motive all along. All this talk about how you still care for me was just to blanket your real purpose."

"Carolina, I want you to know I was sincere in—"

"This is all about gold mines, isn't it?"

"Surely, you don't think that I'd—"

"Sweet Carolina! You wanted to use our past friendship to make a fortune."

"Miss Cantrell," he barked, "I already have a fortune. But I do have a business deal for you. I would like to review your documents. Perhaps I would even make an offer on some of them. Even if I don't, I will pay for the privilege of reviewing the documents. You are a businesswoman. This is a business proposition."

She kept her arms folded under her bosom. "What will you pay?"

"I guarantee I'll vote to name the town Cantrell."

"Just to look at whatever claims I might have?"

"That's right."

"Then you'll ride off on your way?"

"As soon as I'm strong enough."

"You look strong enough tonight." She had an urge to straighten his crooked black silk tie.

"Thank you, I do feel better."

She backed up to the counter at the rear of the store.

"I'll tell you what. You may review the ledger of accounts receivable. The claims are all listed there. Then if you need further information on any, I'll allow you to review the certificates in my presence."

"I'll need to take them over and have my geologists review the actual documents."

"Not without me or an appointed agent of mine present."

"You don't think I would—"

"In the past you stated on more than one occasion that I tempted you beyond your ability to resist. I wouldn't want to tempt you to confiscate my mining company certificates."

"You're a tough woman, Carolina. Your father would be proud."

"Thank you, Mr. Hardisty. I take that as a compliment."

"Then we have a deal?"

"I let you look at the books, and you vote for Cantrell?"

"Yes." He reached out to shake her hand.

She reached out and suddenly found him kissing the back of her hand. Carolina wanted to jerk it away and wipe it on a towel.

"If you want me to go, I'll go."

The words came from the doorway, not from Hardisty. It was a deep, tingly voice.

She pulled her hand back and turned to stare.

Hat in hand.

Freshly bathed.

Clean-shaven.

Hair combed.

New boiled cotton shirt buttoned at the neck.

Canvas trousers still creased from the package.

Worn boots.

Low-slung holster.

Anxious gray eyes.

"Mr. Parks!" she called.

"Yes, as a matter of fact, we *would* like you to depart," Hardisty instructed. "This is private business."

"I noticed." Ranahan turned to leave.

"Ran, please wait! I thought you went to Billings."

"Who said that?"

"Well, July said he thought that's where you went."

"July was wrong. I wouldn't go to town without telling you. I just went to scrub up in the river before I talked to you again. I wanted to be more presentable this time. Looks like I need to wait in line."

"What do you mean by that?" she demanded.

"Do you cast dishonor on my Sweet Carolina?" Hardisty huffed.

"I am *not* your Sweet Carolina!" she bellowed. "Mr. Hardisty, I would like you to leave now."

Ranahan pulled his hat low on his brow. "Yeah, well, maybe I should leave too."

"Here's my brother's ledger, Mr. Hardisty. I believe this was the main reason you came to see me. Now if you'll please go."

Out of the corner of her eye Carolina saw Ranahan step back out onto the porch. "Ran, will you please come here?" she called out. "I'd like to talk to you."

"You don't need to explain," he murmured.

"Of course I do. Even a simple-minded cowboy should be able to see that I'm *your* Sweet Carolina—not his."

With hat in hand, he stepped back inside the door. "You are?"

"Yes, I am. Now come in here and hold my hand and tell me all those nice things before my heart breaks and I die on the spot!"

"Carolina Cantrell, I can't believe you'd talk that way to a man like him," Hardisty huffed.

I can't believe it either. Lord, are You sure this is the way it is supposed to be? Just jump on the bike and ride?

"You ain't just teasin' me, are you?" Ranahan asked.

"There's only one way you'll find out, cowboy. Come here." She winked and held out her hand. *If he rejects me now, I'll kill myself. I really will!*

A smile as wide as Texas broke across his face. "Yes, ma'am!" Ranahan strode across the store. His boot heels tapped and his spurs jingled.

"But . . . but, Carolina," Hardisty gasped, "do you have any idea what you're getting into?"

"No. But I plan to fill my life with joy. You just told me that was what was missing. I believe you. That was the most honest thing you ever told me. Good day, Mr. Hardisty. I will expect you to fulfill your part of our business deal."

"But, Carolina, surely you're just trying to make me jealous. You can't be serious about this . . . this drifting drover."

"Mr. Parks, if Mr. Hardisty doesn't leave the store immediately, would you please shoot him?"

"What?" Hardisty cried.

"Be happy to, Carolina."

The voice laughed.

Tickled.

His eyes teased.

She walked over to Ranahan and slipped her arm in his. They stood like that until Hardisty was out of sight.

Ranahan slipped her hand from his arm. "Were you just toyin' with me to get rid of Hardisty? Is this a game, Miss Carolina?"

"It depends on you, cowboy. Are you serious?"

"About how I feel for you? Yes, ma'am, I surely am. Never been more serious about a woman in my life."

She slipped her fingers into his. "Then it's not a game. We need to talk."

"I reckon we do." He looked around the store. "I was hopin' July would be here."

"Why?"

"Then we could go for a ride, and folks wouldn't interrupt us this time. Figured he could run the store while we were gone."

"That would be nice. He'll be back later. Perhaps we could go then." She tried for her most uncommitted smile, but knew by the sparkle in his eyes she had failed.

"It will be too dark to go for a ride then."

"Are you afraid of the dark, Mr. Ranahan?"

"Nope. Are you afraid of what can happen in the dark, Miss Carolina?"

"Nope." She grinned. *I probably look sillier than July scampering off to see Miss Quincy.*

"Then let's sit and talk until July gets back."

"Would you like some supper?"

"Yes, Miss Carolina."

"If you try not to call me 'Miss,' I'll try not to call you 'Mr.'"

"If I don't call you 'Miss,' I'm liable to blurt out 'Sweet Carolina.'"

"Don't worry about it, cowboy. I'll get used to it."

They ate.

Talked.

Laughed.

Talked.

Went out and sat on the bench side by side in front of the store.

Held hands.

Talked.

Sighed.

And talked some more.

The only light left filtered out from the kerosene lamps in the saloon. The baritone banter of men drinking and playing cards provided a background noise and made their conversation private. Her head rested on his muscled shoulder.

"Did you ever have anything come on you so sudden?" he asked her.

"You mean what's happening between us?"

"Yep. Did you ever see anything happen so fast?"

"Well, when I was six years old, I went to bed feeling well one night and woke up the next morning with the chicken pox."

"What happened?"

She poked him in the ribs. Hard, muscled ribs. "I lived."

"Are you saying this thing between us is sort of like chicken pox?"

"Yes, I think it's a disease."

"Is there any cure?"

"I hope not. How about you, cowboy?"

"Miss Carolina, I have never in my life felt as good as I do at this moment. My body, soul, and spirit seem to be dancin'!"

"You never felt this way before?"

"Well," he drawled, "there was one time I almost felt this way."

"Oh, what was her name?"

"Ginger."

"Ginger? I don't know if I want to hear about this."

"Well, you're goin' to have to listen. See, I was in Virginia City when I spotted her loungin' in front of the Bucket of Blood Saloon."

"A saloon! No, I'm sure I don't want to hear this."

"We got to be honest with one another. I don't aim to keep secrets from you. So anyway there she was—absolutely the purdiest brown hair I'd ever seen and them big eyes lookin' at me. I just couldn't resist."

Carolina put her hands over her ears. "I am not listening to this."

"So you know what I did?"

"No what?"

"So I bought her right there on the spot."

"What do you mean, you bought her?"

"I bought her. Threw my saddle on her and rode her down to Carson City. Ginger was the sweetest horse I ever owned."

"Horse? You're talking about a horse?"

"What did you think I was talkin' about?"

Carolina slugged him in the arm, only to have her hand bounce back. "You set me up for that, Ranahan Parks!"

"I suppose I did, but the point is—"

"This is going somewhere?"

"Yes, ma'am. Right after that, I rode Ginger up to Lake Tahoe. It was a cool fall day. The sky was so clean and cool, it was like you could reach right up into heaven. I didn't want to come down. I just wanted the Lord to scoop me up and take me to heaven."

"You and Ginger?"

"Me and Ginger," he sighed. "But the point is, even that feeling was not as wonderful as how I feel right now. Sometimes you got to sit around a long time and figure out what's right and what's wrong. But me and you—it's just right, isn't it?"

"It's crazy. We haven't known each other a month."

"But it's right, isn't it?"

"Yes, cowboy. It's the most right feeling I ever had in my life."

"I love you, Miss Cantrell."

"And I love you, Mr. Parks."

"Sweet Carolina," he whispered. "I don't believe this evenin'. I keep thinkin' I'll wake up out there in the hay shed, and it will all be a dream."

Carolina leaned back against the wall of the building. "I know what you mean. I thought the same thing."

"That you'd wake up in the hay shed?" he teased.

Her elbow plowed into his ribs.

"You turned my life around, Sweet Carolina."

"You didn't exactly fit into my plans either. Do you think either one of us has any idea what we're doing?"

"I don't think so," he laughed. "You willin' to take a chance with me?"

"What kind of chance did you have in mind?"

"I've been givin' it thought most ever' night. What I'm sayin' is, if you can still stand me by the first of August, we should go to Billings and get married."

"That's a month away."

"Well, I know that's a long wait, but it gives you time for the Lord to bring you to your senses."

"And it gives you time to drift on down the trail."

"Me? Why would I want to slip out of it?"

"Because you hardly know me. I am told that I demand, domineer, and manipulate men." She squeezed his hand. She thought she heard someone riding up the darkened road.

"Well, I've been called a driftin', no-account loner on more than one occasion. But I'm not worried. I'm a good judge of character."

"In horses or women?"

"Horses mainly," he teased. "Miss Cantrell, do you mind if I take a look at your teeth?"

"You don't examine anything until I have a ring on my finger, Mr. Parks!"

"Fair enough, ma'am. I reckon I don't."

"Well," she whispered, "that's not entirely true. You can inspect my lips if you want to."

"They look fine to me," he laughed.

"Kiss me, Ranahan R. Parks!" *Why did I call him that? Now I'll have to explain how I know his middle initial.*

"Right out here in public?" he gasped.

"It's pitch-dark. No one will see us."

With his arm slipped around her shoulder, his chapped lips brushed hers.

Carolina Cantrell could not remember how many boys and men she had kissed over the years. But she knew she had never experienced a kiss like this one. It was one of those I-can't-think-of-any-reason-why-we-should-ever-stop kind of kisses. *Lord, this could lead to serious, serious trouble.*

"Hey, Miss Cantrell! Ranahan! Guess who I've got with me!" July shouted from somewhere near the corrals.

They pulled back in unison and sat straight up. He leaned over and whispered, "I want to finish that kiss later."

You're not the only one, cowboy! "Did you bring Miss Quincy?" Carolina asked.

"Shoot, no. But Molly Mae is comin' for supper one of these nights. I've got the Marquesa!"

"Surprise, Carolina Cantrell! I bet you thought you'd seen the last of me!" A syrupy, almost sarcastic feminine voice danced across the street.

She and Ranahan stood side by side as they waited to view July and the Marquesa in the shadows.

"Has she come to finish the job on Hardisty?" Ranahan whispered.

"We've got to keep them apart."

"Shouldn't be too tough until daylight."

The swish of the Marquesa's full skirt preceded her visibility. When her cascading black hair came into view, Carolina spoke first. "I thought you were in the Billings jail."

"They released me. Isn't that sweet of them?" the Marquesa cooed.

"Why? You did shoot Jacob Hardisty."

"Oh, that. Well, the nice judge said I had extenuating circumstances. He allowed me to go free if I'd leave town. So I did. And here I am." She looked up at Ranahan. "Why is it every time I see you, you're surrounded by handsome cowboys?"

"Oh, Ran, this is Miss Isabel Leon, sometimes known as the Marquesa. Isabel, this is my, eh, my fiancé, Mr. Ranahan Parks."

"He's your what?" July gasped.

The Marquesa grabbed July's arm. "Fiancé, dear boy. That means she plans to marry the man."

"But . . . but," July stammered, "I was only gone a couple hours! You cain't up and decide to marry him in two hours!"

"See what happens when you leave me alone?" Carolina teased.

"I don't believe this!" July exclaimed.

"Neither do I," Carolina admitted. "Do I have your approval, Mr. Assistant Manager, to marry this man?"

July Johnson looked up at Ranahan who towered above him. "Can you take care of Miss Cantrell accordin' to the manner of which she is accustomed?"

"Yes, sir." Ranahan grinned.

"Well, you got my approval then."

"How old is this kid?" Isabel laughed.

"Forty," Carolina replied.

The noise of men exiting the Assay Office drew everyone's attention.

"Come on, let's all go inside. It's too dark out here." Carolina pushed Isabel and July toward the doorway.

Isabel's voice teased and prodded. "Too dark for what? You two were quite chummy when we walked up."

"Yes, well, we'll just have to continue that conversation another time. Won't we, Mr. Parks?"

"Yes, ma'am. I reckon we will."

Within a few minutes all four were gathered around the small table. They sipped coffee or tea and ate English biscuits from a newly opened tin. Carolina sat in a chair, and Ranahan stood behind her, his strong hands on her shoulders. Isabel sat across the table from them. She wore a dark green dress with the high neck and bodice revealing black lace. July, with a cracker in each hand, sprawled across a 100-pound sack of oats.

"Is there any particular reason you came out here after you got out of jail?" Carolina asked her.

"The judge asked if I had any friends around that I could stay with."

"We aren't exactly friends," Carolina reminded her.

"Yes, well, any port in a storm. I needed a destination to tell them. They put me on a coach that stopped at the river, and then Mr. Johnson graciously allowed me to ride with him up here."

"But your belongings—they sent you off without them?" Carolina questioned.

"They said they'd send them out with your next shipment of supplies."

"You plan to stay here awhile?"

"Carolina, I know you don't like me very much. I've certainly done nothing to warrant your friendship. I would like a place to stay until my belongings arrive and I make enough money to take the train to San Francisco."

Lord, I don't believe the audacity of this woman! Stay here! There are no accommodations!

"Miss Leon," Carolina began, "I—"

"Please call me Isabel."

The dark-haired woman's eyes looked very tired. In the shadows of the kerosene lamp, her shoulders slumped and her sneer faded.

She looks old, Lord. A young woman worn out and old.

"Isabel, we don't have a hotel here. There's just a loft, and it's crammed with—"

"She can use my cot," July offered. "I'll sleep out in the hay shed. You've got room for another bunk out there, don't you, Ran?"

"I reckon so. I could use some company."

"It would just be temporary. I just don't have anywhere else to turn," Isabel added.

"What about . . . I mean, you said you needed to earn some money, but there aren't any jobs around here."

"Maybe I could, eh, sing at the saloon. I'll pick up some tip money. I'll figure something out."

This is not good, Lord. I can't have her . . .

"Listen, I'll be happy to lend you train fare to San Francisco. After you get a job there and earn some money, you can repay me."

"You want me out of here that bad?" Isabel laughed.

"Put yourself in my place," Carolina challenged.

"I'd rather be scrunched up with a good-looking cowboy on the front porch without another woman hovering around," Isabel agreed. "I'll take your offer, but I do have to wait for my clothes."

"Will you be an actress in San Francisco?" July asked her.

"Yes, I'll probably work the theater until I run into Hardisty again. Someone in Billings said they thought he went to San Francisco."

"Why, shoot, no," July mumbled through a cheek crammed with crackers.

"July!" Carolina blurted out. "Don't talk with your mouth full!"

He coughed and cleared his throat. "I was just sayin'—"

"Mr. Johnson, I almost forgot a business deal I made while you were gone. I need to talk to you alone. Would you please step out onto the porch with me?" Carolina requested.

Isabel looked at Ranahan. "I do believe she doesn't want us to hear this conversation. I'm surprised she'd leave you and me alone."

"Why's that?" he asked.

"Oh, my, Carolina! He does only have eyes for you."

Isabel's and Ranahan's voices faded as Carolina tugged July to the front porch.

"July, don't mention that Mr. Hardisty is here. She doesn't

know that yet. I'll warn him in the morning, and he can leave before she knows."

"Yes, ma'am. I reckon that would be best."

"One other thing." Carolina looked back into the store. *What are those two laughing about?*

"What's that?" July pressed.

"Don't tell Ran about the man named Cigar."

"You ain't told him yet?"

"No, and if he and Hardisty leave in the morning, I don't need to."

"Don't you reckon he'll be mad if he finds out?"

"He doesn't have to find out."

"But he's been searchin' for over a year for that man."

"If he kills Mr. DuBois, he will be arrested for murder. And if Mr. DuBois kills him . . . "

"Either way, you ain't got no fiancé."

"Exactly."

"Are you really going to marry Ranahan?"

"If the Lord has mercy on us and we don't annoy one another to tears in the next month."

"A month ain't a long time. I reckon I'll have to wait four years to marry Miss Quincy."

"I reckon you will. But in four years you'll only be eighteen. In four years I'll be twenty-eight. Now can you keep still about this?"

"Yes, ma'am, I'll keep quiet if I can."

"What do you mean, if you can?"

"Sometimes my mouth skips right by my brain and jist blurts things out. You know what I mean?"

"Yes, I do. Well, try to keep your mouth from misbehaving."

"Yes, ma'am."

It was well after eleven, and the saloon was at a roar when Carolina, Isabel, Ranahan, and July decided to break off a dominos game and go to bed.

Isabel Leon scooted back to straighten the downstairs cot. July hiked out to the hay shed to build himself a bunk. Carolina and Ranahan stood in the darkness of the store's front porch.

He reached out his hand. She laced her fingers into his. Her voice was low and soft. "Did we really agree to get married in a month, or did I imagine it?"

"You havin' second thoughts already? You lookin' for a way out?" His voice was low. Tingly.

"Not hardly, cowboy. And you? You aim to wake up in the mornin' and ride off?"

"I might."

She dropped his hand from hers.

"Didn't we say we had a whole month to change our minds?"

"Yes, but—"

"Then I could wake up in the mornin' and find you've gotten into your buggy and made a run for safety."

"Well, I guess that's always a possibility."

"It will be an interesting month, Sweet Carolina."

She slipped her fingers back into his.

"You think it's right not telling her about Hardisty bein' here?" Ran asked.

"She can't shoot every man who breaks off a relationship."

"Maybe she has a good reason for takin' a shot at him."

"I can't think of a reason worthy of murder. Besides, he has that bodyguard, Mr. DuBois. He might shoot her before she gets a chance. It's better to keep them apart."

"Some people do need shootin'," he maintained.

"I don't believe that."

"Well, Sweet Carolina, that's where we disagree."

This time he dropped her hand from his.

"Does that mean we don't get to finish that kiss good night?" she asked in a voice much too weak and timid.

Two strong arms enveloped her small waist. His warm lips flattened hers as he lifted her off the ground. Her arms encompassed his neck. Finally he gently eased her back down to her feet and pulled back.

Wait! Don't stop yet! It's way too soon.

"Carolina, I do believe I've waited a whole lifetime to kiss you."

"Cowboy, don't give me a fraudulent line about I'm the only woman you've ever kissed."

"No, I won't lie about that. But I always knew something was missin' before."

"What was missing?"

"You, Carolina. I choose you—if you'll have me."

"You have thirty more days to prove yourself, cowboy."

"Yes, ma'am. And I think I better go tie myself into my bedroll so I don't do something to ruin my chances."

She watched him saunter off toward the hay shed and then turned to go back into the store. As she did, she glanced up at the starlit Montana night. *Everything seems clean, fresh, new—like starting life over. It's been a good day, Lord. A really, really good day. Thanks.*

Isabel Leon, dressed only in petticoats, sorted through a stack of women's flannel gowns on a shelf near the cookstove. "Any chance I could add a gown to my tab?" she asked. "I didn't want to sleep in my dress."

"Those look kind of rough. I have a silk one you can borrow," Carolina offered.

"Are you serious? Last time I was in this store, you threw me out. Now you'll lend me a silk nightgown?"

"I've had a good day."

Isabel raised her black eyebrows and nodded toward the hay shed. "I guess so. I'll take you up on that gown offer."

"Come on up to the loft." Carolina carried a lantern up the stairs.

"So this is Miss Cantrell's boudoir?"

"Isn't this a mess? Those are all David's things."

"David? Who's David? I thought his name was Ran."

"David was my brother, who operated this store before he was murdered."

"Oh, I didn't know. Carolina, I don't do well in conversation with women, as you are well aware. Still I'm curious. Why did you offer your hospitality to me this time?"

"I'll answer that if you'll tell me how you talked the judge into ruling on your behalf."

Isabel stared across the loft and clasped her hands together. "Okay, but you go first. Why your change of heart about me?"

Leon sprawled across the feather bed on her back while Carolina dug in her trunk and held up a long purple silk gown. "What do you think?"

"Other than the long sleeves and high neck, it's beautiful."

"I'm afraid that's my style." Carolina shrugged.

"It's quite nice. I'd say you bought it in Paris."

"Yes. I love to shop there, but I can never afford much. And you?"

"I can never afford to go at all," Isabel replied.

"Oh, well, my father had an import company, and we had to go to Europe on business."

"It sounds wonderful."

"To go to Paris?"

"To have a father."

"Everyone has a father."

"Well, mine decided to go back to Puerto Rico and leave my mother and me when I was five," Isabel sighed.

"I'm sorry your father wasn't around."

"So am I. But you've just evaded the question."

Carolina handed her the silk gown. "When you came by a couple of weeks ago, all you did was stir up old pain. Jacob left me for you. It was hard to live with that at one time."

"And you didn't want a reminder?"

"Yes, and I really didn't care that he treated you poorly. I thought it was a way for me to get even with you. But that didn't sit well with my conscience. I really don't know anything about you, Isabel."

"You can say that again."

"It's Jacob who's a rogue."

"So why did you push me when I was about to shoot him?"

"I just didn't think anyone should get shot over such a thing." Carolina pulled off her dangling earrings and rubbed her lobes. "Besides, the judge might not have let you off so easy if you had actually killed him."

"I imagine you're right about that."

"Anyway, now the whole episode with Jacob Hardisty is in the past. I've got a future."

"And an extremely handsome cowboy to focus your attention on. Aren't you worried I might try to steal him?"

Carolina sat down on a short wooden stool and began to unlace her high-top black leather shoes. "No."

"Why?"

"He's unstealable."

"How can you tell?"

"The kiss."

"That good?"

"That exclusive."

"Then I envy you." Isabel lifted up her head with her interlaced hands.

"I take that as a compliment."

"I intended it as such. So you can welcome me now because you've dealt with the past and have the future secured?"

"Something like that." Carolina sat down on the bed across from Isabel. "Now how did you keep yourself from conviction for attempted murder?"

Isabel ran her index finger across the gown as if she traced a map. "I told him the truth."

"What do you mean?"

"The judge asked me why I tried to murder Hardisty, and I told him."

"So what is the truth?"

"It's a long story."

"I've got all night."

"Well, I'll give you the short version." Isabel looked up, and Carolina could see sadness in her dark brown eyes. "About six months ago I found out I was expecting a child."

"From Jacob?"

"Yes."

"I don't expect that fitted into his plans too well."

"That's a mild way of putting it."

"Did he abandon you?"

"I wish."

"Then what?" Carolina glanced over at the dark-haired woman, who quickly looked away.

"A couple nights after I told him, he took me out to dinner in New York at the Ostrich Club."

"That's a lovely restaurant."

"Yes, Jacob knew it was my favorite. I got this notion in my head that he would ask me to marry him that night. We stayed there a long time. I kept having another drink and waiting for him to ask me."

"He never did?"

"Not hardly. At some point, I passed out from the liquor. I didn't wake up until the next morning—in terrible pain." She looked over at Carolina. "Are you sure you want me to go on?"

Cantrell took a deep breath and held her stomach with her hands. "I think so."

"I woke up in a hotel room on 43rd Street, a nurse by my side."

"A nurse? Were you in an accident?"

"It was no accident. As far as I could learn from the nurse, Hardisty took me to see a doctor friend of his after I passed out. The wonderful doctor kept me knocked out with chloroform and performed an abortion on me."

"He did what?" Carolina's mind began to whirl.

Isabel Leon began to sob. "They killed my baby and removed it from my womb."

"But . . . they . . . I . . . I think I'm going to faint." Carolina lay back on the bed.

Isabel collapsed as well. "Not only that, but the nurse said I would never be able to bear children."

"No . . . no . . . ," Carolina moaned. "That's criminal! Did you go to the authorities?"

"The nurse said she heard me agree to it."

"You were drunk!"

"Anyway, Hardisty paid for room and board in that hotel for a week. Then he sent me $100. He thought he could buy all my children for a lousy $100," Isabel wailed.

Carolina sat up on the bed and pulled the Marquesa closer to her. Both women held each other tight.

And sobbed.

Carolina had no idea how much time had passed. Isabel remained in her arms until neither had any more tears. Then they both washed their faces in silence and pulled on their gowns.

Finally, Carolina nodded toward the feather bed. "Why don't you stay up here? It might be more comfortable," she offered.

"You've been more gracious to me than I deserve. The downstairs cot will be fine. It's much nicer than waking up in a filthy, rat-infested jail cell."

"Isabel, forgive me for judging you so quickly."

"Carolina, I've been sarcastic, bitter, and angry for so long, I don't know if I can act differently."

"We both need some rest. Perhaps we can talk about it more in the morning."

"I'd like that. Now can I take one of the lanterns downstairs?"

"Certainly. Would you like me to come with you?"

"No, Mama, I can tuck myself in."

"Well, do me a favor and check the front door. I don't remember if I locked it."

Carolina hung her dress on the hanger and quickly brushed it. The flannel gown she wore felt rough against her skin. She crawled under the covers of her bed and turned off the lamp. She lay on her back to watch the light die out. The loft felt stuffy and warm, but a cold chill washed over her.

Maybe I should have kept the silk gown for myself. Sure, Sweet Carolina, what an unselfish person you are. Isabel needed a break.

A faint glow from downstairs signaled that Isabel's light was still lit.

Maybe I was wrong, Lord. Maybe there are some people who need to be shot. But not by me—or Isabel. I've got to keep them apart. In a town of nine people, that will be almost impossible.

At least I've succeeded for tonight.

— Eight —

WHEN THE FRONT DOOR BANGED OPEN, Carolina Cantrell sat straight up in bed. When she heard Jacob Hardisty's voice, she fumbled on her dresser for her gun.

"Carolina, I must talk to you! I want to buy these gold claims of your brother's tonight."

She didn't bother finding her robe or slippers but padded down the stairs barefoot.

"I saw the light on back here and . . . Isabel!" Hardisty cried out. "What are you doing here?"

"It's destiny!" Leon growled. "I had just talked myself out of murdering you, and then you burst into my bedroom. Now I can kill you in self-defense! You're an answer to prayer, Jacob Hardisty."

"Bedroom? This is a store! You're supposed to be in jail!"

"And you're supposed to be in Hades! What are you doing here?"

"I own the Assay Office here. Put down that knife, Isabel!" Hardisty screamed.

Carolina made it to the bottom of the unlit stairs in time to see Isabel Leon lunge at Jacob Hardisty, a buckhorn knife with a six-inch blade in her right hand.

He jumped back and slammed his clenched right fist into the back of Leon's head. The knife tumbled to the floor, and Isabel crumpled at his feet.

Carolina stood in the shadows, unable to move or speak.

Hardisty kicked the knife into the dark reaches of the store and slammed his boot heel into the small of Leon's back and pinned her to the floor.

Carolina Katherine Cantrell scooted out of the shadows toward Hardisty. The small gun trembled in her right hand.

"Carolina! She tried to kill me again. Why didn't you warn me she was here?" he cried out. "Give me that gun!"

"He was here all the time?" Leon screamed from her prone position on the floor. "You knew he was here, and you didn't tell me. Give me that gun, Carolina. I have a right to kill him and you know it!"

"Jacob, get away from her!" Carolina shouted.

"What?"

"I said get your foot off her!"

"I most certainly will not. What has gotten into you? This woman has repeatedly tried to kill me."

Carolina stepped within five feet of Hardisty and pointed the pistol at his head. "Maybe she had good reason. Now get your foot off her."

"You wouldn't pull that trigger."

She lowered the barrel to point about six inches below his belt buckle. "Watch me! Seems like this might even the score."

"Wait! What did she tell you?"

"That you got her drunk and had a doctor abort her baby."

"She agreed to that."

"And he botched the job, and she'll never be able to have children. Now keep your hands up and get your foot off her, Jacob Hardisty. So help me, I'll shoot!"

He backed away, which allowed Isabel Leon to roll over and sit up. She leaned against an empty saddle stand and cradled her ribs with both arms.

"Put the gun down, Carolina!" Hardisty blubbered. "You promised to put the gun down."

"I can't believe I ever loved you," she snarled. "How could you do that to a woman?" She stepped closer toward him as he hovered against a shelf stacked with coveralls.

"She would have made a horrible mother. I probably saved society a lot of anguish."

"You what?" Carolina shouted. She could hear Isabel Leon sob. The cocked pistol was now only a couple of feet from Hardisty's head.

"Carolina, you told me to move away from her. I moved away. For God's sake, put the gun down!" Jacob Hardisty's pleading turned to a wail.

"He's right." A deep masculine voice crashed into the darkened store like a wave on a rock.

"Ran? How long have you been there?"

"Ever since the first scream."

Carolina didn't move her pistol. Ranahan and July hovered at the door. Ran had his revolver in his right hand. "Why didn't you help us?"

"You didn't need any help. I figured it was something you gals needed to work out. But you did tell him to back off or you'd shoot. He backed off."

"Do you know what he did to Isabel?"

"I heard."

"Then you know we can't let him get away with it!" Carolina proclaimed. "He has to pay."

"What can you do to even the score?"

"I could kill him."

"That would gnaw at you the rest of your life. Besides, I think he deserves worse than that!" Ranahan offered.

"What's worse than death?"

"Hell."

"You mean, allow God to settle the matter."

"Yep. Besides, you've got to honor your word."

"Honor?" Carolina questioned.

"Yeah, it's important to me to honor my word."

"Jacob Hardisty is not an honorable man."

"I don't think that's the point," Ranahan said. "Are you an honorable woman?"

Honorable? A man with honor? A woman with honor?

Carolina lowered her gun.

Hardisty stepped toward her.

"Back off, mister," Ranahan called out. "I guarantee if you come within two feet of either of those women any time in the rest of your life, I'll have the honor of killing you myself! You've just been given a break you don't deserve. Now get out of here!"

"You haven't heard the last of this!"

"Mister, it's time for you to ride on down the trail. There are only nine people in this town, and three would like to kill you."

"Four," July called out from the doorway.

"Four out of nine want you dead. I'd suggest you leave town tonight. Don't ever plan on coming back."

Hardisty stiffened. "You can't force me out of town."

"Of course I can. You're a woman-abusing coward, and you know it. You're not about to stand up to me face to face."

"I've got a business in this town."

"Let Milton and Ostine run it. They did all right before you arrived."

July Johnson scooted inside the store. "Here comes Cigar!"

"Who?" Ranahan shouted.

"Mr. Hardisty's bodyguard!"

Cigar DuBois stalked to the doorway, his hand resting on his holstered revolver. He peered in through the dark shadows. "You got trouble in here, Mr. Hardisty?"

"Shoot him!" Hardisty screamed.

"Don't draw it, mister!" Ranahan shouted. "Mine's cocked and pointed at you."

"I said, shoot him!" Hardisty screamed.

"Hardisty, I ain't goin' into a fight I cain't win."

"What kind of bodyguard are you?"

"I'd take him in a fair fight, but I'm smart enough to know when I don't have a chance."

"You couldn't take buffalo dung in a fair fight!" Ranahan growled.

"What are you talkin' about?"

"How about when you and a dozen others jumped four drovers in the middle of the night up in Alberta and stole 600 head of prime beef and left the cowboys for dead?"

DuBois leaned forward into the darkened store. "Who are you?"

"The one drover who was too mean to die!"

"I didn't shoot those drovers. It was Swearingen and One-eyed Joe who done the killin'. They're both in Texas now."

"In that case, you can die in their place."

"That ain't fair!" Cigar rubbed his hand back and forth on the polished walnut grip.

"Tell it to Gritman, Wallace, and Perry-boy."

"Who?"

"The three drovers you left dead on Alberta dirt."

"Well, I ain't drawin' on a man who's already drawn."

"Then I'll just have to shoot you all holstered up."

"Ran!" Carolina called out.

"Stay out of this. It's different," he shouted back. "I want justice for my friends."

"I want an honorable husband. You can't shoot a man with a holstered gun. You know that."

Ranahan glowered at the man for several seconds. Then he waved the barrel of his pistol at DuBois. "You and Hardisty get out of here! You two are leavin' Cantrell tonight."

"I ain't never been run out of no town," Cigar protested.

"Get used to it. It beats being buried here."

"We ain't got no cemetery," July blurted out. "Yet!"

"Maybe you didn't understand—I ain't leavin'," DuBois challenged. "Now I'll get Hardisty, and we'll leave this building. But at sunup I'll be right outside waitin' for you."

"You threatenin' me when my gun is pointed at you?"

"You're tryin' to impress the ladies by not shootin' me with my gun holstered. I reckon as long as I leave it there, I can say just about anything I want."

Ranahan bolted the front door after both men left. Then he turned around and motioned toward the others. "Stay away from the windows. I wouldn't put it past them to try an ambush."

"Was DuBois serious about a shootout in the morning?" Carolina asked.

"Oh, yeah," Ranahan replied.

"You should have killed them both while you had a chance," Isabel Leon reprimanded him. "Then we could dance in the street instead of crouch behind the counter."

"Miss Leon, for over a year I hunted for the men who stole my cattle and killed my friends. If I knew I had the right ones, I would have shot them on sight. Until today . . . "

"What happened today?"

He turned to Carolina. "I guess I got somethin' a whole lot more important to think about."

"Sweet Carolina," Isabel observed with a grin, "you've got this cowboy hooked bad. What do you intend to do about it?"

"I guess I'll just have to marry him. If we both live long enough. . . . Ran, why didn't you disarm him and take him in to the sheriff?"

"A man like Cigar won't be led away without firin' a shot. Someone in the room would have to take a bullet. It wasn't worth that."

July peeked out over the counter toward the darkened store. "What now?"

"I think you two ladies should go upstairs and put on a robe and some slippers before you embarrass this boy to death," Ranahan suggested.

Isabel Leon raised her thick black eyebrows and winked at Carolina. "Who got embarrassed?"

Within minutes they were huddled around a kerosene lamp set on the floor behind the thick oak counter at the rear of the store.

"Did DuBois mean he would shoot any of us who came out the door in the morning?" Carolina asked.

"Nope. I think Cigar has me in mind," Ranahan declared.

"And maybe me," Isabel added. "He was hired to keep me from killing Hardisty."

"Perhaps you could . . . ," Carolina began and then stopped.

"I could what?"

"I was going to suggest you slip out a window, saddle up, and ride to town."

"I don't run that easy."

"Well, I meant to get the sheriff."

"The sheriff ain't goin' to come because someone said he'd shoot somebody. That happens a hundred times a night in every saloon," July instructed. "He won't come until someone's dead."

"That's a comforting thought." Carolina shuddered.

"Well, if you need someone to carry a gun, I'm with you," Isabel Leon offered. "Provided I get to select the one I shoot."

"We've got a short-barrel Greener right over there." July pointed. "I can use it as well as the next man. When I took this job, Miss Cantrell said I wouldn't have to shoot no one. But I figure self-defense is somethin' different."

Carolina pulled her two-shot derringer out of the pocket of her robe. "I don't carry this around for decoration. I'll use it to defend us."

Ranahan waved his arms to silence them. "This is my beef. You three aren't involved."

"That's ridiculous!" Leon insisted. "We're in this right up to the top of our dyed hair."

"Dyed?" Carolina asked.

"Sweet Carolina, I've got more gray than Ranahan, but you'll never see it."

"Isabel's right," Carolina insisted. "This is a stand for justice and for Cantrell, Montana. It's all of *our* fight."

"This is no stage play, ladies," Ranahan cautioned. "Those are real guns, real bullets, and people could really die."

"It's my time to take a stand," July announced. "For the first time in my life, I've got friends I care about. I've got a job that I can stick with the rest of my life and a place to call home. If a man don't defend that, he ain't much of a man in my book."

Carolina rubbed the palm of her hand with her fingers. "July's right. Everything's crazy back in the States. I don't even want to go back. This is what I want, right here. You're what I want, Ran. I don't plan on losing you without a fight."

"It's unanimous," Isabel added. "Hardisty left this store humiliated. I like that. I'm not going to allow him the upper hand. You were right, cowboy. There are worse things than dying. My life's been hell for too long."

Ranahan shook his head. "What am I going to do with you three?"

"You better tell us how we can help you, because we're going to do it one way or another. And our way might not be as wise as yours," Leon declared.

"Who will we be facin'?" July asked.

"Cigar . . . maybe Hardisty," Ranahan pondered.

"Only if Jacob hides when he shoots. He's not the heroic type," Carolina added.

"How many more does Hardisty have with him?" Isabel asked.

"Milton and Ostine are geological engineers. I don't think they'll want any part of a gunfight," Ranahan suggested.

"How about Mr. Starke?" July asked.

"He's only slightly braver than Jacob," Carolina offered. "Whatever he can hit from the doorway of the saloon will be about all you can expect from him."

"But how many are in the saloon and will hang around to join in tomorrow?" Ranahan asked.

"Ain't no way of knowin'," July replied. "Have you got a good plan?"

"I got a plan," Ranahan declared. "We'll have to wait until after sunup to see if it's good or not."

When the dark, starry Montana night began to turn gray, everyone in the store was dressed and sat at the table drinking coffee and tea.

Carolina Cantrell surveyed her companions, resting her eyes on a coffee-sipping Ranahan Parks. *Lord, it's like I want this relationship too much. I'm terrified about something happening to Ran. I'm afraid if I don't get to marry him, I'll spend my life in deep depression and regret. I lost Daddy. I lost David. That's all I can take.*

Please.

Lord, if we get through this today, I'm going to marry him. You know I will. I suppose this is a drastic way to discover Your leading. If You have something better in mind, You'll have to show it to me—quick. Because I can't think of any reason not to marry this man.

Except for the fact that we've only known each other a few weeks.

But it seems like we've known each other for years.

The tea in her cup was now cold. July was standing at the stove frying mashed potato cakes.

"Miss Cantrell, you and Miss Leon surely do look handsome," the young cook beamed. "I didn't reckon you'd be wearin' your fanciest dresses and all them rings, earrings, necklaces. It's like Saturday night after the trail drive in Dodge."

"Since we didn't sleep all night, we had a lot of time to talk," Carolina replied. "And we decided if either of us had to have this be our last day on earth, we wanted to go out in style."

"Of course," Leon added with a wink, "we have an idea that hangers-on might have second thoughts about shooting at ladies all decked out."

"You're right about that." Ranahan shook his head. "Aren't many men in the West that would ever take a shot at a lady. Unfortunately, I got a feelin' that Cigar is one of those men."

"When exactly do we get this plan started?" Carolina asked.

"As soon as the sun's up. One advantage to the store bein' on this end of the building is that the rising sun will be in his eyes."

"What if your plan doesn't work?" Carolina asked.

"Then save yourself and put a marker on my grave."

"Don't talk that way, cowboy," Carolina cautioned. "If you think there's a good chance this won't work, let's forget it. Besides, maybe they all rode off, and nothing will happen this morning."

Ranahan rolled the cylinder in his revolver and shoved a bullet into the sixth chamber. "That would be a miracle."

"Lots of miracles seem to happen around here."

July scooted over to the east window. "I think the sun's about up."

"Anyone out in the street?" Carolina asked.

"Nope."

"Are you ladies ready?" Ran asked.

"Yes." Isabel nodded. "I'll cover you from the window over the sink."

"Shall I go out now?" Carolina asked.

"That's the one part of the plan I can't get used to," Ran cautioned. "I hate it that you go out first."

"Nonsense. The Lord will take care of me," she assured him and marched toward the door.

Lord, I . . . eh, I might have gotten ahead of You a little. I don't want anyone shot. But if someone is to take a bullet, it seems like it ought to be DuBois or Starke or even Hardisty. I don't want it to be . . . okay, You're in charge. May Your will be done.

The morning air had an early summer's day coolness to it as Carolina paraded out on the porch. At first she saw no one. With determination she tramped down the stairs and into the hard-packed dirt that served as yard and street. She held her skirt off the dirt with her left hand. Her right hand cradled the derringer in her deep pocket.

Starke's at the saloon door with a carbine. The Assay Office door's open, but I can't see anyone else.

Isaac Milton blocked her entrance to the Assay Office. "What can I do for you, Miss Cantrell?"

"I want to see Jacob."

"Eh . . . he's busy. I'll tell him you called."

The thick heel of her black lace-up shoe crashed into the soft leather toe of Milton's stove-top boot. The geologist let out a pained grunt as she stormed into the office, past the counter, and into the back room.

"Miss Cantrell!" Hardisty called out as he quickly tucked the revolver he carried back into the belt band of his trousers. "You are hardly welcome here. Last night you threatened to kill me. Maybe I should just keep my hand on my revolver."

"You didn't think I would really shoot you, did you?"

"You put on a convincing performance."

"Good. You have my ledger. I want it back right now," she demanded.

Hardisty nodded at Milton. "Give it to her. It will all be mine, Sweet Carolina. I will own that mining property one way or another."

"Jacob, you do not get everything you want."

"I have so far."

"You don't have me."

"A fact, I'm sure, I'll be able to live with. You didn't believe all that stuff I said last night, did you?"

Carolina squinted into Hardisty's shallow eyes. "No, I didn't."

Milton returned from the front of the tent building. "Here's the ledger." He shoved it at Carolina. She took it in her left hand. Her right remained on the small, hidden handgun.

"Now I must ask you to leave," Hardisty insisted.

"Why?"

"I have things to do."

She walked right up to Jacob Hardisty. "I know one thing you aren't going to do." He yanked the revolver out of his trousers only to find her derringer pressed into his ribs.

"Drop the gun!" she ordered.

"My word, men, she's going to shoot me!" he cried out. "Stop her!"

"Wait!" she called out. "I do not intend to shoot anyone, provided he drops his gun. If either of you grab my arm, I might get nervous and pull the trigger out of fright."

"Don't just stand there!" Hardisty shouted.

"I don't reckon I want to cause the lady to pull that trigger," Milton replied. Ostine nodded agreement.

"Well, then go get DuBois!"

"He's already in position."

Carolina marched Hardisty at gunpoint to the front room of the Assay Office. *What position? Where is he?* She peeked out the open doorway. *I can't see anyone at all.*

"Mr. Milton . . . Mr. Ostine, would you men please step out on the porch?"

Ostine hesitated. "No one's going to shoot at us, are they?"

"Not that I know of. Of course, I have no idea what Jacob's friend will do."

With her gun jammed into Hardisty's ribs, she shoved him out the door. Except for their boots on the wooden porch, she heard nothing. "Don't go any further. I think we'll stand right here and watch."

"We could get hit by a stray bullet," Ostine moaned.

"We'll just have to take that chance."

"You ain't got a chance!" Horatio Starke hollered from the doorway of the saloon. Carolina glanced up. Starke's carbine pointed at her. "Put down that gun or I'll blast you."

"I'm afraid he has the advantage, Sweet Carolina." Hardisty lowered his hands. "You are really out of your element here!"

"He ain't got no advantage at all," a young voice shouted.

Starke kept his carbine on Carolina. "Who said that?"

"Down here!" July called.

"Down where?"

"You see those two pipes stickin' up through the crack in the porch?"

Starke looked at his feet. "Pipes?"

"It ain't pipes. It's the firin' end of a short double-barreled shotgun. I figure if I pulled both these triggers, it would divide you into two equal pieces, sort of like separatin' an orange. Drop your carbine!"

"You ain't got no shotgun under there. The porch isn't high enough."

July shouted, "Miss Cantrell, make sure you're standin' back. It's goin' to be pretty messy, and I don't want to stain that beautiful dress of yours."

"I'm all right, July. Go ahead—"

"Wait!" Starke yelled out. "That kid's crazy enough to do it!" The carbine crashed to the porch.

"Now don't take one step, Mr. Starke. They told me if you even hint at movin', I'm supposed to pull both these triggers."

"I ain't movin'. Tell him I ain't movin'!" Starke yelled.

"He's not moving, July."

"Where's Cigar?" Johnson called out.

Carolina kept her eyes and her gun on Jacob. "I haven't seen him."

"You don't really think you're going to pull this off, do you?" Hardisty scoffed.

"I think it's Mr. DuBois's move. Where is that brave man?"

"Where's Parks?" Hardisty asked.

"Right here!"

The deep voice sliced through the summer air like a train plowing a snowdrift. All of those on the porch looked to the east end of the building. Ranahan Parks, holstered gun at his side, stood at ground level and leaned against the end of the building.

Carolina could see his hat pulled down low on his forehead, his right hand on the grip of his Colt. His eyes searched the street, the corrals, the hay shed, and the trees beyond.

"Come on, DuBois! Let's get this over with!" Ranahan yelled.

"Maybe he rode off!" July hollered from beneath the deck. "Shall I go ahead and plug Mr. Starke?"

"Wait!" Starke rolled his eyes to the sky and pleaded, "He'll show!"

His action caused Carolina to glance up at the shingled roof of the building.

"DuBois, I'm waitin'!" Ranahan challenged.

"He won't step out with you hidden behind the building," Hardisty called out.

Ranahan pushed his hat back a little. "Nope, I reckon he won't."

As he took a step forward, Carolina spied a figure raising up at the crown of the roof. The morning sun reflected off a nickel-plated gun barrel.

"Ran! The roof!" she shouted.

Ranahan dove to the dirt. A blast sounded from inside the store, then another from the roof. Before the well-armed audience, Cigar DuBois tumbled down the roof and crashed into the porch in front of the store. Ranahan rolled to his feet and charged to the downed man.

Carolina hurried toward Ranahan. Horatio Starke reached down for his carbine.

"Don't even think of it!" July called out from the front of the saloon porch where he was now perched on the steps.

DuBois struggled to his hands and knees.

"I missed!" Isabel Leon announced from the doorway of the store, a revolver still in her hands. "When you yelled 'roof,' I shot straight up through the shingles."

Ranahan kept his gun on the stunned DuBois. "I reckon it startled DuBois enough to lose his footing and fire a wild shot as he tumbled off."

"My leg! I think I broke my leg!" DuBois groaned.

"Yep, it sure does look like it to me." Ranahan kicked DuBois's pistol off the porch and then stuck the barrel of his Colt in the man's ear.

"You wouldn't shoot an injured man."

"No, but I shoot a leg-broke horse just to take it out of its misery."

"I ain't no horse."

"There's nothin' about your behavior that shows you're a man."

"I ain't got a gun, and you know it!" the man cried out.

"Crawl down there in the dirt and get it!" Ranahan snarled. "I'm tired of this!" The barrel of his gun crashed into Cigar's head, and the man crumpled unconscious on the porch.

"What happens now?" Carolina asked.

"July, go hitch up the carriage. I'll tie up Starke and Hardisty. We'll take all of them with us."

"You ain't goin' to hang us," Starke protested. But before he could lean down and retrieve his carbine, a bullet from Ranahan's gun blasted the door casing and showered him with cedar splinters. Starke stood straight up, his hands raised above his head.

"Why are you taking me with you?" Hardisty protested, his hands still in the air.

"For attempted murder, of course. You, Starke, and Cigar DuBois were in this ambush together."

"That's ridiculous! You can't prove that."

"If I were you, I'd come along peacefully, 'cause if you try to escape, I'll shoot you before you ever talk to the judge."

"You can't be serious!"

"Well, of course if you and Starke left town right now, I suppose there's not much we could do about it."

"I got a saloon to run!" Starke protested. "You ain't going to take away my business."

Carolina walked over to the crate-top fence that separated the store porch from the saloon porch. "Mr. Starke, will you sell me your property for $1,000?"

"Cash?"

"Yes."

"And $250 for the inventory?"

"I don't want the inventory. You may take it with you."

"I ain't got a rig to haul all of that."

"Mr. Hardisty's leaving town in a big rig. Perhaps he could

freight it for you," Ranahan suggested. "You are leavin' town, aren't you, Hardisty?"

"There's no reason to stay in this loathsome hole a day longer," Hardisty grumbled.

"Good. How about it, Mr. Starke?" she asked again.

"I want $1,500," he demanded.

"Okay," Carolina agreed.

"Have you got that kind of money?" Ranahan asked.

She looked down at the two geologists. "Mr. Milton, would you or your employer be interested in purchasing my interest in the Eureka Claim at Devil's Canyon for $1,500? I believe according to my brother's ledger, that's a bargain."

"Yes, ma'am, it is," Milton called back. The mining engineer looked over at Hardisty. "How about it, boss? You want to buy her claim? Because if you don't, me and Mr. Ostine will buy it ourselves."

"Why such sudden generosity, Carolina?" Hardisty puzzled.

"It's simple. I'm just that anxious to get you out of this area. So I want it understood that the deal comes with the restriction that you can never enter this town again."

"I have to move my Assay Office?"

"Oh, no, I would enjoy having Mr. Milton and Mr. Ostine stay. It's just you I detest."

July drove the carriage up to the front of the store.

"What is it, Hardisty?" Ranahan demanded. "Shall I coldcock you and haul you to town with Cigar?"

"I'll buy the claim. It's the best deal I've made all week, the only deal I've made all week."

"Draw up the papers, Mr. Milton," Carolina instructed. "Then give Mr. Starke the $1,500. Mr. Ostine, could you help Mr. Starke load his things?"

"Yes, ma'am."

Ranahan packed Cigar, who was tied up securely, out to the carriage.

"Are you sure you want to sell that gold mine claim?" Isabel asked Carolina as she stepped back into the store.

"I've got a gold mine right here."

"The store or the cowboy?" Isabel winked.

Cantrell locked her arm in Leon's. "Need you ask?"

"Miss Isabel! Sweet Carolina," Ranahan called out.

They both strolled out to the porch. "I've got a favor to ask of you."

Carolina stared at his dancing gray eyes. "Yes?"

"I would like July and Miss Leon to run your store today."

"Why?"

"I figured you'd like to ride with me into Billings to take DuBois in."

"Well, yes, but why?"

"First of all, it's the only way I can be sure I won't drive down to the river and put a bullet in Cigar's brain. I don't trust myself. Those were good men that died in Alberta. But I'm tryin' real hard to let the Lord have the vengeance. I do know that DuBois has a $300 reward on his head in Deadwood if brought in alive. I found that out last month but didn't figure I would want to cash it in. Now I reckon that would be enough to order up a mighty nice weddin' ring."

"A wedding ring? But it's still a long time until August 1. Are you sure you want to risk it?" Carolina challenged.

"I spent the last hour prayin' that you and me would get through this ordeal so we could get married."

"You did? So did I," she admitted. "I think the Lord answered our prayers."

"Do you two make everything sound spiritual?" Isabel prodded.

They looked at each other, then back at Leon—and nodded agreement.

"Come on, Sweet Carolina, climb into the carriage," he requested. "You've got a wedding ring to select."

Isabel Leon looked over at Carolina and grinned. "Go on, Miss Cantrell. July and I will take good care of your store."

"But we ain't had the votin'!" July called out. "We was supposed to vote at noon."

"All those in favor of this settlement being called Cantrell, please say 'aye,' those opposed, 'nay.' . . . Ayes have it!" Ranahan declared to the surprise of those gathered on the porch. "Well, do I hear any objections?"

"I don't want my name on no petticoat town anyway," Starke growled.

Carolina smiled. "Was that supposed to be an insult?"

"Go on, get up there with your cowboy," Isabel Leon urged.

"But won't I need to pack a few things?"

"Grab your purse and coat. Miss Isabel, if Hardisty and Starke aren't out of town by dark, I reckon the only right thing to do would be to shoot them."

"It will be my pleasure to take care of that, Mr. Parks." Leon flashed her wide, professional smile.

Within a few moments Carolina scooted out the front door to the carriage. She clutched her coat and purse. A straw hat was now tied on her dark brown hair. "When will we return?"

Ranahan pushed his charcoal gray hat back. "By midnight if we don't get lost."

"Lost? How could we possibly get . . . " It was Isabel Leon's elbow that jabbed her ribs. *You are blushing like a schoolgirl, Sweet Carolina.* "Yes . . . well, fortunately I'll be in the presence of an honorable man."

Her throat tickled, and her heart raced as he put his hands around her waist and lifted her into the carriage. Ran swung up beside her and immediately placed a strong arm around her shoulder.

July flipped his shaggy brown bangs out of his eyes. "So if you two ain't home by midnight, we'll figure you're lost."

"If we aren't home by midnight, you can surmise we found a preacher," Ran called out as he slapped the reins on the horse's rump and trotted down the road toward the river.

Carolina Katherine Cantrell brought his right hand to her lips and kissed the back of it gently.

A preacher . . . today? Now that is an intriguing honorable idea, cowboy!

Look for book #2 in the

Heroines of the Golden West Series

by Stephen Bly

The Marquesa

Follow the exploits of Isabel Leon
as she constructs the Hotel Marquesa in
Cantrell, Montana Territory.

For a list of other books by
Stephen Bly
or information
regarding speaking engagements
write:

Stephen Bly
Winchester, Idaho 83555